*Find[...]*

Ann Stevens took up [...]
working and bringing up [...]
career took off quickly, with numerous sho[...]
published and winning competitions. She lives with her
solicitor husband in a thatched cottage in a Devon village.

*Finding Maggie* is her second novel, and follows the
successful publication of *November Tree* in 1995.

# FINDING MAGGIE

## Ann Stevens

HarperCollins*Publishers*

HarperCollins*Publishers*
77–85 Fulham Palace Road,
Hammersmith, London W6 8JB

A Paperback Original 1997
1 3 5 7 9 8 6 4 2

A catalogue record for this book is
available from the British Library

ISBN 0 00 649899 X

Set in Linotype Postscript Meridien by
Rowland Phototypesetting Ltd,
Bury St Edmunds, Suffolk

Printed in Great Britain by
Caledonian International Book Manufacturing Ltd, Glasgow

For my children

# ONE

She knew she had arrived when she opened the flaking front door into a cool dim hall that smelled of lavender and onions and old wood. And when, later, her bare white feet touched the sun-warmed tiles of the terrace – cracked tiles, a deep rusty red, a little dusty but glowing hotly – she said out loud, 'I have made it. I am here!'

Margaret hadn't exactly said that she was running away, but she was.

Harriet had said, 'Well, if you're sure . . . but it doesn't sound like you.'

And Margaret had said, 'Exactly!'

Her daughters had responded with an equal doubt. Sheila, bossy as ever, told her she must be mad. 'Think of the risk, at your age. Suppose you get ill? And you'll be lonely – who will there be to talk to?'

Clinging Cassie wondered mournfully how she would manage without her mother. 'Who will I get to babysit?' she complained, adding, 'I shall miss you,' and looking miserable.

To them she had made little attempt to explain or justify; to Harriet, her friend, she had said, 'I know it may appear astonishing to you, but after all I have nothing to lose. There's nothing to keep me here. And it's not for ever. A year perhaps . . .'

'Nothing? You have two daughters and a darling grandson.' Did Harriet's voice hold just the merest hint of envy? 'And this house. How can you leave the garden for a year . . . ?'

'Mr Blake will do it as he does now. It's all taken care of.'

'But suppose you're ill? There'll be no Dr Gibson down the road, no NHS.'

'I'll take out insurance. As for the NHS, I don't have much faith in that any more. It's nothing but cuts and waiting lists . . .'

'You were glad of them when Robert had his stroke.'

'Maybe. Not that it did any good in the end.'

'Oh Margaret! I know it's lonely for you now, but it will be even more so miles away . . .'

'But don't you *see*, that's what I want? I can try my wings . . .'

'At fifty-three! Surely by now you know how far you can fly!'

'No, Harriet, I don't. Because I've never tried. And if I crash to the ground I've only myself to blame, and nobody gets hurt but me.'

'But *I* shall miss you, Margaret,' said Harriet sadly.

Margaret gathered herself to say, 'Nonsense, your busy life, when do we ever see each other anyway?' but, noticing for the first time a certain drawn and suggestive pallor, said instead, 'Oh my dear. It's sweet of you to say so. And I shall miss you too. But you must come and pay me a visit. When I've found my feet.'

In the imperceptible shake of Harriet's head she read a denial of her plans.

'Anyway I'm going,' she had said, obstinately. 'Because it's all arranged.'

And now here she was, in Spain.

It had all been very easy really, once she had made up her mind. Feathers and Forster, the estate agents by the car park, had begun to specialise in properties in Spain. 'But not just a holiday let,' she had stressed. 'I want something

2

with character, not a purpose-built apartment. And I want it for a year. And not the south, with all the rest of the Brits. Something in the north-west, preferably not too far from Santiago. Such a fabulous city. I shall want to visit there.'

And without too much ado Mr Feathers had come up with a two-storey house in Gondomar, just two hours south of Santiago and half an hour from the sea, and here she was, after two days on the road and the long crossing to Santander.

She knew she had arrived when her overloaded car drew up outside in a cloud of dust and squawking Latin chickens and she looked into the dark toffee eyes of a little girl in a pink satin dress, with pink satin bows in her hair, and when she opened the flaking front door into a cool dim hall that smelled of lavender and onions and old wood. And when, later, her bare white feet touched the sun-warmed tiles of the terrace – cracked tiles, a deep rusty red, a little dusty but glowing hotly – she said out loud, 'I have made it. I am here!'

She had thrown off her sandals as she pushed wide the door onto the terrace and now she breathed, rapturously, gasping in the glory of the southern air, taking huge gulps of the warmth and the light and the view of hazy distant hills so that she felt already at one with the golden evening and the little white-painted home that she had so miraculously acquired and the huddle and tumble of other houses, the houses of her neighbours, all around. And she loved them all already.

Then she put her feet sensibly back into her sandals and went downstairs again, through the dim hall and out into the late afternoon scorch of the still street to her car. The chickens had returned, pecking round the seed heads of the weeds which grew along the wall of the house and spilled out into the dusty road in a resilient green mat. The little girl was still there, drawing idly in the dust of the car bonnet with a brown finger. When Margaret came out she dropped her hand, then raised it again to sweep away the shiny red lines on the paintwork.

'Hello,' said Margaret. *'Cómo te llama?* What is your name?'

'Madrilena.' The toffee eyes were solemn but fearless. Margaret held out her hand and the child, after a long hesitation, took it in her own dusty clasp as if to follow, dutifully, wherever Margaret led. Such trust touched Margaret deeply and she loosed her hand and said, 'And I am called Margaret Fairbrother. Señora Fairbrother. I am very pleased to meet you.'

And now Madrilena smiled and the toffees melted and shone and white teeth slashed the smooth olive cheeks, and Margaret knew that she had made her first friend.

She unlocked the boot of the car and began to pull out the bags and parcels and loose packages which had been stuffed round her big trunk. Madrilena was still there, watching with interest. On an impulse Margaret said, 'Will you carry this inside for me?' holding out an open canvas holdall full of shoes. She waited tentatively; was her rusty embryonic Spanish understood? Yes. The child stretched out and with both hands took the bag, which reached nearly to her feet. She must only have been six or seven. Without waiting she staggered in through the front door and up the stairs, with Margaret following carrying a box of groceries and her portable stereo. Madrilena had opened a door at the back of the small landing which led into a bedroom. She set the bag of shoes down carefully by an elaborately carved wardrobe and gave Margaret another melting smile. 'Those will go in there,' she said, her accent clear and comprehensible.

Margaret breathed a sigh of relief. She had understood, and was understood. 'You know this house?' she asked

4

carefully, feeling for the words. 'Have you been inside before?'

The little girl looked shy. 'Yes. It is Señor Velasquez's,' she answered, as if that explained everything. Then, bolder, 'He is my uncle. He told us you were coming.'

Margaret nodded. Hence the little welcoming committee of one. 'Then can you please show me where the kitchen is? For the food.' She nodded again, towards the box in her arms.

Madrilena pointed down the stairs and they descended together.

The kitchen was in the front, beneath the flat roof that formed the upstairs terrace. It looked out onto the dusty street and the car, melting in the sunlight which filtered in through half-closed Venetian blinds. Setting down her box, Margaret swished up the blind with a mental whoop of joy. Now she could see everything: the village street, the church with its three bells hung in the crumbling façade, the equally crumbling houses of at least six of her neighbours, and two shops. Standing at the little stone sink beneath the wide window-ledge, she would watch the world go by.

She heard a bustle and a shooing from the entrance hall. Three of the chickens had come in and were pecking at the rush matting which covered the tiles. Madrilena was swooping them away with little rushing movements of her hands and a combined shooing and hissing which Margaret joined in with until, laughing, they watched the fowls scurry away down the street. The child and the woman's eyes met in a complicity of achievement, and a simple happiness she had not known for months, for years, filled Margaret's heart to bursting. So soon, and she had surely found part of what she had come for.

Between them they had soon emptied the car, apart from the trunk which Margaret had always known would be unmanageable, was a ridiculous and unreasonable thing to

5

take with her, several smaller cases would have been far more sensible. But she had not wanted to be sensible. The metal trunk, unused since Sheila's college days, had seemed to her in fact eminently suitable for a journey such as hers. Tourists took suitcases; travellers took trunks. It was as simple as that. Not so simple, however, was how to get it out of the back of her car and up the stairs.

Together, they stood looking at it. Margaret shook her head and saw Madrilena do the same in imitation. Then the child shot out a taut hand. 'Wait,' she commanded, and ran off down the road in a whirl of pink satin and satin hair, scattering the chickens as she went.

Margaret leaned against the hot car, content to wait for as long as it took. She had thought, during the last hours of the long drive and in her English way, that she could do with a nice cup of tea. Now, nothing was further from her thoughts, from the reality of this Spanish street where half-past four meant not tea but the slow awakening from a siesta that had lasted since the long late Spanish lunch-time.

The waspish whine of a motor scooter gradually disturbed the silence until it drew near enough for her to see the creased brown features of the old man who was driving it. The panniers on the back were loaded with shaggy bundles of grasses and perched across them both was a wooden cage containing two rabbits who gazed impassively from their precarious captivity as they passed. Encouraged by Madrilena's welcome, Margaret raised her hand in greeting, smiling widely, but was rewarded with no more than a passing glance. Chastened, she turned back to look after the girl and saw her skipping back along the road, followed by a swarthy young man so typically Spanish he might have walked off a poster advertising a bullfight. His dark brown eyes, she was sure, had the capacity to flash. He was tall and muscular and lean, and his arms below rolled-up white shirtsleeves were both silky and chestnut brown. He had the appearance of an artisan, but the expression and bearing of something else.

Madrilena said, 'This is Marcos. My cousin. He is a student and helps my father sometimes.'

'In the garage. I am afraid I am rather dirty.'

'Never mind.' Margaret could forgive him that. '*De nada*. Have you come to help me move my things?' The word for trunk escaped her but she nodded into the back of the car.

'Certainly. Is it as heavy as it looks?'

'More, I think.' She laughed, nervously, biting her lip. Marcos leaned into the back of the car and she could see the muscles rippling under his shirt. He managed to get one end up over the lip of the boot. 'Take this please,' he said, then courteously, 'but be very careful. It is certainly heavy.'

Together, struggling, they managed to get the leaden trunk out of the boot, and Madrilena clapped her hands together in delight. Margaret gasped as she took the weight; at home, in Surrey, her good neighbours Ralph and Derek had done the job for her. Now she felt horrified at how she had imposed, at what they must have thought.

'We will leave it downstairs,' she gasped as they entered the hall. 'Madrilena, please open that door there.'

The doorway facing them at the end of the hall led into a long dining room which itself, she could see when they had lowered the trunk to the tiled floor, opened onto a patch of shady green inside a white painted, deep-tiled wall. So she had a garden too – was there no end to happiness? Good neighbours, a room with a view, and a garden. All in the space of half an hour. She turned to thank Marcos and shook his greasy hand, wondering if she ought to tip him but unwilling to convert a neighbourly gesture into a service. He smiled, and his eyes did indeed seem to flash.

She was delighted, and regretful. Why couldn't she have had a dashing, dark-eyed son like Marcos to help her carry her burdens instead of her burdensome daughters?

Both of them dull, conventional and ordinary. As Margaret had been, up until now.

Locking up the car and straightening to ease her back, she watched as Madrilena and Marcos walked away, the evening sun behind them and the dust of Spain rising round their feet. She looked down at her own feet, which were grimy with the same dust, with the further proof that she had indeed arrived, and her heart sang a proud incredulous song.

There were five rooms; the kitchen and dining room downstairs and, upstairs, a sitting room leading out onto the tiled terrace at the front, and the bedroom with a tiny bathroom leading off it at the back. From the bedroom window she could look down on the small walled square of her garden, shaded by the house and, she guessed, completely private from ground level. Beyond the white walls to one side was a small patch of scrub with some wooden sheds round which more chickens scratched and pecked; on the other a larger garden with a paved patio overgrown with weeds which merged indefinably with a patch of scruffy grass, a stunted cactus and a clump of last year's sweetcorn, pale and dessicated as old bones. The house itself had looked derelict; at least there would be no problems with the neighbours. Beyond the gardens to the rear was a field of young sweetcorn with someone bending low, weeding, in the slanting golden sunlight. A donkey was tied to a post in the corner of the field and as she stared it lifted its heavy grey head and gave its squeaky-hinge of a bray as if in distant greeting. Beyond the cornfield was a huddle of grey, tiled buildings, and a *hórreo*, a rectangular Galician grain store on stone mushroom legs, with farm machinery clustered underneath and a little cross on its gable end. With the view came a sweet heavy scent of blossom.

She washed her hands, slightly alarmed at the banging in the pipes as she turned on the large brass taps, and wondering how she would get them to produce hot water. She wondered too about washing her feet, and decided not to. This wasn't Surrey, after all. This was Spain. There were no fitted carpets to worry about. In confirmation of her decision, she kicked off her sandals and opened the large, ornately carved wardrobe with them hanging in her hand. A smell of camphor and sandalwood gushed to meet her and wire hangers clanked gently on their rail as the air moved round them. The wardrobe was huge, and all to herself. Impatience to hang her clothes in its fragrant recesses overcame the sudden urge to eat, the longing to sit on the terrace and watch the world wake up outside, the urgent desire to tell someone about it all which meant starting her first letter to Harriet.

There was so much she wanted to do, excitement burst inside her in a flood of energy and soon she was running up and down the narrow stairs with armfuls of clothes, hanging them in the wardrobe, folding them proprietorially in the depths of the matching chest of drawers, arranging the shoes in lines beneath her dresses and skirts and trousers. Her raincoat, looking shamefacedly of England, she hung up along with the rest. Despite the hot bright stillness of the afternoon, she knew she would need it eventually. Northern Spain wasn't called the Costa Verde for nothing.

Lastly, she unpacked her blue Terylene-cotton sheets and made up the high carved double bed, pulling up the unaccustomed blankets – she had been used to sleeping under a duvet – and drawing up the thick white fringed coverlet. She lay her nightdress on the end of the bed and set her pink slippers beneath the bedside table on which she arranged her travelling clock and a pile of paperbacks specially purchased on the ferry. Satisfied, she thought that, now, it was time to get herself something to eat.

It was darker in the kitchen as the sun had moved westward and sunk behind the high façade of the church. Experimentally, she pressed the switch inside the door and, to her delight, three spotlights came on simultaneously, lighting respectively the sink, the small work surface, and a round wooden table on which she noticed for the first time a letter addressed to herself. Inside, in the careful English in which her correspondence with Señor Velasquez had been conducted and as usual sent from an address in Vigo, was a formal welcome to 'his house' and various instructions including those for hot water 'by depressing the small switch in the cupboard for linens in the bathroom' and for lighting the furnace in another cupboard in the kitchen 'for such times as when the weather is inclement'. The letter closed by announcing that he would pay her a visit when next he came to Gondomar, and wished her much happiness in his country.

Happiness? Sitting at the table holding the letter in her hands Margaret asked herself, not for the first time, what was this happiness that she had come to find? Was it the happiness of independence, for the first time in her life of doing something that was her own idea entirely, and of doing it alone? Was it the satisfaction of breaking the mould, of kicking over the traces, reneging on her responsibilities, throwing caution to the winds, of casting herself off into the unknown as she cast off her old life . . . ? Was it the challenge of living alone in a foreign country, of getting by with her rudimentary Spanish and hopefully improving the same? Or was it simply that she and Robert had so often toyed with the idea for later, when he had taken early retirement, and she was merely doing it for him?

At that moment it seemed to her that it was something

of all these reasons; and that whatever the reason it was something she had had to do.

And she had done it.

She unpacked her box of provisions, carried carefully all the way from Sainsbury's, the Grade A eggs coals to Newcastle with chickens pecking at her very threshold. She washed some lettuce and tomatoes carefully in the sink, reassured by Señor Velasquez's firm statement that 'the water in the cold tap in the kitchen is completely suitable for drinking' and put some of the same suitable water in a copper kettle on the little gas stove to make some coffee. While the water boiled she rooted about in the cupboards unearthing treasures: a red enamel coffee jug, a small china teapot with matching jug and bowl decorated in ethnic red and blue squiggles and splodges that couldn't have been more different from the pale blue and grey flowers on her tea set at home in Godalming, and six wine glasses each engraved with the figure of a bird. In a drawer beside the sink she found a blue linen tray cloth and some napkins and she set a tin tray and whipped up an omelette while the coffee brewed. She buttered some chunks of a crusty loaf she had picked up when she stopped for lunch and, humming to herself with satisfaction, took the whole lot up onto the terrace where she had noticed a pair of white iron chairs and a small table, with a wilting geranium in a pottery tub.

Really, she should have brought some wine, she thought, sipping water from a wine glass and crunching lettuce which had kept fresh and crisp in a cool bag. Bringing wine to Spain had seemed senseless – now she had nothing better with which to drink to her good fortune than coffee and 'completely suitable' water. Even so, she raised her glass to the darkening sky and said, 'To Spain – and freedom. *Viva España!*' and, giggling a little as if it really was wine she was drinking, she sipped the water and watched the sun go down.

Later, sitting up in the hard, high bed with the blankets tucked round her knees against a night that was surprisingly cool, she began her letter to Harriet.

My dear. Well here I am, installed in my little *hacienda* and I can't wait to tell you all about it. Everything is far, far better than I expected, and my worst fears (of snakes and spiders and damp beds! which I didn't admit, even to you!) have not, so far, been realised. I have already made a friend – she is called Madrilena and she has the most beautiful Spanish eyes. I think the Spanish girls are at their best before puberty. Madrilena is certainly a little beauty. She helped me to unpack, and introduced me to another, occasional, neighbour, called Marcos, who helped me with the dreaded trunk. Marcos is – well, I suppose the archetypal Spaniard – swarthy, with flashing eyes and that peculiar Latin grace and arrogance. If anything could make me believe I was truly here it was the combination of Madrilena's beauty, and Marcos's stereotypical good looks.

My other visitors so far have been chickens!

I can hardly believe I will wake up here in this strange bed with the sun shining in and everything new and waiting for me. I don't think I will sleep at all, so I will now describe the house. I have a lovely sunny terrace which I shall fill with tubs of flowers, and a dear little kitchen, partly modernised but with a quaint stone sink and a slate draining board. There seems to be everything I shall need in the cupboards – more than enough for a lonely old widow like me. I have a charming sitting room with cane chairs with pretty floral seats and a rather flickery television set which seems to need some adjusting – and a large, quite formal dining room leading onto the garden. I am saving the garden for tomorrow's treat! I can't see me ever using the dining room, at the

12

moment it is just housing my trunk which I shall have to cover with a cloth and leave there. My bathroom is en suite – just like home! – the plumbing noisy, but adequate, and the water hot and very soft. My bubble bath produced a positive mountain of foam!

Here she paused, suppressing a huge exhausted yawn.

Oh dear – perhaps I am rather sleepy after all, it was a long journey, twenty-four hours on the ferry and two days on the road. I shall pick this up again tomorrow when I have explored further. Goodnight, dear Harriet, I hope you are not missing me too much . . .'

She switched off the light and slid down beneath the covers, smelling the reassuringly familiar smell of her own sheets, washed long long ago in England, at Heathercote. From long sad custom she thought of Robert and the cold space where he used to be. But it didn't seem to hurt so much in this strange bed in a foreign land, and perhaps after all that was why she had come.

# TWO

It had been just over a year ago that Robert had died, suddenly, of the stroke from which, at fifty-six, he had never recovered. It had been a Sunday; he had been playing golf while she prepared the lunch. Cassie, Anthony and their baby had come for tea; it was little Robert's second birthday and Margaret had made a cake. They never ate the cake, which she found in the tin days afterwards. Watching the little boy unwrap the rocking horse they had bought for him, she was conscious that her husband was in some sort of distress. He couldn't tell her what it was, nor could he lift himself from his chair. One side of his face was twitching uncontrollably, and soon, waiting interminably for Dr Gibson and then the ambulance, he had begun to dribble. It was the dribbling that she remembered most; the shame and discomfiture of it and her own desperate tender attempts to wipe it away while trying to comfort and reassure, though she already knew the worst.

Anthony had followed the ambulance and stayed with her through the long night, and by Monday morning, Margaret had been a widow: at fifty-two and quite unprepared for it. 'But I hadn't finished with him yet' was her first reaction, railing against a God in whom she didn't believe and a fate which had done the dirty on her. 'He wasn't ready to go, and he couldn't even say goodbye.'

Six months later, she began to admit that she was feeling rather better. She had been fond enough of Robert – once she had loved him, passionately – but over the years, without her realising it, passion had turned to custom, intimacy

14

to an easy friendship within which they had been increasingly going their own ways. They still played bridge together once a week with Ralph and Doreen from next door, and she accompanied him to Bank functions and Rotary Club dinners, and hosted little dinner parties for their friends, but she no longer played golf with him at weekends, preferring to potter in the garden, doing the light work that Mr Blake left to her. Robert was no gardener, neither was he a handyman though in a good-natured way over the years he had put up bookshelves, wired up some spotlights and even built a wardrobe into the smallest bedroom. His hobby was the pursuit and collection of nineteenth-century detective stories, the volumes of which had gradually filled most of his home-made bookshelves, and when he wasn't reading and cataloguing these he was poring over other people's catalogues or, latterly, placing telephone bids at auctions with the growing audacity of increased affluence. The adequate disposal of his collection at the best possible price, in defence to his enthusiasm, had taken Margaret several months to face and then achieve, and after that the bookshelves had stood empty and accusing so that she had either to take them down or fill them with something of her own. Never a collector herself, she then began to collect jugs; old jugs and new jugs, of every shape and size and colour. Under the spreading tide, the shelves began to fill up nicely, and at the same time Margaret began to learn about jugs, and to look for pieces that might be collectable. Thus, part of her memory and her grieving was transmuted into china – shapely and colourful and sometimes even valuable, as fragile as her recently acquired independence.

Of her daughters, Cassie had been the most openly shocked and distraught at the loss of her father. True, she had been there at the time, seen him slumped and slobbering in his chair while she clutched her child protectively to her breast, the half-unwrapped rocking horse forgotten along with his birthday cake and jelly. She had had to stay there alone in the house all the long night, waiting for news, waiting for Sheila to arrive from Liverpool. Sheila, arriving in the small hours, had bullied her into courage, then put them both to bed with the sensible suggestion that there was nothing they could do. It had been Sheila who calmly took the call from Anthony at the hospital next day confirming that there was indeed nothing that anyone could do, now. She hadn't cried, though Cassie had wept and wailed until Robert wailed too, in fright and sympathy, and Sheila, preparing strong coffee and brandy to greet her mother's return, had to talk quite sharply to Cassie, and not admit that her own hands were trembling so that she could hardly lift the kettle.

Gradually, the pain of waking in an empty bed had eased and instead of rising through a black gum of despair Margaret found herself anticipating the day ahead with pleasure. She was forced to acknowledge that for a long time she hadn't really needed Robert – nor perhaps her two daughters either. What was more, neither did she need to feel needed. The realisation introduced an element of liberation into her bereavement which was not without its associated guilt. It seemed to cast a doubt on her worth as a wife and mother, as a human being. To counteract the guilt, she doubled her voluntary work commitments; where she had done Meals on Wheels, now she did Books on Wheels too, taking library books to the elderly and house-bound where she found a new interest in discussing their likes and dislikes, and took a quite extraordinary pleasure in searching the shelves for something that they would especially like to read.

She still played bridge. Ralph and Doreen's plain unmarried daughter, Janet, took Robert's place and, indeed, played rather better than Robert had. Despite or maybe because of his fastidious banker's brain he had been unimaginative and lacking in daring in his play; with Janet as a partner Margaret either won, or lost, with flourish and flair. The idea appealed to her, for flair and flourish was what her life had lacked so far. She began to think of ways that she could change it.

On her first morning in Spain she was woken not by the sun stroking her face as she had so fancifully imagined the night before, but by the donkey braying. The persistent beast was answered in triplicate by the cockerels on the adjoining land and somewhere, in the near distance, several dogs joined in the chorus in the savage feral manner peculiar to dogs south of the English Channel. She rolled over and reached for her clock. It was half-past seven, and just light. Although it was early May, the double summertime in which the Spanish indulged themselves meant that one paid for the long light evenings with late dark mornings. Fortunately, she was familiar with this particular aspect of the Spanish summer and was unsurprised, and anticipation of the day lifted her from her bed in high spirits.

It was bliss to put on a thin skirt and sandals and not to bother with tights. 'This is the life,' she told herself, brushing her hair in front of the dressing-table mirror, which was encompassed and intimidated by its huge scrolled wooden frame. She pulled her hair back behind her neck – it was almost long enough to plait. For years she had had a short, well-cut bob – suddenly, six months ago, she had decided to grow her hair, which was still dark and glossy with only a suggestion of grey. 'I'm not too old for long hair,' she told herself firmly; and she had told Sheila so, too, when she had remarked that her mother needed a haircut, or perhaps a perm.

'I'm fed up with how I look,' she had said. 'For years I have looked the part – your mother, Robert's wife, the wife of a successful banker. Now I'm going to look like ME.'

17

Surprisingly, she had found there was more truth in the defiant words than she knew. She had always thought that 'me' was the person she saw in the mirror every day, the woman who presided over a tasteful and immaculate house, did good works, gardened, played bridge, babysat for her grandson and knitted him pullovers. Suddenly, to her unsettling surprise, she had found that it wasn't.

So she had let her hair grow, winding it up into a tortured bun as soon as it was long enough, or letting it brush her shoulders, held back with combs above her ears. It pleased her, the variety and the combination of freedom and elegance. Worn loose, it slimmed her face which she had always thought plump – swept high, it added interest to her eyes, which were an indeterminate shade of blue. And, she realised, it made her look more like Harriet. Harriet had always worn her hair long, smoothed into a graceful chignon or hanging in a long thick plait down her back. Harriet's hair was quite grey now, but it didn't matter at all. With her long hair and tinted glasses, Harriet always looked artistic, feminine, creative. Yes, there was no harm in looking more like her.

Over breakfast she wrote a few more lines to Harriet, telling her in an amusing way of her noisy awakening and describing the life that passed the kitchen window. In fact she was none too pleased at the convoys of heavy lorries that thundered by; it was after all the main road, though she had been able to ignore this fact on the previous evening, which had also been a Sunday. She didn't mention the lorries to Harriet, telling herself that countless people at home lived quite happily with a similar inconvenience, which she would surely get used to. It must be preferable to living on the flight path to Heathrow, in Kew, as Harriet did. Or rather, as Harriet usually did.

For Harriet had surprised her, less than a week before she left for Spain. It had been about nine o'clock in the evening and Margaret was already dressed for bed, having spent the day turning out the loft and the cupboard under the stairs, having for some complicated reason associated with her flight decided that now was the time to remove the accumulated detritus of the years. She took the call in her bedroom with her feet tucked under the top of the duvet for warmth. It had been a slow, cold spring and the central heating had already switched itself off.

Her friend's voice had sounded different, somehow, as if she were waiting for something.

'Margaret – how are things going?'

'Fine, thanks. The clearing-up's finished, I shall start packing tomorrow. What does one need for a year, I wonder? And do you think I would be mad to take a trunk? It will be so heavy . . .'

'Probably, but then that won't make any difference to you. We're all quite convinced you're off your rocker anyway.'

'Hmmm.' It was as much of a snort as she could make it.

After a pause Harriet said, strangely, 'So you're all set, are you? You really are going?'

'Of course I'm going. I can hardly wait.' Margaret pressed down the flicker of apprehension to which, had she been braver, she would have admitted.

There was another pause. Margaret suppressed a yawn. It had been a busy day. Then Harriet said, 'Well, I was wondering if you could do me a favour actually. I mean, I don't think it will put you out at all, in fact it may actually be a help to you. For a while at least, I don't expect it would be for long . . .'

'Harriet? It's not like you to beat about the bush!'

'No. Well, the fact is, I have to go into hospital.'

'Harriet! My dear – what's wrong?'

'Oh the usual. Woman's troubles.' After a moment she

added, 'Actually I have to have a hysterectomy.' She sounded apologetic as if admitting to a crime.

'Oh, poor you. But that's not the end of the world. Not at our age, anyway. And you'll feel so much better afterwards – your sister did, remember. You've never said you've been feeling ill,' she added accusingly. 'You should have told me.'

'I haven't. Not really. There were just other symptoms – you know, bleeding, all that inconvenience.'

'I know,' Margaret commiserated, though she didn't, never having had a problem and her own bleeding having stopped spontaneously with the shock of Robert's death, when she had thought, Good riddance to all that. 'But what bad timing, just as I'm going away. I can't even come and visit you. And I could have looked after you when you came out. When will you be going in?'

'On Friday. The day you leave, can you believe? But don't worry about visiting. I shall have plenty of visitors. I was wondering, though, if you could help me in another way.'

'What's that? You know I'll do anything . . .'

'Well, can I come and live at Heathercote for a while to convalesce? It would be so much quieter there, and I wouldn't be tempted to "get on with things" as one always is at home. I promise I wouldn't make a mess.'

'A mess! Of course you wouldn't and anyway, what does it matter if you do. And of course you must come. For as long as you like. As you say, it would help to have someone in the house. I was going to give all my houseplants to Cassie to save getting Doreen to water them. You can't ask that of someone for a whole year. But I'll leave them here for you, to cheer the place up a bit.'

'Margaret, you're a love. That's a great relief. I shall look forward to it.'

'And I'll get Cassie to call and keep an eye on you. Are you sure you'll be all right on your own?'

'Actually, I can't imagine anything better. I shall just sit in your lovely garden and listen to the birds sing. And in the evenings I shall play music, and read, and gather my strength. Perhaps I won't even miss you, after all!'

Margaret didn't quite believe her. 'Harriet, you're not worried are you? I mean, it is all quite straightforward, isn't it?'

'Quite straightforward. No cause for alarm. And as you say, it will be a good thing over and done with.'

But Margaret didn't feel quite easy in her mind as she went to bed. For a start, she would have to spring-clean the spare room and make up the bed. Or would it be kinder to let Harriet have the big double bed in her own room? On such perplexing thoughts, she had finally fallen asleep.

She had telephoned the hospital to ask for news, and been blandly assured that all was well, but that Harriet was asleep. Maggie finished her letter with best wishes for her early recovery and signed the letter 'Maggie' with a flourish of bravado, for Maggie it was that she now intended to be called. She addressed the envelope to the Nuffield clinic where Harriet was receiving private treatment. She was glad that over the years Harriet had kept up her BUPA payments; now, she would be indulging herself in the luxury of a private room and a choice of menu without worrying about the stringencies imposed by the cuts in the National Health Service. She finished her own breakfast of coffee and muesli, wondering if such a thing as muesli could be purchased in Spain. She remembered the breakfasts served in most of the hotels she and Robert had visited as comprising lots of fruit but also sweet, sticky cakes and buns, which was a habit she had no intention of getting into.

Then, like a child savouring a present, she passed through the cool, sombre dining room with its heavy carved furni-

21

ture and shiny red and brown tiled floor, and opened the door into her garden.

The air was fresh and sweet with the heady scent of lilac which hung in a white drift against the wall of the house and whose scent had filled her room during the night. Now, standing on the uneven stones of the little paved patio she looked into its branches and breathed deeply in pure delight. Leaning against the house wall was a stiff and faded canvas sunbed which she opened with difficulty and much creaking of its joints, and set it in the patch of early sun which was still sneaking round the end of the house. She judged that there would not be much sunlight on the patio; if she wanted to sunbathe here in private, it would have to be in the morning.

Smiling with satisfaction, she took a few steps down the garden, stepping off the patio onto a patch of uneven weedy grass which dissolved into an untidy tangle of unfamiliar shrubs among which she did recognise a hydrangea, its new leaves tired and wilting, and a pink rose already breaking into bloom and rambling its rampant way up a gnarled apple tree in full blossom. The mingling of pink in the morning sun, the smell of the blossoms, the secret privacy and the tingling possibilities of the little plot made her feel quite weak with happiness and she wanted to cry, to dance, to tell somebody. 'Oh Robert,' she said out loud, suddenly and unreasonably. 'It's so good, like we thought it would be.' But, she told herself, with Robert it wouldn't have been the same, and she knew it to be true.

Just then there was a strange rhythmic sound from the bushes, like a low hoarse bark. Parting the branches of the hydrangea she saw eventually, though disguised by the broken sunlight, a small, thin tabby cat. Its sides were heaving in time with the sound and its head was outstretched, its mouth open and straining. Then it was convulsively sick onto the dry earth. 'Oh,' she said, turning away in pity and disgust, but when she looked back the little cat was sitting facing her, unconcernedly washing itself with a narrow white paw. 'Hello,' she said in English. 'Hello, puss, where do you live I wonder?' The cat ignored her; perhaps it only understood Spanish. *'Cómo te llama?'* she asked, knowing herself to be foolish and wondering if she wasn't already showing signs of loneliness if she was forced to converse with a cat. But now, as if in comprehension, the cat approached her, winding itself round her legs in a slalom of greeting. She felt the silk of its fur against her bare skin with a sensuous pleasure and stooped to stroke it. Through the soft fur she could feel a knobbed backbone and the brittle cage of its ribs. 'Poor little thing,' she murmured. 'Whoever you live with doesn't feed you well. And now you must have found something that disagrees with you. Or perhaps you're just a stray. Like me . . .'

She had a sudden longing to pick the little creature up and take it indoors but knew too well the penalty for feeding a cat. Then, they never left you alone, and maybe someone, somewhere would be looking for it. She stepped back and shooed it gently away. Then she went inside, regretfully closing the door behind her.

As she stepped through into the entrance hall, there was a knock at the door. With a little puzzled thrill of excitement, she opened it and there stood what was obviously the postman. He was holding out two envelopes to her, both bearing English stamps.

'Good morning, señora. You have two letters on your first day. You are a fortunate lady!'

'Fortunate, yes.' She smiled. *'Buenos días, y gracias.'* Still smiling, she closed the door. How many other people, she wondered, knew about her arrival? She glanced down curiously at the envelopes and was unsurprised to recognise the writing of her daughters. Unsurprised, yet strangely not pleased and at the same time guilty at her displeasure. She opened Sheila's first. It was a blank card, with a picture of roses on the front. Inside she had written, 'You're bound to be feeling strange and homesick, and not surprisingly. Don't worry – no one will mind if you just pack up and come home. Meanwhile, I hope the journey went smoothly, it was a lot to take on on your own. Take care of yourself and let us know how things are going. Love Sheila.'

Margaret snorted scornfully. So she was homesick, was she? She couldn't wait to tell her daughter otherwise. She opened the other envelope. Cassie had chosen a picture of a thatched cottage with a cat sitting at the gate, and 'Welcome Home' printed across a blue sky of puffy white clouds and smiling birds. 'Hi, Mum,' she had written in her rounded scrawl. 'I hope this is there to greet you and that you are feeling marvellous. You are *so* brave, I wish I could be as brave. It will be horrible knowing you're not there on the other side of town. Robert and Anthony join me in sending lots of love and kisses – Cassie. PS, I think I am starting flu, or perhaps it's just a summer cold.'

Margaret sighed. She didn't really want to know. She didn't want to be missed, she didn't want to be reminded that if Cassie was ill she would need some help with Robert. She didn't want to be told she felt strange and homesick – nor, perversely, that she was brave. She didn't want the obligation of feeling marvellous either. She left the cards on the kitchen table then, ashamed because they were after all from her daughters, fetched them and stood them in the living room beside her radio. She had to admit that it made it look like home. Into her irritation mingled a confusing mix of love and gratitude. She went into the bedroom and screwed her hair into a high, scrawny ponytail. So what if she was trying to look sixteen? Who was there here to care? She picked up the large canvas shopping bag she had last used in Sainsbury's in Guildford and, with neither a shopping list nor a cardigan, slammed and locked the front door and set off in search of some provisions.

The first shop she came to was a butcher's. She stood outside examining the few strangely cut slabs of meat. The lamb looked dark and tough but there was veal, pallid and fine-grained, and some large purplish legs of something that may well have been dog, though she thought not. She studied the prices, mentally converting and comparing and deciding it wasn't cheap. But then small shops in small towns never were. She passed on down the street, nodding and smiling to other women who nodded and smiled back without comment save a slipped '. . . *nos días*', which she returned. Further along the road there was a familiar red sign reading 'Spar' above the cluttered window of a grocer's shop. Inside, all was superficially familiar; the customary pile of bent blue baskets, the freezer cabinets and stacked tins and packets. She took a basket and began to browse thoughtfully along the shelves, sifting and sorting, finally settling for biscuits which she knew would be a poor imitation of McVitie's, some tins of tuna, red beans in oil and soup which promised to be tomato.

The bread was all packaged and limp so she passed on by and came to the cheese counter. Here, a bewildering array of unappetising-looking cheeses lay on straw on wooden pallets. '*Cómo se llama?*' she asked of the young pale assistant, pointing at a creamy slab. '*Es bueno?*'

'*Si, muy bueno. Es queso Teta Larsa*. A Galician cheese.'

'*Vale*. Okay. Half a kilo, *por favor*.'

The cheese was cut and wrapped, the little transaction completed and she went on her way with pride. She may not like the cheese, which was sticky and soft, but she had made her purchase. At the checkout she asked the woman, timidly, where she could find some bread and was directed back towards the shelves at the rear of the shop.

Margaret shook her head. 'No. Thank you. I would like

25

some different bread. Without the . . . paper.' She waited, hopefully, while the woman gazed at her without comprehension.

Then, from behind her and entirely taking her by surprise she heard a masculine voice, unmistakably British, saying, 'You want some proper bread. Not this plastic stuff! You'd best come with me and I will introduce you to our baker.'

She took the strange coinage of her change and half turned to look at the speaker. She saw a grey-haired man of military bearing wearing a crisp short-sleeved khaki shirt and long white shorts. Meeting her eye he gave a half-salute.

'Major Tyson at your service, madam. We heard you were coming, so allow me to be of help.'

Outside the shop, the Major bent to release a dog who was lying patiently in the shade, his nose on his paws. The dog leaped up eagerly, his upcurved, feathery tail waving. He was a foxy creature with thick reddish fur and a pointed face.

'Oh, a Finnish spitz,' said Maggie in delight. 'Such an attractive breed.' She held out her hand and the dog nosed it.

The Major sounded pleased by her approval. 'His name is Finn. Been with me a long time. Don't know what I'd do without him.'

Grasping the lead he set a brisk pace along the dusty edge of the road, Finn keeping admirably to heel and looking as military as his master.

'Edna and I came out here nine years ago,' the Major told her. 'When I retired. Then she went and died on me. I decided to stay. Used to the sunshine and all that – can't see myself now in an English winter somehow.'

'But the weather can be quite rough here, I believe.' Margaret was puffing like a new recruit on the parade ground. 'I've seen it rain cats and dogs, even in July.'

'Yes – well it's not like English rain. And the wine's cheap! Now here's our baker chappie – it's the best you'll get round here. Quite a choice as you can see. So long as you get here early.'

It was true. The small dark window was piled with crusty loaves, round and square, long and flat. Margaret took her turn among the small gaggle of women inside. The insistent flow of their conversation stopped briefly as they regarded her with dark curious eyes, and one or two of them smiled.

'*Buenos días*,' she said, looking friendly.

When it was her turn she chose a flat round yellowish loaf and some white bread rolls because there didn't seem to be any wholemeal. Outside the shop she said, 'Bother, I meant to get some wine. I'll have to go back to Spar.'

'No problem, dear lady. Let me carry your bag.' He took it without waiting for a reply. 'You managed that very well, very well,' he went on. 'Got on top of the old lingo, eh? Can't say I've ever really mastered it. Edna was the one, prattled away like a native, she did. Is your husband joining you out here?'

She was taken aback, still not used to having to explain her widowhood. 'No,' she answered finally. 'My husband died last year, I'm afraid.'

'Ah. I'm sorry about that. Rotten business. It's been nearly three years now for me and I still find myself looking for her. Still, you're obviously a gutsy woman, coming out here alone.'

'Oh, I don't know about that . . .'

'If there's ever anything you need, just let me know. Do you have a telephone?'

'There is one, yes . . .'

'I'll give you my number. You must come round some-time, have a drink. Or a swim. I've got one of the new villas up the hill. About two miles out of town. Walk in every day – have to have my little constitutional.' He patted his flat stomach with satisfaction. 'Keeps me in trim. That, and a few turns of the pool each day. Do you play bridge?'

'Bridge? Yes, I do as a matter of fact.'

'Good. Splendid. We've been wanting a fourth since Edna died. Can't get any of the locals interested. Would you care for a hand sometime?'

'Well . . .' It wasn't something she had been expecting

28

but it would seem ungracious to refuse outright. 'Well, if you think . . .'

'Of course I do. And you'll need something to do with your evenings. How about tomorrow? I expect the Erskines will be free. They can't get about much now.'

'Oh?' It seemed polite to show an interest in the Erskines.

'Chloe. She's an invalid, poor girl. Multiple sclerosis. Or muscular dystrophy – never sure which is which. Some such thing. Lovely girl! Only forty-three. But she plays a good hand of bridge – or she used to. I'll ask them. Now – which wine do you fancy?'

When he finally left her at her door Margaret's head was buzzing from his questions and advice, and her feet ached. She reflected reluctantly that it would be polite to ask him in for coffee but he said, 'Must love you and leave you. I've shopping of my own to do. I'll pick you up tomorrow, about seven, in case you can't find your way. There'll be a light supper first, that suit you?' She nodded. 'By the way, name's Nigel. Nigel Tyson. And you are . . . ?'

'Maggie,' she told him experimentally. 'Maggie Fairbrother.'

He held out his hand. 'Suits you,' he commented, looking at her appreciatively. He gave her hand a firm clasp. 'Until tomorrow, Maggie. *Hasta la vista* and all that!' And he turned on his heel with military precision and marched away, his plimsolls puffing up little rhythmic squirts of dust.

She put on the copper kettle and unpacked her shopping, opening the cheese paper and pulling off an experimental corner with her finger. It was good; creamy and cool. She wished she had a cold larder to keep it in, rather than the fridge. The kitchen would get hot as the sun moved round. She dropped the Venetian blinds and as she did so saw Madrilena running by. The child smiled and waved but didn't stop. Margaret was curiously disappointed.

*       *       *

29

She was sitting on the first-floor terrace with her bare legs stretched out in the sun and a Spanish dictionary on the table beside her when she saw the little cat again. Suddenly aware of a scrabbling below her she looked over the railing and there it was, clawing and pushing its way up the gnarled vine which had spread along the railings from the adjacent house. Its persistence had an edge of desperation as it fixed its huge green eyes on hers and struggled the last few inches to the top. Then it balanced there, calm and relaxed, its scruffy tabby coat shining in the sun.

'Well, there's nothing much wrong with you, is there, puss?' She reached out to stroke the taut back and the cat arched with pleasure. A vibrant purr out of all proportion to its small frame reverberated beneath her fingers as she scratched its chin. Then, with a fluid leap, it was on her lap and reaching up towards her chin.

'You're very friendly. I wonder who you belong to?' Experimentally, she repeated it in Spanish, feeling for the words. She reached for the dictionary, unsure of the word for cat. '*Gato. El gato.* Well . . .' she laughed to herself. 'Well, *gato* – I shall call you Cake! That will confuse you good and proper.'

Looking anything but confused, the little creature curled into a ball and fell instantly asleep, which seemed to settle the matter. He – or she – was here to stay, and would later be sharing her tuna fish supper.

She had forgotten to post Harriet's letter, though she remembered seeing the little post office as the Major had marched her by. Not being sure of the opening times she decided to join the natives in a siesta after lunch, stretching out luxuriously on the high bed and feeling not in the least bit guilty. After a while Cake joined her, leaping lightly up onto the coverlet and pressing against her hip in a warm vibrating ball. Gently, they slid together into sleep, from which Maggie was eventually awakened by the raucous squawk of chickens being fed. She looked at her clock, amazed to see that it was four o'clock. The sun would already be sliding down the sky. She had been here just twenty-four hours! The cat stretched alongside her, yawning pinkly, showing sharp teeth, looking as relaxed and at home as she felt herself. Live and let live, she thought generously, ignoring the intrusive noise as she splashed her hands and face in the bathroom. At least the convoy of lorries seemed to have ceased during the course of the morning; and her siesta, surely the most civilised of customs, had been uninterrupted.

She made herself lemon tea, giving Cake a saucerful of milk, which he lapped eagerly, and some crumbled biscuits. Then she took Harriet's letter and her purse and let herself out of the house, waiting for the cat to follow, which he didn't, and later, turning back as she crossed the street, she saw him watching her from the table on the terrace. It was strangely comforting to know he would be waiting for her return.

At the post office she posted Harriet's letter and bought a quantity of stamps for England, telling herself she must write soon to Cassie and Sheila. She asked the clerk where she could buy some postcards of the town and, eventually understanding her, he shook his head. There were no postcards in Gondomar, but at the coast, in Baiona perhaps, there she could buy beautiful postcards of her holiday. 'Oh, I am not on holiday,' Maggie explained, smiling. 'I have come to live here.'

'Ah,' acknowledged the clerk. 'In Señor Velasquez's house, of course. You are welcome in our town, señora,' and he leaned over the counter and shook her hand vigorously as if priming a pump. 'If there is anything you want, please ask me or my wife. We live upstairs.'

'Thank you. You are very kind. My name is Maggie Fairbrother.'

31

The clerk nodded, but did not offer his own name, perhaps preferring the anonymity of his official capacity. Walking back along the shady side of the street, Margaret wondered what it must be like for him, to spend his days in the small, quiet office with its ageing piles of official forms and documents and the old brass letter scales. Other people's lives, spent in such various ways and such diverse settings, far from her own experience, fascinated her, the more so for being impossible to imagine. Equally intriguing was the thought that her own erstwhile life back in Surrey in the pleasant detached house with its fitted carpets and lined curtains, surrounded by carefully tended green lawns, would be equally unimaginable, strange and probably unappealing to the residents of Gondomar with their crumbling façades facing the dusty, weedy road, their dark interiors secretive behind rampant vines and roses.

Punctually at seven the following evening the Major drew up outside in a dusty 2CV which had once been bright yellow, was now as khaki as his shorts. Maggie waved to him from the terrace. 'Come on up for a moment. The door's open,' she called, feeling pleasantly informal.

'Right. Yes!' he agreed briskly, bounding in through the door and up the stairs. She met him in the sitting room where he took her hand with a flourish. 'Maggie. Delightful to see you again. And how well all this suits you.' He glanced round the room and out onto the terrace which was now adorned with several red and pink geraniums in stone tubs which she had bought that morning. His appreciation seemed to include her own sun-rouged skin and the long cotton skirt she had wrapped beneath a white cotton blouse. 'Our little town is obviously agreeing with you, you look quite at home.'

'And I've been adopted,' she laughed, nodding down at Cake, who was curled on one of the floral chairs, sound asleep after a tuna supper. 'Cake has come to live with me, it seems.'

'Cake?' The Major was mystified, but he had told her he had never mastered the language.

'Just a silly idea of mine,' she explained apologetically. 'Perhaps the sun has gone to my head! Would you like a glass of wine, the Sauternes we chose was excellent . . .'

He shook his head. 'Another time perhaps. I have left the Erskines drinking my own and they are eager to meet you. Do you have a wrap? The evening will be cool.'

She had considered a cardigan, now picked up instead an Indian shawl and her bag in one hand, and the sleeping cat in the other, putting him gently onto the terrace and closing the doors. Then, feeling both curious and faintly anxious, like a teenager on a date, she following Nigel Tyson out to his car.

The road rose swiftly up into the low hills outside the town between pungent drooping eucalyptus trees and small oaks. After a mile or so, white villas appeared among the trees, crisp as sugar cubes with a backdrop of the little town in a rosy haze below. At the third, the Major stopped the car. 'Here we are, Maggie. A small thing, but my own. No, stay where you are a moment. Manners maketh man!' He got out and came round to her door, ceremoniously opening it and helping her out. Maggie stifled a smile, feeling grateful for his warm hand under her elbow as she eased herself out of the little car. They walked round the house onto a terrace which was catching the last of the sun and where the Erskines were waiting beside the blue water of a small swimming pool.

Chloe Erskine, she saw with a shock, was in a wheelchair. Lorne, standing up to introduce himself, was a broad six foot or more which seemed to swamp even Margaret's five foot nine and towered over his seated wife.

'We're very pleased to meet you. Maggie, isn't it? We are somewhat starved of new company. This is my wife, Chloe . . .'

Chloe held out a thin hand with a surprisingly strong grip. 'As my husband says, I'm very pleased to meet you,' she said with an undercurrent of irritation. Margaret guessed she was suffering from the 'does he take sugar' syndrome which afflicted the disabled. She gave her a wide smile which she hoped conveyed her understanding of the woman's predicament.

'And I am more that delighted to meet you. I hadn't expected to find company quite so soon.'

'Oh, we're not company, we're just us.' The Major filled a glass and handed it to her.

'But would you have minded? If you hadn't?' Chloe was looking at her curiously so that an answer seemed to be required.

'I don't know.' It was true; in all the excitement and anticipation of her escape, Margaret realised she had never seriously wondered how, and with whom, she would spend her days. It had been enough to be doing something of her own, and on her own. But had she expected to remain alone? And could she have coped, after all? How eagerly she had welcomed the cat into her home, how wistfully she awaited Madrilena's return.

'Perhaps you came here to be alone?' It was Lorne, also looking at her seriously over his glass. He had fine grey eyes under thick greying hair and his face looked drawn and used, more so than his wife's whose skin was smooth and strangely untroubled despite the dark stains beneath her brown eyes.

'I don't think so. I came because I *am* now alone. I don't know what I was expecting. Perhaps – adventure?' She gave them all what she hoped was a mischievous and daring grin, not yet ready for the confessional.

To her relief the Major added, 'And the sunshine and the wine – like the rest of us,' which satisfactorily lightened the tone. She suppressed a smile as he added, 'Bottoms up,' before tilting his glass and draining it dry. She might have expected 'Cheers' and a universal ceremonious clinking of glasses which she deplored; the Major's injunction spoke more of the bar parlour than the officers' mess and she risked a glance sideways at the Erskines. Finding no reaction she told herself that they were, of course, used to him. The unkind word 'buffoon' filtered into her mind, to be suppressed guiltily along with the smile. If he was, then he was a harmless one, and it was to him that she owed her seat by the pool with the fine view of the town, and the prospect of a pleasant evening ahead.

In the event, it didn't turn out quite as expected. First, they didn't play bridge, though it was mentioned once or twice both by Lorne and by the Major. Chloe however did not seem enthusiastic, and watching her handling her glass clumsily with long uncertain fingers Margaret guessed that to manage a hand of cards was now beyond her. She felt a sadness for this woman whom she didn't yet know, despite the challenge in her eyes that she personally found rather off-putting. Catching Lorne's expression as he rescued the glass which seemed to be slipping from her fingers, she was surprised by an even stronger feeling of pity for him.

The Major was entertaining them with a story which the Erskines had clearly heard before but which they politely endured. 'Well, the poor chap obviously hadn't understood a word I said because he came back with a can of oil – when all I wanted was the windscreen washed. It would make life a lot easier if the natives spoke English!'

'You're a great one for proverbs – haven't you ever heard of "when in Rome"?' interrupted Chloe with surprising tartness.

Margaret looked at her in alarm but the Major merely beamed affably, responding quickly, 'But I'm never actually in Rome, my dear. I'm just a rolling stone, gathering no moss.'

'Well, you seem to have gathered quite a bit about you here,' joined in Margaret quickly, glancing round at the pool and the terrace and the neat sloping garden dropping away from them towards the village, which was now just a small glitter of lights.

'Ah, that was Edna, not me. She was always the home-maker, on our travels. Making little nests here and there.'

'But you're going to stay here? I mean, do you feel you've put down roots?'

'As far as I have roots anywhere, dear lady. Anyway, where else is there to go?' For a moment his crisp, amiable face looked genuinely perplexed, a little lost.

Suddenly Lorne interrupted, 'It's getting late. Didn't you say something about some supper, Nigel? Only we didn't eat. Chloe will be getting hungry.'

'No she won't, and I'm not. If you're hungry, just say so. I can speak for myself.' Chloe was gripping the arms of her chair with her thin fingers and her dark eyes seemed to flash out in the faint light. Unperturbed, Lorne leaned towards her, smoothing the thin hair back from her fore-head. 'But you must eat, my darling. You need to keep your strength up.'

Margaret was unable to see his expression but something about his hand on Chloe's head and the closeness of their faces made her unable to look and she got up quickly saying, 'Perhaps I can help you, Nigel. And I'd very much like to see indoors . . .'

He leaped up with alacrity. 'Certainly, my dear, certainly. Though you'll find it sadly lacking, I'm afraid. Sadly lacking . . . Are you hungry too? My apologies for not thinking. I've made some sandwiches. Or I started them at least . . .'

36

She followed him through the sliding patio doors into an unlit room where she stopped, uncertain of her route until he turned on the light in a doorway at the far end, enabling her to follow him into the kitchen. At the door, she stopped, shocked and surprised, but quickly covering her astonishment in the face of his embarrassed expression as he followed her gaze.

'I don't seem to manage things very well on my own, as you see. I did try and warn you . . .'

'Indeed . . .'

'You see what I mean?'

His discomfiture made her uneasy. 'Yes . . .'

'I don't suppose . . .' He nodded towards the table where there was evidence of some attempt at sandwich making. Realising to her surprise, both at her own perception and at his helpless audacity, that this was precisely what he had intended, Margaret found herself agreeing to complete the sandwiches, but with a spurt of resistance she heard herself adding briskly, 'I'll do that if you clear up a bit. There's no room to move. And fetch me a plate to put them on.'

She moved from the table the plates from which presumably he had eaten his last meal and squeezed a space for them on the draining board. Sheepishly offering her a willow-pattern plate he said, 'Need a woman about the place, don't you see?' His expression was entreating as if asking for allowances to be made.

'Nonsense, you're quite capable, I'm sure.' She was surprised at her lack of sympathy, her almost rudeness. Nigel – for she supposed she must think of him as that – was after all her host, however ineffectual. More kindly she continued, 'It only takes a bit of organisation, you know. Certain places for certain things, keeping up to date. The sink, for instance . . .'

'Ah yes, I was seeing to that when the telephone rang.'

Obediently, he turned hot water onto a pile of crockery

and began stuffing limp lettuce leaves and a mouldy cucumber into a plastic refuse sack. She wrapped a crumpled tea towel round her waist to protect her skirt and busied herself with knife and butter greasy from the heat, laying chicken and tomato neatly between the unevenly hacked bread and hoping that the Erskines were used to the Major's rough-and-ready hospitality. Images of Chloe's uncertain fingers clasping the thick sandwiches were interspersed with memories of the tense anguish in Lorne's voice, the way he had stroked her hair . . .

'Where do Chloe and Lorne live?' she asked.

He crumpled the sack shut, leaning it against a cupboard door. 'Have to wait another week for this lot to be collected. You'd think they'd manage more than once a fortnight in this climate . . . Another mile or so up the road. An old farmhouse. Lorne paints, made himself a studio. Good light . . .' His voice trailed off vaguely. Then, glancing at the loaded sink, he said, 'I'm afraid I'm not a very good housewife!' The grin he gave her then was roguish, inviting tolerance, complicity, assistance . . .

'So it seems.' She looking reprovingly at the bags and packages squabbling for space on the worktop. 'You could put that shopping away perhaps?'

Obediently once more he began to unpack the tins and bottles and packets, stuffing them into cluttered cupboards at random, and once more she was surprised that she should speak to him so, surprised and uneasy that she could care that he lived in a disorder that verged on the unwholesome. She had come away to be free, irresponsible, uncluttered. Already, she was taking control, meeting a need. It wouldn't do, it wouldn't do at all.

When finally they carried out onto the verandah the sandwiches and a pot of coffee and a sticky shop-bought cake of indeterminate age and quality, the light had faded completely. The Erskines' faces under the verandah lamps were etched with the lines and shadows of a tension which bristled round Margaret as she moved the empty glasses and set out plates and cups on the wrought-iron table. She thought, How different this is. At our bridge evenings the supper was always carefully prepared beforehand, dainty sandwiches with the crusts removed set out on a trolley with home-made cakes and biscuits, embroidered napkins and pretty bone china. There were no insects gathered in a death dance round the lights, just the hiss and sigh of a log on the fire, an amiable postmortem on the last hand played. But then, we haven't played a hand, which is per- haps just as well . . . Pouring coffee for Chloe she met the fierce eyes with a glance she hoped was understanding. There seemed to be a rage inside the younger woman, a rage and a frustration which was understandable. 'Can you manage?' she heard herself asking, then, irritated at her own question, added, 'Of course you can, I'm so sorry,' pushing the cup towards her and offering a sandwich, which Chloe took with a smile and no surprise.

Lorne on the other hand took his without a smile, staring past her at the lights below them in the valley. Annoyed, Margaret said, 'I hear you're an artist, Mr Erskine. What medium do you paint in?'

'Oils, watercolour . . .' Seemingly reluctant he swivelled his eyes towards her. 'And please call me Lorne, Maggie.' Then he smiled and the craggy lines of his face reformed into a more youthful warmth. She felt she saw him briefly as he must have been, before things had gone wrong for him and Chloe.

'And what do you paint? The scenery here is wonderful . . .'

'It is. And the light. But really I prefer portraiture. It's what I used to do, before.'

'Before we came to live in Spain.' Chloe's interjection was final, delivered in a flat, firm voice that brooked no argument. 'Can I have another sandwich, Nigel? I am hungry, after all.'

Nigel said, 'Maggie made them. They're good, aren't they? I left her to it. Too many cooks, and all that!' He beamed as he passed the plate, but then sat back, silent, in the shadows.

Margaret struggled to keep the conversation going. In society as she knew it, convention dictated that one took an interest in one's companions, contributed something to the gathering in which one found oneself. But this was not like the society she knew and she felt she was struggling alone. 'So what do you paint now?' she asked, thinking that after all it only succeeded in sounding nosy, not interested at all.

After what seemed like an unnecessary time spent chewing and swallowing Lorne did grant her an answer. 'I'm doing a series of still lifes. And landscapes. I'm hoping to have an exhibition in Santiago. One of the hotels stages them occasionally. It's something to work for, at least.'

He reached out a long hand and took another sandwich, delivering it direct to his mouth hungrily. Margaret did so too, deciding that to help herself was quite in order. Nigel was sitting quietly, drinking a glass of wine which he had filled from somewhere. His coffee sat untouched before him.

Summoning enthusiasm Margaret said, 'It must be wonderful to be creative. I wish I was . . .'

'Nonsense!' It was Chloe who, after making tentative approaches to her second sandwich now put it down on her plate which she pushed away dismissively. 'All women are creative in some form or another. Do you have children?'

'Well, yes . . .'

'Well then. Motherhood is the very essence of creativity. You gave birth, for a start. And don't tell me you didn't mould your children, try and turn them into something you wanted them to be. Even if it was for the most selfish of reasons.'

Margaret was startled. 'Yes, I suppose so. But then that's just instinct, isn't it? And the lowest life form can give birth, there's nothing so very consciously creative about that.'

'But isn't it enough that you have done it? Made a life, where there was none before? It seems to me that should be cause for satisfaction in itself.'

'Not always.' Margaret thought resentfully that over the years there had been precious little satisfaction in her daughters. Rather, disappointment, guilt, anxiety and regret and questioning; latterly, resentment at a responsibility which seemed never to be lifted from her, and from which, finally, she had run. Resenting too Chloe's aggressively critical manner she asked, 'Do you have children? Has it been enough for you?'

Chloe said quietly, 'No, we don't have children.' She picked up her cup and pretended to drink.

'But Chloe is a poet.' Lorne spoke quietly too, but with a definite defensive pride. 'She has had several volumes published, and still writes now . . .' It was obviously a mistake.

Chloe bridled once more. 'Is that so very amazing? I do still have a brain, even if I sometimes can't hold the pencil!'

There was a silence. Margaret shifted uneasily, unused to scenes and innuendos, to washing one's dirty linen in public. She caught Nigel's eye. Rising suddenly to his responsibilities he said, 'Chloe has a word processor! Most amazing thing I ever saw. Always prided myself on my typing, but this knocks the old Remington into a cocked hat. Have you ever seen one in action, Maggie?'

'No, I can't say I have. And I never really mastered typing anyway.'

'But you don't need to with a word processor. Do you,

Chloe?' Lorne looked at Chloe, cajoling her into benevolence. He turned to Margaret. 'Chloe wouldn't be without it anyway. Would you, darling?'

'No,' she snapped. 'No, not if you say so. And I think we should be going.' Without waiting for his agreement she moved her hands across the wheels of her chair, easing it out to pass behind Margaret, who pulled her chair obligingly nearer the table to let her through. The wheelchair passed perilously close to the edge of the pool but Chloe didn't appear to notice.

'I'm sorry,' Lorne seemed to whisper as he stood up and took Margaret's hand in a brief farewell clasp. 'She gets tired. It was pleasant to meet you. Perhaps you'd like to come to us sometime. See the studio?' He lowered his voice still further. 'Chloe's not always like this, she has her better days. We both do.'

'I understand. Really I do.' She smiled brightly to reinforce this. 'And I should be delighted to come. Will you invite me sometime? It would be better, I think. My telephone number is three six three, which is easy to remember. It's so nice having a three-figure number, after all those awful digits at home!'

Lorne's answering smile was another reminder of how things must have been, once. Watching him grasp her chair and guide her into the darkness Margaret thought that Chloe had been a very lucky woman.

She still was.

# FOUR

A letter arrived from Harriet. It began with expressions of pleasure at Maggie's 'happy landing' and touched briefly on her own slowly recovering health. But to Maggie's surprise there were several more closely written pages, and she read on curiously. What, in the circumstances, could her friend have found to say?

You will forgive me, if I indulge myself in some nostalgia, for I am full of sentimental thoughts about us both. Maybe it is being here alone in your house. Maybe it is feeling weaker than I am used to, or perhaps it is because I feel obscurely that I have lost you, that I find my mind wandering back to how we began.

Did I ever tell you how you seemed to me, that first day at the grammar school – you all crisp and neat in your new poplin blouse and regulation navy skirt – me in my sister's castoffs, my hair cobbled into plaits as a concession to 'big school'? They were fastened with elastic bands – how I longed for crisp navy ribbons like yours!

I was delighted when I found us sitting next to each other in that shiny classroom, smelling of paint and hot radiators. In those days, schools got repainted fairly regularly – not like now. I remember introducing myself and asking you your name. Do you remember?

Maggie smiled and found herself nodding. Yes, she remembered. Harriet had then asked her if she had brothers and sisters. 'I have four, two of each,' Harriet had told her, and Margaret, as she then was, had felt a wild envy for she

43

had only had one brother, but he had died in infancy of a congenital heart disease. She had told Harriet this hesitantly, wary of her pity, but Harriet had only smiled and asked, 'Shall we be friends?' and Margaret had said, 'I should like that very much.'

She returned to the letter. There was much to come and she was both curious and moved.

> That was over forty years ago. It seems impossible that we can say that – it seems longer than I have lived. I marvel at my longevity – at our joint longevity. At our sheer staying power. And now, when I seem to be failing, you have given me your home to hide in, to lick my wound while it heals, and regather my resources. Oh Margaret – Maggie – I wish I could feel it would be as easy as that. I wish I could feel that they are telling me the whole truth, those men in white coats with notes and clipboards who advise me to give it time, be patient and take things easy. I'm not used to pain or weariness. My body has gone slack, my brain too, atrophied from a wilful neglect.

Maggie lowered the pages, her face creased with concern. This was not like Harriet. Harriet had always been the purposeful, positive one, forging ahead with her law degree, while she, Margaret, had opted out of her A levels. Her parents and her teachers had told her she was wasting herself, she should pursue her plans to go to art school and be an art teacher, but she left school none the less, got a job in a bank where she met Robert, and married him when she was just twenty-one.

Did she regret it? Staring aimlessly down into the street from her sunny terrace, Maggie remembered that she had enjoyed being a counter clerk, dressed in crisp blouses, flicking through notes with a deft precision before passing them over to the customer with a bright smile. Robert had encouraged her to take some banking exams, but she lost interest. Maybe it was because she didn't need to work, and was happier in their neat little house on an estate in Reigate, furnishing it in tasteful conventional style and, later, adorning her children with the same care.

The thought of the girls brought her back to reality. Was that where she had gone wrong – right back at the beginning? Not wishing to pursue the thought, she returned to Harriet's letter.

In the past, whenever I've felt down, I could always rely on you and Robert and your restful, quiet home for consolation. In the crowded house I grew up in, peace and privacy were at a premium. For that reason, I loved visiting your parents' house. Your own home was just the same. I envied you, of course – your husband, your children. Did you realise that? Robert was such a support to you, his only interest other than his family being his books. I remember them now, and rather regret their absence from your house – the ranks of red, gold and green, with pictorial and decorated blocking on the spines, a few half-bound in leather. I learned quite a lot about those books from Robert. Did you?

I remember when I came to tell you about Jake, almost mad with shock and disgust, you burst into tears of sympathy, but Robert provided a steadying hand. It was hard to admit that Jake had left me – worse still that it was for another man! What I never told you, Maggie, was that I had been falling in love with that other man myself. A bitter irony, almost funny! I have waited all this time to share the joke.

Maggie felt pain but only mild surprise at her friend's revelation. It was so long ago. Cassie had been about two. Sometime during the evening she had woken, troubled perhaps by some disturbed vibration in the air. To her surprise, Harriet remembered it too.

Cassie suddenly appeared at the door, wearing a pink fluffy sleeping suit I had given her for Christmas. She looked like a warm soft peach, and do you know, Maggie, that gave me an ache that had nothing to do with a man, for I suddenly knew that I would never have such a succulent treasure of my own. I was thirty-two. A successful solicitor with a partnership on the cards. But I would never be a mother – and sadly I have been proved right.

Thinking about Cassie – that was one surprise you sprang on us all – not her birth, which had been planned, announced and eagerly awaited, but her name. You simply insisted on Cassandra. After Sheila, it seemed a little odd! I never mentioned it at the time, I supposed you had your reasons.

Oh yes, thought Maggie, I had my reasons all right. I was nearly thirty and was drowning in a sea of respectability and conformity. Cassandra was a last grasp at a glamour and excitement which I had never wanted until then, and had seen the door closing upon irrevocably.

Harriet asked me once if I was content. She meant without a job. It was true that I sometimes wondered if Robert would find me more interesting if I was like Harriet, with a career. But my pride made me answer, 'Robert likes to feel he's looking after us all. And I have my voluntary work. I'm not entirely useless.'

Stretching her legs to the sun, Maggie tried to pull her mind back to the present. Such introspection was making her feel unaccountably depressed and anxious. She didn't like to think of Harriet, alone and sick, full of maudlin thoughts of the past. She didn't want them herself. But there was one more paragraph to read.

Just as you have your reasons now. You have become someone I don't know, who stands barefoot in the sun-

shine stroking a cat called Cake; who writes about somebody called Nigel who lives in squalor and whom I shall
probably never know. While I am lying on your sofa,
with the purple fringed shawl you draped over the back
now lying across my legs. Since when have you gone in
for fringed shawls? Since Robert died, it seems to me.
Since you sold his books, and grew your hair, and started
putting garlic into everything.

My dear – since you became Maggie!

Indeed, thought Maggie, smiling with satisfaction. Harriet,
at least, has understood.

# FIVE

Each time she came to write to Sheila and Cassie, Maggie experienced a paralysing reluctance to reconnect. It was as if by acknowledging them, she was acknowledging too their claims on her. To write to them, to let them into her new life, would also be to reopen the pipeline through which flowed the pain and complexity of both her love for them and her disappointment. She would be reminded once more of her failings as a mother, her own growing inclination to opt out which had culminated in her rebellious disaffection. She had put hundreds of miles between them, yet the cords of commitment and contention were hard to break. The thinner they stretched, the tighter they grew.

Even while she prevaricated, her guilt grew. Sheila might be twenty-seven and Cassie twenty-three, but she was still their mother. And while Cassie had Anthony and Robert, Sheila had nobody.

Not that she would ever admit she needed anyone. Sheila would have everyone believe that her case-load as a social worker was all the commitment she needed in her life. She didn't need to 'justify her space'; neither did she need support. Margaret wished she could completely believe that this was so. Remembering herself at that age she knew she had been profoundly grateful for Robert and her safe and ordered family life. She had been happy, then, to be loved. Only now, since Robert's death, did she really doubt that she had actually needed any of it at all. She had found she could be surprisingly self-sufficient on an emotional level, to the point of resenting the claims of family and friends.

Apart from Harriet. But then she had never felt that Harriet made claims upon her. Harriet had always been so admirably self-assured, so much to be envied, so completely at ease with herself. Even during the dreadful days after Jake had left her, Harriet had exuded an air of flamboyant suffering so far removed from anything that Margaret had ever experienced that it was almost impossible to pity her. In fact, a small secret part of Margaret had actually envied this disaster which, if nothing else, was out of the ordinary. Trust Harriet to have her marriage collapse with flair, with style, with drama. Oh it had been shocking, disgusting even, and Margaret remembered the easy tears which had flowed initially on behalf of her friend. Looking back, she wondered sometimes if some of the tears had in fact been for herself, locked as she was in her safe impermeable casket of security.

It was ridiculous to find that, after all these years of knowing her daughters, it was now hard to decide how to address them on paper. She had been used to seeing Cassie several times a week, more often than she herself would have chosen, but others thought her fortunate, especially when young Robert arrived. 'You've no idea how lucky you are to have your grandson near enough to come to tea,' Helen Armstrong had told her as they lugged the heavy wire baskets of library books round a sheltered housing estate. Helen's daughter lived in Scotland, and when she visited, it was for a week at a time. 'I'm always exhausted after two days, and unable to enjoy any of them.'

'But at least you're not landed with them when they're teething, or grizzling with a cold.' Margaret had known by the looks when she dared to express such sentiments that she was deemed to be unnatural, selfish even. That was what mothers and grandmothers were for, the looks told her. Just as she had to endure Sheila's weekly perorations over the telephone from Liverpool. The iniquities of the social services system, the loopholes in the welfare state,

the profligacy of the recipients and the impossibility of keeping up with her work-load were all grist to Sheila's mill.
When asked, tentatively, if she didn't find the work
satisfying none the less, which was after all the impression
she always strove to create, Sheila would answer brusquely,
'There are various forms of satisfaction, Mother, and struggling to fill an infinite need with finite resources is hardly
one of them. But then you couldn't be expected to know
that really.'

'Why not?' Margaret would bristle. Bristling seemed to be
her customary reaction to Sheila. Always on the defensive,
while at the same time feeling a deep, wordless pity for the
girl which she was unable to give expression to.

And Sheila would answer, 'Well, you've always had
things very easy, haven't you?'

'I do my voluntary work.' It annoyed Margaret that she
should feel the need to justify herself. 'I've been lucky, I
know. But I do try to do my bit.' The silence on the end of
the telephone spoke volumes. 'Sheila? Are you still there?'

'Yes, Mother. I'm sorry you don't understand. I know
I'm a bit of a bore on the subject, I won't go on about it
again.'

But next week, of course, she did.

Picking up her pen yet again Maggie asked herself, not
for the first time, how Sheila would manage without her
receptive ear on the other end of the telephone. She had
purposely and rather guiltily been vague as to whether or
not she had a telephone in the Spanish house. Now something told her that when writing, she must give them both
the number. After all, there might be a very real emergency.
She would have to think of a tactful way of indicating that
she would not welcome calls on any other basis. If she
wanted to talk to them, she would call home. Cassie in
any case would be bound to reverse the charges. She and

Anthony never seemed to have two pennies to rub together. Furthermore, Cassie was used to frequent discourse with her mother, both in person and on the telephone. Everything from Robert's nappy rash to the cracked exhaust on the car and the injustice and enormity of the Council Tax must be brought home and mulled over, the whys and wherefores, pros and cons aired and ironed out, reassurance sought or comfort extracted, possibly even a little financial help offered by Margaret from a vague feeling not that she wanted, but that she ought, to help.

Maggie had already received a letter from her. The washing machine had broken down, flooding the kitchen on a Sunday morning when, naturally, Anthony was out, and Robert had caught her cold which thankfully hadn't been flu after all. Thank goodness for small mercies, Maggie had thought to herself. It was not often that Cassie was positive about anything. Rereading the letter, which was written in a large childish hand across a pictorial notelet depicting a red squirrel the like of which Maggie had never seen, she decided to write to Cassie first.

She began in a jolly, affectionate way, realising as she did so that there had been few occasions to write to her younger daughter, who had never lived more than a mile away, in some ways in fact had never left home. An excited note of mutual congratulation when the baby was born and annual postcards from Robert and herself while on their holidays did not exactly constitute a lively correspondence. 'Dearest Cassie' was what her daughter would like to hear and she supposed, in all honesty, that the girl was very dear, and seemed more so *in absentia*. She was after all pretty enough if only she'd watch her weight, and affectionate. It was always Cassie who remembered birthdays and anniversaries with extravagantly sentimental cards too lavish to throw away. It had been Cassie who had cried with her after Robert's death, when she had arrived back at the house without him to find the rocking horse still unclaimed, though young Robert could hardly be restrained from climbing up onto its painted back. Together they had torn off the rest of the wrappings and installed the little boy on the saddle. Holding him while he rocked, tears pouring down their cheeks while Sheila banged angrily in the kitchen preparing something sustaining, Margaret had been grateful. She had not cried so well or easily since.

So 'Dearest Cassie,' she began, knowing she was setting a precedent for Dearest Cassie it must now always be. 'It sounds silly to be saying I'm having a marvellous time, as if I was just on holiday, but in fact I am so I shall say it after all. I wish you could see my dear little house . . .' Here she stopped for if she were truthful she didn't wish anything of the sort. The last thing she wanted at the moment was any intrusion on her privacy. Not that Cassie was exactly in a position to take her up on it, to read any sort of an invitation into the casual remark. It was just the sort of thing one said, after all. She went on cautiously '. . . and perhaps you will one day, who knows? I always said it would make a lovely holiday for you all, when I'm settled and know my way about a bit.'

She was interrupted by a clawing at the verandah door which she had closed against a brisk breeze blowing in from the sea. Cake was outside, his fur blown forward and out so that he seemed twice his normal size, a tabby dandelion clock with urgent eyes. As she opened the door a gust swept in with him, sending her papers to the floor and causing the heavy petals of a yellow rose to fall onto the bookcase in a silken pile. She picked them up, smelling the last of their fragrance and exulting in the satin warmth of them between her fingers. They were still too lovely to throw away. Tenderly, she spread them in a china bowl. She would enjoy the last of their beauty, which was after all irreplaceable.

She went downstairs to make some coffee, Cake tearing past her on the stairs in expectation of being fed. Waiting for the kettle she wondered what to say next to her daughter. She could describe the Major, but it seemed indecently soon to admit to having a suitor who brought her flowers, had indeed brought her the yellow roses from his garden. She most certainly couldn't confess to lusting after Lorne, whom she had seen only twice and hardly knew. He was a married man, with a sick wife; though she suspected that abrasive Chloe was not entirely helpless. But the remembered ache between her legs told her that Lorne had awakened something in her that she had conveniently forgotten. She had remembered what it was like to want a man, but she most certainly couldn't tell Cassie that.

To her surprise it had been Chloe, not Lorne, who had telephoned her. Maggie had been in the garden planting petunias and French marigolds in a shady corner. She had purchased the plants in the forecourt of the garage in the village. There she had seen Madrilena again, hanging around after school, bouncing a ball idly in the dust. Maggie had smiled at her, unaccountably pleased. Without a word the little girl had dropped the ball and picked up one of the plastic trays, following Maggie back down the street and into the garden, and it was Madrilena who heard the telephone as, together, they dug holes in the powdery soil and separated the delicate roots of the plants.

'*Teléfono!*' Madrilena inclined her head towards the house like a tense, satiny bird, her brown fingers stilled in the earth.

'So it is!' Maggie jumped up automatically. It was only as she ran up the stairs that she recognised the unexpectedness of the intrusion. It was nearly two weeks since a telephone had rung for her.

'Hello,' she said, unable for the moment to summon up

the number in Spanish. Irrationally, she expected it to be Cassie and it was with a liberated sense of pleasure that she learned that it was Chloe.

'That's nice,' she exclaimed honestly. 'How are you today?'

Chloe's reply was unnerving. 'No better for having to think about it. I just take each day as it comes.' When Maggie remained silent, debating an apology, she added, 'Actually, you could say I'm in a bit of remission at the moment. That's why I'm ringing. We wondered if you'd care to come to lunch tomorrow. Lorne seemed to think you'd like to see the studio. Anyway, it's good for him to show it off.'

'I should like that very much. The lunch and the studio. I still have some English biscuits. I'll bring them with me . . .'

'You know where to find us? About a mile past Tyson's place. Crumbling grey stone ruin, but it's all right inside. It's called Serenidad, though it's far from that sometimes. About twelve thirty?'

'Thank you. I shall look forward to it.' Automatically, Maggie reached for her appointment diary which had always hung on the wall beside the telephone, then realised that it wasn't there. Appointments, like responsibility, had been left behind in England. 'But at this rate I shall be needing one,' she told herself, and was not entirely displeased.

Serenidad looked every bit a crumbling ruin in the thick mist which had closed around her as soon as she began the ascent into the hills. She was beginning to wonder if she had missed it when the white painted sign announced the presence of a house somewhere beyond a line of dripping conifers and young eucalyptus trees. She turned down a sloping stony drive, driving cautiously. The ground seemed to drop away in front of her but the drive gradually curved to the right and deposited her safely in front of a high stone façade. Two enormous urns of geraniums spilled blood-red blooms into the enfolding white bandages of mist.

After the echoing slam of the car door she was met with total silence. No sound penetrated upwards from the main road or the town below, no bird or insect twittered or buzzed. Despite the gloom all the windows at the front of the house were in darkness and a heavy wooden door which had once been painted white was tightly closed beneath a complicated fanlight of wrought iron and coloured glass. There was neither bell nor knocker.

Irritated at the lack of a welcome Maggie was inclining towards resuming her seat in the car when a crunch of wheels was followed by Chloe, rounding a corner of the house with a deft manoeuvre of her chair.

'I thought I heard the car. That's what we usually rely on. Come round this way. We don't use the front door, it's too heavy. I'm sorry it's so wet.' She turned back the way she had come, leaving Maggie to pick her way carefully over uneven stones. The white sandals and light dress which she had put on in the sunlight down below looked as incongruous as the McVitie's digestive biscuits in her hand.

Chloe glanced at her dress as she pulled back to allow her into an open door. 'I can see you're not used to reading the weather. If you can't see the church of San Miguel, you can expect to find mist and rain up here. If we can't see it, we know it's raining in town. It's very simple really.'

Maggie laughed. 'I'll remember that. Fortunately, in true English fashion, I have a cardigan in my bag!'

'Oh you won't need that. Lorne has lit a fire.'

The wheelchair rattled over uneven flagstones into a long gloomy room with a beamed ceiling. There was a low sink and range of pine units along one end, two deep sofas drawn round an open wood fire and in the middle a refectory table with two oak benches. On an old carved table at the far end glimmered a word processor, white and incongruous.

'We find it easier to concentrate all our living into the one room now. The units were specially built for me. Lorne had his studio, I had my sink.'

There was a bitterness which embarrassed Maggie. She would have liked to sympathise but feared a rebuff. 'What do you do with all the other rooms?' she asked instead. 'The house looks huge.'

'Some of them are uninhabitable. We never intended to use it all. There's our bedroom of course, and a couple of guest rooms, all downstairs in the front. Mainly we bought it so that Lorne could build his studio. That's taken three of the rooms at the back. He's up there now. He likes the light, there are no shadows.'

She reached up awkwardly and lit a large oil lamp on an elaborately carved chest beside a sofa. 'Sit down and get warm, won't you. I'll see about the food.'

Maggie sat down, and looked about her. Between greyish vertical beams the walls were painted white and liberally hung with paintings. They were difficult to see from a distance; outside the slope of the hillside brought the wet trees close to the house robbing the small windows of light.

'Are all the pictures Lorne's?'

'Mostly. Some are from friends, a few we bought. I'll let him show you himself.'

'Can I help you at all?' She went over to where Chloe was stirring something on a black cooking range which alone among the kitchen equipment was really too high for her to manage. 'I could stir that if you like.'

'I'm used to it.' She stirred in a silence which went on uncomfortably long, then said, 'I'm not very good at accepting help. It's bad enough needing it at all.'

'I can imagine.' As Chloe spurned sympathy, Maggie

56

offered her none. None the less she was curious. 'How long has it been? Since you became ill?'

'Three years. But I've only been in this damned thing for one of them.'

'You didn't think it best to return to England?'

'No. Of course we might not have come had we known, but Lorne had just finished his studio and was getting commissions. And I was writing well. Things were cheaper here. And we have the sunshine. Sometimes.' She grimaced towards the grey windows.

'You don't miss England? And your family and friends?'

'We neither of us have family, and our friends come and visit us here. They're only too glad of the holiday. I fly over to see my specialist, and there's a doctor in Santiago whenever I need him. Anyway, it won't be for ever.'

'You mean you're getting better? That's wonderful.'

'No, I don't mean that.'

The wooden spoon thudded rhythmically in the pot like a beating heart. Chloe's expression was defiant and Maggie said obligingly, 'That smells good. What is it?'

'Herb soup. I used to gather herbs on the hillside, now we have a raised herb garden outside the back door. Lorne built it for me with stone from the walls he took out to make the studio. He's good with his hands.'

Maggie remembered his hands. She remembered them smoothing Chloe's hair back from her forehead. 'What's he painting now? Is he working on a commission?'

'I don't know. I don't think he has any at present. And I never go up to the studio, of course, not now.'

'And do you still write?'

'Sometimes. When I'm feeling good.'

'Do you work anywhere in particular? I always imagine poets and authors having special, private places. Like Dylan Thomas and his boathouse.' Then she remembered the word processor. 'It's a bit naïve perhaps . . .'

57

'Perhaps. I used to be able to write anywhere, if I was sufficiently moved. Now I prefer to compose outdoors. I can breathe out there. Then I type it out in here.'

Exhausted, because it did seem to be turning into an inquisition, Maggie asked, 'I should like to see some of your poetry. I mean the published works, of course. Lorne did say you had been published?'

'If you want to.' Chloe looked neither pleased nor interested. 'It must be one o'clock, I'll call him.'

She wheeled herself through a double doorway into the house. Maggie waited with interest. Would she call just 'Lorne', or 'darling' perhaps, though that seemed hardly in keeping? Instead there came the clanging of a bell, followed after a while by heavy footsteps on wooden stairs. Lorne came into the room, pushing Chloe's chair.

'Forgive me, Maggie,' he said. 'I had some paint to finish up.'

'You shouldn't have stopped just for me.'

'But I always try and stop for visitors. We don't have enough as it is. Do we, Chloe?'

Chloe didn't answer. She wheeled away towards the table and started cutting bread. Maggie looked at Lorne as he crossed the shadowy room. It was then that she thought, My God, he's a beautiful man. I wonder when they last made love . . .

He was pulling out one of the benches. 'Maggie? Would you like to sit down?'

'I'm sorry. How rude of me. My mind had gone off at a tangent. It does that, these days.' She busied herself with her napkin, reeling with shock at the quick discomfort of desire, at the audacity of imagining him naked against Chloe's debilitated grey flesh. Her own body, sunburned and rejuvenated, crawled and clamoured. But she took the heavy bowl of soup from his hands and met his eyes with an uncomplicated smile. 'I told Chloe that this smelled delicious. I'm longing to try.' Her spoon banged against the china and the soup seared her tongue, peppery and tangy with sage and marjoram. The onslaught of heat and flavour mercifully stilled her other senses.

Lorne was breaking his bread onto the linen tablecloth, pressing large pieces into his mouth and washing them down with soup like a peasant. It was impossible not to notice his physicality yet his voice and eyes were fine and his fingers long and supple. Watching them hypnotically, she imagined them exploring her body. Struggling for normality she asked, 'May I come up and see your studio, or are you too busy?'

'By all means. I expect Chloe will be having her rest.'

Maggie looked at Chloe. She was crumbling bread into her soup and didn't answer. 'Are you working on anything in particular?'

'A seascape. South of Baiona on the coast road. I did the initial sketches on a day just like this so the light is right for filling in the detail.'

There were several seascapes on the wall opposite her. 'Are these all yours?'

'Only the watercolours. The gouache are David Bellamys. Do you know his work? He's another Welshman, quite delightful.'

'No, I'm afraid not.'

'Don't sound so apologetic. I don't suppose you've heard of me either!'

'I'm sorry. I used to be interested, but modern painting is a closed book to me.'

'By which you mean you are a specialist in the Old Masters?'

'No. Not that either.' Maggie wished Chloe didn't have to be so challenging. She was well aware of her limitations. 'I was studying art at school – long enough ago, of course!

I'd thought of becoming an art teacher, but changed my mind.'

'Why?' It was Chloe again. She had every right, Maggie had questioned her methodically, but somehow she felt she herself had enquired partly out of interest, partly for something to say. Chloe seemed to expect an answer of some significance. It was like being orally examined.

'I'd had enough of school, I wasn't a natural student. As simple as that really.'

'And have you regretted it?'

'Sometimes I suppose, yes. I don't seem to have done much with my life since then.'

'But you had your children.'

'Yes.' Maggie had no wish to cover the same ground again. 'Is there any more soup? It's as good as it smells.'

'There is, but I've a baked ham and jacket potatoes. Have you room for both?'

'No, well perhaps not.' She allowed Chloe to remove her bowl, staring at the table like a reprimanded child. Then, crossly, she lifted her head and looked straight into Lorne's eyes across the table.

He said, 'Were you good at painting and drawing, when you were at school?'

'I suppose I must have been if I was taking exams. I would have had to have gone on to art school. But I've never done any since so it couldn't have been a true muse.'

'Even so, it can be a source of great pleasure. I could help you if you like.'

She thought for a moment. 'Well, the scenery is very beautiful. And there's a lovely child in the village, Madrilena. She lives at the garage. She seems to have befriended me. She's at her best at the moment, like all the little girls. Spanish women don't seem to wear well, generally. I must say I'd like to try and capture her. Photographs don't mean quite the same. Perhaps it would be a good idea.'

60

'You've forgotten the wine,' Chloe interrupted, clumsily transferring a heavy iron casserole onto the table with gloved hands.

Maggie felt guilty. 'Oh let me help.'

Chloe said, 'I've done it now,' which neither blamed nor exonerated her. Lorne drew the cork from an unlabelled bottle and poured red wine into a heavy glass before her.

'Bottoms up – as the Major would say,' exclaimed Chloe unexpectedly, giving a loud laugh. It was the first time Maggie had heard her laugh. With relief she joined in, swallowing the harsh liquid and watching Lorne's deft hands slice the pink flesh of the ham.

'He – the Major – arrived one day with a bunch of flowers,' Maggie said for no particular reason, and immediately regretted it. She seemed to be inviting a continuation of their mirth at what, after all, had been a courteous and curiously touching gesture.

She wrote to Cassie:

> I have made several acquaintances already, all of them English, though I believe Lorne has some Welsh blood in him somewhere.
>
> There's Major Tyson, or Nigel, a widower who lives up in the hills. He's a strange mixture, well-meaning but a bit of a buffoon. But I mustn't be unkind. He is taking me to the coast tomorrow.
>
> Lorne is an artist and lives in an old stone farmhouse. His wife, Chloe, has some debilitating illness and is in a wheelchair. It is tragic, she is only forty-three and a poet. I do feel so sorry for them both. Lorne is going to help me start painting. I really feel quite excited. He has a studio at the top of the house. He showed me his work and we drank tea and ate McVitie's digestive biscuits just as if we were in England. He enjoyed them so much,

perhaps you could pack up a box sometime and send it out? I expect there will be things I miss too, before long.

I have been very lucky so far, I do realise that. Everything is working out far better than I could have expected. I can't believe it really.

She could have added, 'Leave me alone. Please don't spoil it.' Like a child at boarding school, having found her feet, she wanted no interference with her new and joyous independence, no reminders of home to undermine it.

# SIX

Maggie wished she had suggested they take her car for the trip to the coast. She hadn't liked to hurt Nigel's feelings but the little Citroën was rattly and uncomfortable and, rather to her disappointment – for was she not now a free-wheeling spirit? – she also thought it a trifle undignified.

The Major arrived in holiday mood, his khaki shirt replaced by pink poplin, open at the neck and with the sleeves rolled up. His stiff moustache and military bearing were uncomfortably at odds with this attempt at laid-back leisurewear. Maggie was reminded of a childhood game of Cassie's where an odd assortment of heads, bodies and legs had to be assembled into their proper sequence. Today, the Major's head didn't seem quite to match his body.

Finn was installed in the back seat, staring eagerly out. The roof of the car was open, rolled back and fastened down against the dusty bodywork. Maggie's initial thought was that this would be fun. She had never driven in an open car and it was, she felt, indicative of her new-found freedom, her casting aside of conventionalities. It was not long, however, before her hair had been torn out of its restraining band behind her neck and was whipping uncomfortably across her face and inside her sunglasses. It had seemed to her that women in open cars always had their long hair streaming conveniently and glamorously behind them; in reality a perverse air-stream seemed to carry it both forward and sideways so that she could neither talk nor see the view. Besides that, the noise of the wind and the engine made conversation impossible and intruded further on her enjoyment of the passing scene.

'Nigel,' she felt compelled to shout at last. 'Please stop a minute.'

He braked obediently, pulling into the verge though the road was narrow. 'What is it, Maggie? Forgotten something?'

'No. But I do find this wind rather uncomfortable. It's very boring of me I know, but do you think we could have the roof up? If I'd thought I would have brought a scarf,' she finished apologetically, acknowledging her own carelessness.

'Not at all. *Mea culpa*, as I believe they say. Edna didn't like it either. She said it made her eyes water and her head feel like a plumped pillow. Yes.' He gave a dry cough. 'Did you have a good day at Serenidad?' He began unpopping the roof.

She said guardedly, 'Yes. It was interesting. I did wonder about Chloe though. I don't think she really wanted me there. It must be an effort for her, after all. I can sympathise with that, though she doesn't want sympathy, of course. I find it difficult knowing just how to be with her.'

'She can be off-putting. She frightened poor Edna to death, though she wasn't sick then. But she has such very strong views on everything, and expects everyone else to have them too.'

'Quite. Somehow I feel like an awkward schoolgirl who must be on her best behaviour. Yet you'd think she'd welcome company. They must be so isolated . . .'

Nigel edged back into the little car. His own hair was ruffled and he smoothed it down, touching his moustache automatically. Amused, Maggie found herself waiting for him to give a salute. He said, 'They've never seemed to mind that. They always had their work. And each other.

Lorne just worships her. I really don't know how the poor fellow's going to cope . . .'

'And he's so nice.' Maggie spoke quickly. She didn't want to think about it. 'Quite charming. He made me feel very welcome, enthused madly over some biscuits I had taken and spent a long time showing me his work. He's offered to help me to paint, though I doubt if I'll be much good.'

'Nonsense. Look, there's the sea. How about that, eh?' He sounded as if he were personally responsible for the glitter of blue which stretched across the horizon as the road began to run through scattered houses. 'Wonderful sight, isn't it? Perhaps I should have chosen the navy not the army. But too late now.'

'But surely you don't regret a whole lifetime?'

'You sound like Chloe! She always challenges the odd remark.'

'God forbid. Forget I ever said it. It's just that I felt genuinely sorry . . .'

'Nothing to be sorry about. We make our beds and we lie on them. I've had a good life. No regrets.' He coughed again. 'We're nearly in Baiona. Would you like to stop and have a look at the parador? We could have lunch there. Named after our Count, I believe. The Parador Conde de Gondomar. He was Ambassador to the Court of James the First. Some of the walls are much older. There's been a stronghold on the mount since before Roman times and the Moors and the Portuguese had their turn in residence. Now it's even more international, of course.'

'I can imagine. Robert and I used to stay in paradores when we felt like a bit of luxury. Some of the buildings are superb. Is this one original?'

'I think not, though it looks and feels authentic. Supposed to be a typical Galician *pazo*, or country manor.'

'You seem to be very well informed.' Maggie was surprised.

65

'It's only what I've read in their leaflet. Like to know a bit about where I am. When you move about the world you get used to finding out about places. On a superficial level, anyway.'

They were running along a coast road with bright sandy beaches to their right and ahead a steep peninsula crowned with battlements on top of tumbling cliffs softened with vegetation. Maggie was impressed. 'It's quite a site. I can see why it was fought over.' Passing through an outer gate-house they had to declare their business before completing the climb up a steep drive. Pedestrians were toiling up in the midday heat. Maggie regretted for a moment having had the roof replaced. There would have been a nice theatricality in arriving windswept and abandoned at such a place.

Above them on the ramparts other people were strolling, looking down at the view.

'Can we walk up there? It seems to be the thing to do.'

'It is, and we can. It was my express intention, though I doubt if you'll want to do the whole three kilometres.'

'Try me!' Suddenly she felt frivolous and girlish. She hadn't felt so carefree for years, and if it was because she had to think of nobody but herself, what did it matter after all?

'Tell me about your family.'

Finn was on the lead and they had begun their walk, turning left in an anticlockwise direction out towards the sea. She could hear it sifting and sighing out of sight beneath a tumble of rocks and brambles. She gave a little uncalled for sigh herself. Her family. Sheila and Cassie. After all she was not alone, detached, without tie or commitment. Resentment at being reminded was followed by the weightier pain of guilt. Chloe and Lorne had no family. She had been twice blessed. Such ingratitude deserved to be abhorred and punished. A swift rush of fear followed the

66

habitual guilt. Was retribution waiting for her round the corner? Was disaster even now like the Sword of Damocles poised over the heads of her daughters, even little Robert? Would she return to find the telephone ringing, tragedy or bereavement on the other end? She shook herself. As yet, nobody had her telephone number. She had only that morning posted the letters to the girls. For a day or two, she was safe . . .

'Maggie?' Nigel lay a hand on her arm as her pace quickened involuntarily. 'Did you hear me? I was asking you to tell me about your daughters.'

'So you did. I did hear you. It just set me worrying for the moment.'

'About them? Have you any cause?'

'No. Nothing specific. I suppose it's just that parenthood seems to be synonymous with worry. For me, at any rate. That's one of the reasons . . .' She stopped, ashamed at the confession she had been about to make. 'Well – Sheila is twenty-seven and she's a social worker in Liverpool. She's single and pretends not to mind, though I suspect this is now a problem for her.' She stopped, turning to look at Nigel who was strolling beside her looking out towards the sea. Was he really interested? And why was she choosing to offer him even this small insight into her concern?

'Go on,' he said, without turning. 'I am listening.'

It occurred to Maggie that his turning away indicated a shyness, a difficulty in taking on board the personal intimacies of family and emotional life. His life had been constrained and regulated by rules and discipline, his every decision dictated by necessity. If she was right, then to feign an interest indicated at least a willingness to please, a wish to find some common ground. Not wanting to deny the gesture she forced herself to go on.

'Cassandra – well, we call her Cassie though I never intended to – Cassie is twenty-three. She's been married for three years and has a son, Robert, named after my husband. My late husband.' It seemed necessary to be precise. 'She's a pretty little thing, always had plenty of boyfriends. We would have preferred it if she'd waited before marrying, done something more with her life.'

'And what did she do with it?' He was now looking straight ahead, his back held ramrod straight, arms swinging easily at his side. She judged that he had come halfway to meeting her and it loosed her tongue with a strange gratitude that he should be bothered.

'She left school after her A levels – which she failed pretty dismally – and did a secretarial course. We'd always hoped she'd go in for journalism, her English was good and she seemed keen. But nothing we said would persuade her to retake her exams and try for university. Any more than anything my own parents had said to me . . . but that's another story. As you say, we make our own beds . . . the difficulty as a parent is letting them do just that, especially when you see history repeating itself. I don't think, now, that Cassie would have been suited to university life. She's not a stayer. Neither would she have coped with the cut and thrust of journalism. So maybe she knew best. We were expecting too much of her, I suspect. She's just a simple, ordinary girl and I suppose that's what I find hard to forgive.'

That was going too far. Swiftly she added, 'Forgive *myself*. I fear it's me that's made them dull.'

'Dull? I find that hard to believe. You're anything but dull, Maggie. Uprooting yourself and coming out here, on your own. And anyway, is dullness such a crime?'

He could hardly be expected to think so, she thought unkindly. 'Not a crime, no. I'm sorry, I didn't mean to say all this. Why should it interest you? We've come out to enjoy ourselves.'

He didn't try to draw her out. Embarrassment perhaps?

Or was it tact, an unexpected delicacy of feeling? They walked in silence for a while, stopping now and then to look back at the receding view of the bay until they rounded the headland and saw only heaped rocks and a restless sea drawing out the seaweed as it sucked at the shoreline. Perversely she found she now wanted to talk. His very indifference, his lack of comprehension or condemnation tempted her to speak out. With this simple, well-meaning rather boring little man, she felt, her words would sink into a bottomless pit. There would be no comeback, only the catharsis of having spoken. She had never put into words her disappointment, her guilt, her regrets over how the girls had turned out. It would have been shameful, disloyal, ungrateful. Not even Robert had known how she had longed for Cassie to fulfil the gift of her name and branch out, break the mould, expand into something different, something interesting, even become a problem. But Cassie's only problem was that she was no trouble at all. It was laughable. Many parents, indeed many of Maggie's friends and contemporaries, would have given anything for children as painlessly conventional as Sheila and Cassie. How could Maggie have told them that she took their very ordinariness as an indictment of her own, that her disappointment in them was disappointment in herself?

But she didn't speak. It seemed uncivil to presume on the Major's goodwill, neither could she think of anything trivial to talk about. To her intense relief, for the silence was becoming a weight beyond the merely companionable, he said at last, as if also seeking something to say, 'It's a splendid view.'

They had rounded the point. She could see the coastline stretching south towards Portugal some thirty kilometres away. 'Lorne was finishing a picture when I was there. He said it was along this stretch of coast. It was wonderful, I could almost hear the waves breaking.'

'He's a very talented man. His exhibition will be a success. Will you take up his offer and have a go yourself?'

'Yes, I think I will. It will be another interest.'

'That's important, when one's alone.' His moustache seemed to droop a little and his shoulders sag. Maggie felt both pity and a touch of fear for, after all, weren't they both in exactly the same boat?

Prompted by his remark she asked, 'Do you have children? Do they come to see you?'

His shoulders seemed to sag lower before he braced them and brushed his moustache in the way she had come to recognise.

'Sadly no. I mean no, we never had children. My fault, I'm afraid. It was a blow to Edna, but she stuck by me.'

Touched at his confidence she commiserated, 'I'm sorry.' Uncomfortably she went on, 'You must think me so ungrateful, complaining about mine. I suppose I don't know when I'm well off. I just took babies for granted.'

'People do. We thought we might adopt, but I was moving about such a lot. And I wasn't entirely convinced . . . Edna seemed to accept that too. Marvellous woman . . .' His voice failed him.

Bracingly Maggie said, 'Well – you have Finn,' glancing down at the dog who was pulling ahead on his lead, bushy tail swinging.

'That's why I love him so much, I expect. We always had dogs. Used to walk miles. Still do. It's a good discipline.'

Abruptly he called the dog's name. Finn stopped in his tracks and turned round enquiringly, allowing the lead to slacken. 'See – well trained. You wouldn't get that obedience from a child.' Reaching the animal, the Major ruffled the thick hair on his head. 'Who's a fine boy then? Who's Daddy's pet?'

The revealing words brought a lump to Maggie's throat. It was about time, she told herself, that she got things into perspective. She had her girls. She should be grateful, but unfortunately gratitude didn't come on demand.

That night she found she was thinking of Robert. The familiar ambience of the parador, its spacious rooms and cool tiled floors, the remembered layout of the elaborate menu and even the flavour of the food had reminded her of their holidays in Spain. Over such meals they had talked of settling there when Robert retired, or maybe buying a holiday home. Now she was here alone, and the Major's brave attempt at independence was a poignant illustration of how it was going to be for her. She had been relieved, almost exhilarated at the discovery that she could live alone, that she welcomed the freedom of being entirely selfish. It was astonishing how quickly she had got used to the silence of empty rooms, the roominess of their familiar double bed. Now suddenly in this still-strange bedroom which Robert had never shared she missed the comfort of his presence with a sharp physical ache that made her cry out. Desperate, she got out of bed and went to the kitchen where Cake was sleeping curled on one of the chairs. He gave a grunt of protest when she lifted him but, once under the bedclothes he pressed against her body roaring with pleasure and, eventually, she slept.

Filling up the car with petrol next day she saw Madrilena again. Maybe it was the shadow of the night which made her say to Señor Vara, her fat and swarthy father, as he plunged the nozzle into her tank with an almost phallic symbolism eyeing her greasily with Madrilena's brown eyes, 'Would you mind if Madrilena came out with me today? I am going to Vigo. She could help me with my shopping.'

The child's face blazed and she grabbed her father's arm. *'Por favor, Papá!'*

He grunted, his eye on the petrol gauge.

'*Papá?*'

Screwing on the petrol cap with oily fat fingers he nodded towards the house. 'Ask your mother.' The child sped inside the little office where Señora Vara presided over an outmoded cash register and a counter of sweets and canned drinks. Maggie watched Madrilena gesticulate excitedly to be rewarded with a peremptory nod. The woman watched as her daughter ran across the forecourt and climbed into the car. Maggie smiled at her and called '*Gracias*. We shall be back by four o'clock.' She wondered if either of the parents was much interested.

They crossed a small open square in front of the shabby grey church. Children were swarming there, kicking and throwing balls, running with the inexhaustible energy of those used to the sun. Spanish children seemed to run and jump from the moment they got up to the time they went, belatedly, to bed. She thought of her own girls when they were small, playing quietly in the garden with their dolls and bicycles until they were ushered up to bed at the appropriate hour, largely unprotesting and long before darkness fell in summertime. Children in their Surrey commuter belt did not congregate in the street. Churches were not for throwing balls against, they were for Sunday school and Brownies. Likewise, the evenings were for the adults. One did not go to a bar or a restaurant and expect to see children swarming over the furniture and running between people's chairs as she had seen all over Europe. She remembered a particularly irritating incident when a white-faced boy of about six, silly with fatigue, had upset and broken a large table lamp in their Algarve hotel lounge. The parents had not been greatly upset, simply peering into the carrycot at their feet to make sure no damage had been done. Maggie had expostulated angrily to Robert and he had agreed. There were times when children should neither be seen nor heard. They had left the bar in mute protest, walking along the beach on still-warm sand. They had been bound together in indignation. He had held her hand, she remembered. They had often held hands, being easy together. She couldn't understand how she could have become so easily accustomed to his absence, but now her hands ached and she gripped the steering wheel to relieve them.

'Wouldn't you prefer to stay and play with the other children?' she asked Madrilena, who shook her head emphatically.

'I would prefer to go to Vigo.'

It was obviously to be quite an excursion for her. 'Do you often go to Vigo?'

'No. Sometimes, we visit my uncle. Señor Velasquez, who owns your house. I can show you where he lives if you like.'

'Thank you. But I don't think we'll call on him today. I have written to tell him how pleased I am with everything. I watered our plants this morning, they are looking very well.'

Madrilena looked puzzled, sifting through some dubious grammar, then smiled in comprehension. Maggie thought again how beautiful she was, the swarthy sullenness of puberty still far ahead. Madrilena had told her she was seven. She had an unconscious grace and a shine that transcended the dust on her feet and clothes. Today she was not wearing her satin Sunday best but a red cotton skirt and a white blouse, unknowingly seductive with its elasticated top sitting crooked and low over her brown shoulders. She had the confidence that came from being so much with grown-ups, from being allowed carelessly to share their time and their pleasures. Maggie thought again how much she would like to paint her.

'I want to buy some paints in Vigo,' she told her.

'For the house?'

'No. To paint some pictures. Señor Erskine is going to teach me. Do you know Señor Erskine?'

She shook her head.

'His wife is sick. She is in . . . a chair with wheels. Perhaps you have seen her?'

'Ah!' Obviously Madrilena had. 'It is very sad.' Her face moulded into mawkishness; perhaps she had heard other people talking.

'Do you know the shop where I can buy paints?'

Madrilena shook her head again, dark hair gleaming and swinging.

'Then we shall just have to find it together. And we'll have some lunch.' The girl's eyes widened. 'And on the way back I want to stop at Carrefors for some provisions. Major Tyson told me about it. Do you know Major Tyson?'

Madrilena pressed her hand against her lips which escaped into a smile. She sat bolt upright in her seat and pressed her arms into her sides. Maggie laughed. The Major could have been sitting there beside her. 'That's exactly right, but a bit . . .' she fumbled for the word, settling for 'bad' and the child looked chastened, letting her shoulders fall though her eyes meeting Maggie's sideways still held a wicked smile.

Why should I feel so carefree? wondered Maggie. Why should I be so easy with someone else's child? Surely it's not that I am lonely? Surely it has more to do with not being ultimately responsible; I am only responsible for giving her a nice day, buying her lunch and ice cream, which quite obviously is a treat for her. We are not answerable to each other, we take each other as we come. She enjoys the novelty, perhaps a certain kudos in being my companion. The English lady's friend. Perhaps she will be honoured if I ask to paint her picture? I would enjoy that.

Just as she enjoyed feeling a hand slip warmly into hers

as they crossed a narrow hooting street and yes, there was an artshop now, as Lorne had promised, with frames and easels in the window.

The postman had called while she was out. Maggie could see the envelope stuffed behind a geranium pot as she unloaded her boxes of shopping. She ignored it until she had carried everything inside, acknowledging a reluctance to investigate. When she did so, it was to see Sheila's writing on the envelope. The missive inside felt thick and threatening. A little knot of worry twisted prematurely round the pleasure of the day, but there was nothing to be done but open it.

# SEVEN

The English newspaper Maggie had bought in Vigo was the first she had seen for over a fortnight. Predictably nothing much had changed. Rows and speculation still raged over Government sleaze, the European Union, juvenile crime. She felt sublimely detached from them all.

But she couldn't remain detached from the headlines on the second page: 'Child Abuse Case Blame Focuses', 'En Masse Resignations'.

Sheila had written,

I never for the moment felt I had any choice in the matter. The condemnation of Leonard Hawkins for what people choose to see as negligence is so unjust that the time has come for everyone to take a stand. What do people want, after all? If we are too cautious we are accused of acting beyond the call of duty in a manner injurious to both privacy and the rights of parents. If we exercise considered judgement based on the facts as we see them we are accused of putting people at risk by letting them slip through the net. And all this censure is directed at people with a crippling work-load, ludicrous hours and derisory pay. So, its horrific that Sharon Murdoch had to die like that but I ABSOLUTELY REFUSE to be held corporately responsible. I hope you can understand this.

Maggie could understand it. It had always seemed to her that social workers were between a rock and a hard place, even before Sheila had belaboured her regularly with the cruel facts of life as she saw it; life from the underside, very often dirty and unseemly, intimate and disgusting. To be fair and compassionate and at the same time keep sane and whole oneself seemed to be asking for the impossible. She had marvelled at Sheila's apparent strength while at the same time shrinking from her aggression. She had cause to wonder, sometimes, if that same aggression might not be equally off-putting to those she was trying to help. But Sheila maintained you had to be tough to be just. It was no good getting involved or you would go under. Now it seemed she had had enough, though Maggie asked herself if she would have had the courage to act alone. The question was in no way pejorative. She had never imagined her daughter to be a heroine despite a certain formidable aspect to her nature. It was sufficient that she had had the guts to join her colleagues in their statement of defiance. Let the needy go without if all the thanks the social services got was criticism and blame founded on emotion not on reason. Maggie felt proud. Clearly, now was the time to say so. She would write at once, giving her support and sympathy, though not too much of the latter. Like Chloe, Sheila was likely to bite a proffered hand rather than cling to it in gratitude.

She posted her letter the following day. She was pleased to find that on her daily excursions through the town she was able increasingly to nod and smile in recognition at the women she passed. Sometimes, waiting in the queue for her daily bread she would be engaged in casual conversation; was she comfortable in her house, was she enjoying the sunshine, perhaps it was raining in England as usual? The women seemed pleased that she answered them in Spanish. None of them attempted to speak in English. That morning, however, there was a stranger in the queue, a woman perhaps a little younger than Maggie. Like her, she was dressed in a long cotton skirt and a tee shirt. Like

Maggie, her hair was long, though wiry and blonde and untidier. There was a scar on the front of her throat. The gold crucifix which hung below the blemish served not to disguise but rather to draw the eye. Conscious that the woman was looking at her, Maggie averted her gaze.

'Excuse me, are you the English lady?' It was spoken in English.

'Yes.' Maggie was unsurprised. Everyone seemed to know of her existence.

'I was a teacher in England. I taught Spanish and German. Ely? Do you know it?'

'No, I'm afraid I've never been there.'

'It is strange country. Very flat. But the cathedral is beautiful.'

Maggie smiled politely. 'So I believe,' she said, thinking how very English that sounded. English and constrained. 'And now do you live in Gondomar?'

'On the outskirts. Oh, it is your turn, please. Buy your bread . . . Now I teach classical dance. And the flamenco. I come from Granada.'

Now it was the woman's turn to purchase. Maggie found herself waiting while she paid, and following her from the shop. Outside, the woman said, 'My name is Lilli,' and spelled it out. 'It is good to be able to speak English again. Are you here alone?'

'Quite alone. And my name is Maggie. I'm a widow.'

'So I have been told. But you have children?'

'Two daughters, though they are grown women now.'

'So you are free!'

Maggie smiled, thinking of Sheila. 'Is one ever free?' she asked, but lightly. She could hardly burden the woman with the problem.

'Yes, I think. At least you are free to come home with me now, and take a cup of coffee?'

78

Maggie had planned to clean and water, then lie in the garden and write to Harriet.

'Thank you. I'd like that.'

'It is rather a walk. I prefer not to drive. Will you manage?' The younger woman was solicitous. Maggie wondered how old she seemed to her. She had been feeling so young of late. She pushed back her hair which she was wearing loose. She liked the feeling of it now that it was long enough to brush her shoulders and the back of her neck.

'I shall manage,' she said. 'I like to walk,' which was not entirely true. A post-prandial stroll in the Surrey woods, perhaps a walk to the swings with Robert in his pushchair was one thing. Pacing briskly across the fells or, as now, toiling up a sloping dusty road in the full glare of the morning sun, scorched by the breath of passing lorries and pestered by flies, was quite another. She was grateful when they turned off onto a narrow track which ran downhill. The roar of traffic receded to be replaced by the buzz and hum of insects. Young brambles and bracken tangled in the verges and she was reminded of the summer trail to Cornish beaches when the girls were young.

It was the homely similarity to the English countryside which had attracted them to northern Spain. The mix of familiar and strangely exotic had been just rich enough to satisfy without giving indigestion. One did not need to feel an exile in so benign a landscape. There were cider apple trees and quaint haystacks like pepper pots clustered in the orchards. Solitary cows chewed thoughtfully knee-deep in grass. And yet Lilli's garden when they reached their destination was strange enough; a stiff mix of palms and cacti clumped unsympathetically in a spread of arid fawn grass, no leafy trees to offer shade or respite, no splash of colour from petunia or geranium. Lilli had lived in Ely; it seemed peculiar.

Lilli said, 'It's not quite like an English garden, but it was like this when I came.' Her tone implied that there was nothing more to be said about it. Changes could not be made.

'Is it your own house?' Perhaps, as a tenant, she could make no alterations.

'Yes, eventually. At first I rented. Come and see.'

It was modern, crisp and white, blinds tightly drawn against the sun. The roof was a scarlet corrugation against the sky. Set as they were in a wasteland of sandy soil and ugly scrub both house and garden were an anomaly. Piles of building blocks and concrete pipes evidenced that other building has been contemplated and abandoned. Once inside the impression changed from one of crispness and order to a lush and complicated confusion which delighted Maggie. She had the impression of walking into a bazaar, of wading through fans and feathers, huge vases of garish imitation flowers intermingled with dried grasses and seed-heads, castanets hanging in bunches like conkers from curly hooks carved out of bone, intricate shawls decorated with sequins and pearls and dangling slivers of shiny metal, lace mantillas hanging in a row on a brass rail and a pile of combs of tortoiseshell, mother-of-pearl and ivory. Three guitars stood against a wall; tapes and records were scattered on the floor which was partially covered by a luridly coloured and patterned carpet.

Lilli sat her on a deep red plush armchair with curly arms, whisking aside a froth of scarlet frills. Waiting for her coffee Maggie let her eyes wander round the room in delight. She was ravished with the colour and complexity of what verged on chaos but managed instead to be ebullience. Modern chain-store prints of Spanish dancers hung on the walls against a noisy patterned paper. Amidst the gregarious scramble a simple Madonna surmounted by a cross struck a thoughtful note. It was lovingly decorated with a bunch of carnations. The sunlight filtered in through the lowered blind showing dust thick on the strongly grained veneer of a loaded table, on the pale wood blocks of the floor.

There was a felicitous sense that the room was Lilli. With-out wishing to, Maggie compared it with her home in Godalming. Once, she would have dismissed Lilli's room as tasteless, untidy, restless. Now, in retrospect, the unclut-tered space she had shared with Robert failed to satisfy, the neutral colours and sparse ornaments telling nothing about herself except perhaps that she, too, was neutral and sparse. It was small comfort to remember the shelves of china, the rampant plants, the purple shawl which she had latterly gathered around her to replace her husband, to prove to herself perhaps that she existed after all.

The coffee arrived. Lilli had tied her springy hair on top of her head. It thrust out rebelliously like the leaves of a pineapple. 'It's hot today. Far too hot for May. But the weather is no longer reliable.'

'That's true. It's the same at home. We haven't had snow in winter for several years. Somehow, its unreliability makes one insecure. Not that English weather was ever very reliable, of course.'

She had forgotten for a moment that her companion was Spanish but Lilli seemed to have no difficulty in understand-ing. 'In Ely, the one thing you could rely on was the wind! In summer, everything was dusty. In winter, it was always cold. Did you know that there is nothing between the tower of Ely Cathedral and the Russian Steppes?' She passed coffee, black and strong, without offering milk or sugar. The cup was chipped. But there were little almond biscuits in an effusive floral tin. Maggie took two.

'This is a wonderful room. Where do you teach your dancing? I am surprised there is demand for it up here. It's very much of the South I should have thought.'

'Actually, it's becoming popular even in England. There was quite a thriving club in Cambridge. I teach several little girls individually. I have another room which I use as a studio. Also, I take an adult class at the Institute in Vigo. We are giving a performance in August. Some of the children will join us. Perhaps you would like to come?'

'Oh yes, I would. I've never seen proper flamenco. I've always been sceptical of the sort of evening one is offered as a tourist.'

'My grandfather was a gypsy. My flamenco is certainly "proper" if you mean by that authentic.'

Maggie was impressed. 'Well, I don't mean "nice", or "well-behaved".' She stared at Lilli's bushy blonde hair. 'Forgive me, but you don't look as if you have Spanish gypsy blood. Your hair . . .'

'My hair is a cross I have to carry. My grandmother was English. She fell in love with my grandfather on a European tour she made when she was twenty-one. He carried her off, and they lived happily ever after!'

'Do people ever do that?'

'They do if they marry a gypsy, it seems. I have been looking for one for years!'

Was she joking? Maggie asked, 'Are you married?' Lilli's lean, large-jointed fingers were devoid of rings. Now they touched the scar on her neck.

'I was. He was English. He left me. I have one daughter, Miriam. She is not married but she has a son. I call him Pepe but his name is Peter. They live in London, on social security, in a council flat. Sometimes when I can send her the fare they come and stay with me. So – now you know all about me. Have another biscuit.'

Maggie took one. 'It's difficult to know what to say to all that. Obviously you have your problems. Life can't be easy, for you or for Miriam. Don't you worry desperately about her?'

Lilli gave a shrug. 'No. She manages. And it was her own doing.'

Maggie found her detachment enviable though hard to

believe. 'But she's your daughter.' There was accusation in her voice, in her appalled expression. And disbelief. Was it possible to remove oneself so far? Was it possible that, by putting the miles between, one could also sever the ties, cut oneself free, cast off the heavy burden of responsibility?

'And I am my parents' daughter, but they do not worry about me.'

'Perhaps they do, but don't show it. It would be another burden for you. It is a terrible responsibility, being worried about! Sometimes, it's easier to say nothing about one's problems. It causes anxiety, and that in turn becomes another worry. I wonder sometimes, wouldn't it be easier just to go into a convent? Absolve one's guilt by praying for the world in all its impersonal grief and need, and let God take care of everything?'

Lilli looked at her thoughtfully, her cup held poised. 'Do you really think that? Do you find your life so very difficult?'

Maggie felt constrained to admit, 'My own life has been very comfortable. You will think me both selfish and feeble. Perhaps I don't have enough to worry about, so I make mountains out of molehills. Do you know that expression?'

'No, but I can understand it. Are there many molehills in your life? I know you have lost your husband.'

'Yes. But that was surprisingly surmountable.' She thought of Sheila, anxiety twisting at her heart. It was too soon to confide in Lilli. Good heavens, they had met barely an hour ago. She had said too much already.

The heat was uncomfortable as she walked back up the track. It was not yet June and she wondered how she would find it by midsummer. Would the sun that had seemed such a blessing become an enemy? She thought with envy of Nigel Tyson's swimming pool. He had made it clear that she was welcome, any time. She had not so far taken him up on it. Maybe it was the pathos of the neglected kitchen, his touching unawareness of his own simplicity or his childish pleasure when he had handed her the bunch of roses, but something was holding her back. They had not much to talk about, she and Nigel, yet she was aware of the temptation to talk too much. It would be ludicrous to unburden herself to this man who couldn't possibly understand, still less care. She would make herself as pathetic as he was. And yet he had his own dignity, was kind and anxious to please. And he was lonely. Was there any harm in giving him a little of her time? She felt a familiar withdrawal from the thought that he might have need of her. She had no wish to be needed.

She decided to go indoors and have a cold shower before her lunch, afterwards to lie on her bed and read until she fell asleep. But when her house came into view she saw parked outside it the dusty little Citroën. Leaning against her door in his familiar shirt and shorts was the Major. He straightened up when he saw her, brushing down his moustache. He was holding a bunch of roses.

'Maggie, I thought you couldn't be far away since your car was here. You look very hot.'

'Yes.' It was pointless to deny it. 'And thirsty. Would you like a glass of beer?'

He positively bounced into the hall after her. 'I wondered if you would care to come and have a swim? It is exceptionally hot for May.'

After all, the thought was irresistible. She accepted his roses and his invitation gracefully.

That night she wrote to Harriet.

I have spent a delicious afternoon swimming in Nigel Tyson's pool. He is a strange man, so stiff and pompous in some ways, so absolutely slovenly in others. The pool was pristine clean yet the bathroom was a disgrace, I

84

had to resist getting busy with the lavatory cleaner and scouring powder! And the kitchen's not much better. I suggested, tactfully, that he gets somebody in to clean, but he said he can't afford it. He's a strong swimmer with a good body for his age, which must be about sixty. I felt horribly flabby and out of condition, though thank goodness I have been acquiring quite a tan in the privacy of my own little garden.

I have bought my paints and brushes, and report for my first lesson in two days' time. I hope I find Chloe Erskine a little more welcoming. She is quite an alarming person, despite her vulnerability – or maybe because of it.

But how are you, my dear? You said very little in your letter about how you are feeling. Stronger, I hope. When will you be returning to work? Not that you aren't welcome to stay in the house for as long as you like, but I guess you will be anxious to pick up the threads again. You were never one for doing nothing.

I am very disturbed by Sheila's news. I expect you will have assumed (correctly) from the papers that she is one of those that have resigned. While I applaud her solidarity with her colleagues, and the motives behind it, I do wonder how long she will stick it out. She has never been one for trouble or aggravation. Despite her brave face, she likes to keep a low profile, if you will excuse the hotchpotch of metaphors!

It would be good to have you to talk to. How are Cassie and the family? I expect another missive from her any day. It's funny to think of her visiting you, not me. Don't let her lean on you too much. Give them my love – and my love to you of course, as always. Maggie.

When the telephone rang, she was just setting out for Serenidad and her painting lesson. She had gathered up her paints and brushes, a pad of watercolour board, a shawl and an old shirt which she proposed using as a smock.

85

Everything had to be put down again to pick up the receiver. She hoped it wasn't Chloe, ringing to put her off.

It was Sheila.

'Mother? I got your two letters. Thank you for replying so fast. Things are obviously going well.'

'They are.' Maggie drew a defensive wall about her equilibrium. She had no wish to be unbalanced. 'But how are things with you? Has anything changed? I've been trying to follow it in *The Times*, but I'm never quite up to date.'

'Nothing's changed. It looks quite hopeless. They're determined to make an example of Leonard. Consequently, of course, he's becoming a martyr to the cause. There's no alternative but to fall in behind him.'

'But you don't really want to?' It sounded as though Sheila very much wanted to.

'That doesn't really come into it. There's a principle at stake. All our positions become untenable if we can't have confidence in our own decisions. Or in the support of the Department.'

'But how will you manage? Are you being paid?'

'Mother! Of course not. Technically, I'm unemployed. But having made myself so, I can't draw benefit either.'

Maggie was nonplussed. Her heart sank like a stone, there was the familiar feeling of sickness. Like when Sheila had repeatedly failed to obtain the jobs she sought, before being offered the one she had now apparently thrown away. Like when Cassie had thought she was having a miscarriage in the middle of Marks and Spencer and Maggie had had to hold her hand while she lay among the shelves of matching kitchenware too frightened to move until the ambulance arrived. She wondered what Robert would have said to Sheila. Would he have offered her money, told her not to worry, she could always turn to them? He had certainly given her money while she was trying to find a job, but she had been living at home then, with no rent to pay.

'What about your rent?' she heard herself ask, unwillingly.

'It's paid up till the end of the month, and I've got next month's already. But I have to eat of course. Maybe I shall find out what it's like to be on the receiving end of charity!'

'Sheila! Are you sure there's nowhere you can turn to?'

'There's Income Support, if one can live on peanuts. But I have to sign on to claim it. I'm not sure I'm ready for that. Don't worry, Mother. I've no wish to spoil your idyll. And we're all in the same boat, it isn't as if I was the only one.'

'But all the same. Listen, don't go without. You will let me know if you need help, won't you? You're doing the right thing, I'm sure you are.'

'Thanks, Mother. I expect I shall manage. I'll have to go. You're sure you're well yourself? I can't believe you're coping alone. You've no regrets?'

'No, dear. I've no regrets and I've never felt better.'

'That is, until now,' she added silently, replacing the telephone.

She regathered her things and set out up the humming noonday hill to Serenidad.

# EIGHT

Another letter arrived from Harriet. It was not as thick as the last, but Maggie found herself opening it with unusual curiosity. She had been thinking of her friend with some concern. Now perhaps she would learn if this had been unfounded.

It began enthusiastically.

> *Thank* you for the little painting of the Monastery of Santa Maria de Oya. I have hung it conspicuously over the mantelpiece – in place of that old print of Clovelly. You haven't lost your touch – it's lovely. I suppose one day you might be back to see it.
>
> Well, here I am, reinstated in Kew. It was so good to get home. Six weeks is a long time. It will be better still to get back to work.

Here, Harriet had put down her pen, reflecting on the consolation that work brought her. She knew some people thought the law dull – but she found freedom in the very discipline it imposed. At work, she could do what she liked within the bounds of contracts and conveyances, registrations, legal charges and restrictive covenants. Everything was cut and dried. It was the kind of framework she had missed as a child, which Margaret had and which she had envied. While, perversely, Margaret had seemed to envy her.

She continued,

> Cassie used to come and see me often while I was at Heathercote. She brought me magazines and fruit, and

88

fussed about the house watering plants and arranging cushions. She is an endearing girl, so pretty in her plump way.

But she is demanding! For the first time I began to understand how you need to pull away. No decision is either too trivial or too personal to share, to chew over and examine and be reassured upon. I don't mean this so much as criticism of your daughter, as an indication that I sympathise with how you feel. It used to annoy me, if I'm honest, your embarrassed reticence when I congratulated you on your good fortune in having a daughter and grandson near at hand. I used to think you ungrateful. Now I begin to see.

But I feel sorry for her too. She said to me one day, 'I hate having to tell people my name is Cassandra. I mean, I'm just not a Cassandra, am I?' And I suppose I have to agree. She's never going to set the world on fire. But I shouldn't be saying all this to you, you are her mother.

It's a pity she won't make more attempt to share Anthony's interests – his love of Indian food which she resolutely refuses to learn to cook – his passion for that pink Capri with its leopard-skin upholstery which he takes to shows (though I confess I'm rather with her there!). Fortunately he seems to adore her. He certainly thinks the world of Robert.

Robert is a delicious little boy. I got very fond of him, but it was not without pain. I don't mean when he climbed on my lap and hurt my scar – I mean the other scar which never heals, which has been reopened as my body was opened and all possibility of becoming a mother was finally and irrevocably snipped away. I hadn't anticipated that it would hurt so much. I had filled the vacancy and closed the door. There was no longer any room in my life for a child. This is another reason for wanting to get back to work. I must rediscover my *raison d'être*.

But I do still feel wretchedly tired, and there is more pain than I expected to feel by now. A sort of deep down indefinable soreness and exhaustion, though the doctor tells me 'not to worry', to rest and 'take a little holiday'. But what have I been doing if not having a holiday?

Write again soon – I long for news – love Harriet.

She couldn't bring herself to ask if she could come and stay. Why was it that she felt now that she would be in the way?

Having read the letter in one gulp, Maggie lay it on the coffee table and picked thoughtfully at her lip. It was not like Harriet to be so revealing. Her talk of pain – both in the emotional and the physical sense, brought pain to Maggie. Furthermore, she was not sure she liked her shrewd assessment of Cassie. It was one thing for her, Maggie, to find fault. Quite another for someone else, even her oldest friend. And Cassie's own plaintive complaint against her name cut her to the quick. It was true that her hopes of her second child, presaged by her name, had been unfulfilled – but she had never intended Cassie to suffer from her expectations. Guilt rose in a hot flush against the anticipation of a day spent painting in the hills, and cast a shadow over the sun. She picked up Cake and fondled his ears in an ecstasy of tenderness that she realised was meant for Cassie. She must ask her to come and stay – soon – but not yet.

# NINE

As the Major had predicted, Maggie found in her painting both solace and stimulation. She also found that she had retained what little talent she had possessed and, egged on and inspired by Lorne's encouragement, her confidence grew. How much of her pleasure was due to Lorne she had no wish to investigate fully. The realisation that she was now a single woman, but by no means past her prime, had disturbed her. The terms she had thought to have come to over her life seemed, distressingly, to have been amended. The goalposts had been moved. She had taken for granted the rewarding and simple sex life which she had shared with Robert. His lovemaking had, like Robert himself, been generous, good-natured and satisfactory. Since his death she had felt no desire, a phenomenon she had gratefully attributed to shock and then the menopause. Now, in the heat of midsummer, she was plagued by a twittering rest-lessness which manifested itself in turgid dreams which left her ashamed and dissatisfied. More dangerous, it was lead-ing her into foolish fantasising over Lorne.

It was late June. The days were long; Lorne had suggested that they paint the battlemented headland at Baiona in the protracted evening light. At half-past ten the sun had finally sunk into the smooth sea, its crimson path reaching to their feet and then diminishing, fractured and dissolved. They sat together on a stone bench still warm from the day. Regretfully Maggie said, 'Chloe will be wondering. Did you say we'd be out this late?'

'No. But Nigel was calling in, remember? He's not exactly

glittering company, but it will have passed an hour or two. And I do need an escape, just occasionally.'

The sensation of hope was dangerous, and disconcertingly naïve. 'I'm sure that's so,' she said carefully. 'It must all be a terrible strain.'

'She's so brave about it. Usually. I can see that you find her uncomfortable but it's only her way of coping.'

'You know another side of her I'm sure. Vulnerable, frightened . . .'

'We're both frightened. Of when, and how . . . but then, you've been through it yourself.'

'But I had no warning. No dread. I wasn't called upon to be brave and supportive, to keep cheerful. I couldn't have done it, I'm sure.'

'And I'm sure you could, if you'd had to.'

They each stared at the strawberry sea.

She mused, 'People these days aren't really called upon to do very much at all, are they? I mean, in the usual run of events. When you think what our forebears had to cope with. Especially the women. Helping at births, nursing the sick, laying out their dead. I've never even skinned and cleaned a rabbit, let alone strangled a chicken! Sometimes, I feel quite inept. Life has been too easy. Nobody is put to the test any more. Somebody else always does the dirty work.'

'I'm sure you could strangle a chicken if your life depended on it, which it largely did, in those days. And we do what we have to do, don't you think? These brave forebears you so admire would surely balk at the idea of using a computer, driving a car through the London rush hour, even facing Gatwick airport on a summer Saturday! We are all people of our time. It just happens that our time seems a little bit cleaner. The bad things are hidden away, obligingly dealt with or taken off by somebody else. But we have created new problems for ourselves – rubbish, pollution, climatic change. We cope with these, just as they coped with pneumonia and smallpox and doing everything by hand.'

'That's all very well, but I can't use a computer, and Robert always drove when we went to London. So, you see, I am really very useless!'

He laughed. 'Well, useless you may be, but you wield a fine paintbrush. Your landscapes are very promising.'

He stood up and she followed him to the car. It was a green Peugeot, a large estate model to accommodate Chloe's wheelchair. Their paints and easels were already in the back.

She got in and he slammed the door.

'Even so,' she said when they were on the road, 'I really prefer painting buildings. Houses, churches – and boats. I like the man-made things. Landscape is too – vague. I like to be more precise. And then again I really would like to try a portrait. Yours are so impressive. Madrilena would be such a perfect subject. I wonder if she'd sit for me. Do you think her parents would mind?'

'I should think they would be honoured.'

'I'm not so sure. Her father's pretty boorish and the señora is positively daunting.'

'But they probably idolise their children, all Spaniards do.'

'I don't think that I'd want to give them the picture though. It would be for me.'

Away from the coast the road was suddenly dark. She couldn't see him as he said, 'I've been wanting to get back to some portraiture myself. I don't suppose you'd sit for me, would you?'

She was startled, excited, ridiculously flattered. 'But I'm not beautiful, like Madrilena.'

'No, but you have an interesting face, mature and well-boned.'

Foolish to be so disappointed. 'Thank you. I sound like a piece of well-hung game!'

'No, I meant it to be a compliment. From one painter to another. I thought you'd understand.'

'Oh I do.' Very much, she wanted him to know she understood. 'And I do take it as a compliment and I would be delighted to sit for you. As long as Chloe doesn't mind.'

'Why should she? It will hardly be the first time after all.'

'No, of course not.' Why should Chloe mind, indeed?

She prepared her request carefully then walked up to the garage to see Madrilena's parents. She wanted it to be a special visit, not incidental to purchasing oil or petrol. Señor Vara was busy at the pumps, his greasy face leering into the window of a new Rover with GB plates, whose driver, a cool blonde in a silk headscarf, was obviously impervious to his charms. Maggie suppressed a feeling of revulsion. It was inconceivable that those fat oily hands might handle and caress Madrilena's smooth brightness. With a nod and a smile she bypassed the father and headed for the mother, seated in her little office behind the ancient till, surrounded by oily bills, spanners, wrenches, dirty mugs and blackened engine parts scattered like the droppings of some prehistoric bird.

'*Buenos días, Señora. Cómo estás?*'

The woman looked surprised. Usually she was only visited by customers settling accounts or complaining about the dubious servicing of the mechanic. '*Muy buen, gracias. Y usted?*' she responded in a tone which implied obligation rather than interest. She waited, suspiciously.

Maggie said carefully, 'I have come to ask a favour. Did you know that I am a painter?'

It seemed a silly question. How could the woman possibly know? Also it rather overstated the case. However, there seemed to be no better way of approaching her request.

The woman's thin lined face was inscrutable, the dark eyes unhelpful. Maggie stumbled on, her accent and her grammar going all to pieces.

'Your daughter Madrilena has become quite a friend. She often calls in to see me, and play with the cat. I hope you don't mind this? She is a very beautiful child. Very beautiful! I would like to paint her. I would need her to come and sit for me, for an hour at a time perhaps. Would you be agreeable to this, now that school has finished?'

'You wish to paint a picture of Madrilena?' The woman looked interested. 'How much would you charge for this?'

Maggie thought she had misunderstood. Perhaps payment was being asked of her? 'Well, I hadn't thought . . .'

'A portrait is expensive. We hadn't considered having one of Madrilena until her first communion.'

Maggie felt absurdly nervous. 'Well, I really wanted the picture for myself. To keep. There would, of course, be no charge in that case.' She sensed disappointment, possible resistance. 'But if you like it, perhaps I could do another one for you.' Boldly she added, 'We could discuss the price at that time.'

There was a pause. '*Sí*. That would seem a good arrangement. And it will keep the child off the streets for a while. I will send her to you. When do you want to start?'

'I'd rather ask her myself, if you are agreeable. I expect I will see her soon. Thank you, señora.' She smirked her gratitude, almost genuflected as she left the dreary little room. Despite her shabbiness the woman had a presence. Maggie could not imagine a more unlikely pair than the Varas, one so pruriently greasy, the other formidable and enigmatic. She felt anxious for Madrilena at the mercy of such diverse forces, such negligent care. Walking home she thought of Sheila, allowing a coil of worry to wind through her mind.

She had heard nothing since her telephone call. As far

as possible she had followed the news but English papers were unobtainable in the town. Nigel Tyson, who had the *Telegraph* posted out to him from England, had let her see it once or twice, but the news was always out of date. An inquiry had been initiated, questions were being asked and iniquities unearthed. Leonard Hawkins had been suspended indefinitely. The resignations still held. How was Sheila living? The worry expanded into fear.

'Maggie! A penny for them, eh?' Nigel bounced purposefully out of the shadows. She felt an irritated pleasure. He was always so deliberately cheerful, so flattering and eager to please. He carried a carrier bag of fruit, a loaf of bread and a rolled up newspaper. 'Brought you another copy of the paper. And some pears. Not as good as English ones, of course, but you may like them. Nothing wrong with the car I hope?'

'Nigel! I do have legs and I do use them sometimes.'

'And very attractive they are if I might say so. No offence. Only it's so hot. Nothing much in the paper today – case seems to be taking a back seat. More interesting news to report from Lithuania.'

She asked him in, got beer out of the fridge, settled them both on the terrace in a shady corner. Cake crawled out of the vine and onto her lap, kneading the blue and purple fabric of her skirt, his purr a miniature helicopter. She slid her hand into his fur, comforted by his welcome, his unquestioning friendship. As, unwillingly, she was by the Major's. Not for the first time, she felt she should be keeping him at a distance, but faced with his genial flattery, she didn't quite know how.

'How is the painting coming along?' he was asking. 'Erskine tells me you're a model pupil.'

'Hardly. A beginner really!'

'Nonsense. Your stuff is excellent. Excellent.' He sipped his beer. '*Cerveza*.' He was looking at the label on the empty bottle. 'Strange language. Why on earth should beer be *cerveza*?'

'Why should it be beer?'

He looked at her uncomprehendingly.

'I'm going to paint Madrilena. I've just been to ask permission. Bearded the lioness in her den, so to speak.'

'A formidable lady, Señora Vara. She needs to be, with that man of hers! And did she give it? Her permission?'

'Yes, I'm pleased to say. Actually, she seemed prepared to pay me to paint the child, but I think it's rather early days to be taking commissions, don't you?'

A lorry thundered past, its load of produce rattling on the back; tomatoes and aubergines, peppers and lettuces enfolded in a cloud of dust. There were market gardens a few miles up the road; Maggie had established that the morning onslaught was principally their delivery to Baiona, Vigo and Pontevedra. When the racket had subsided she heard the summons of the telephone. It was Sheila. And she wanted to come and stay.

'She didn't say very much, but obviously she just wants to get away. It's understandable.' Maggie smoothed the rug over Chloe's feet, ignoring her tetchiness. Lorne had said she was under the weather. He had to drive to Santiago, something about his exhibition. He didn't like to leave her for a whole day. Would Maggie come? Eagerly, for motives she didn't care to examine, Maggie had agreed, had purchased peaches and a potted plant. Brushing aside objections she had made tea and brought it to where Chloe lay on the sofa. It was blistering outside but the sunless room was cool and a small fire flickered in the huge hearth.

Surprisingly, Chloe had been sympathetic when she told her about Sheila's situation. 'It's preposterous,' she had blustered. 'How can they expect people to work under such pressures?'

97

'Obviously in this case they have reached the point when they can't. But I worry, naturally, about Sheila. Her work means so much to her. You could say it's her life, really. Now the ground has been knocked from under her feet.'

'I know the feeling.' Chloe closed her eyes suddenly. She did look dreadfully ill, Maggie thought. She bristled at the sound of a car engine at the front of the house. Chloe had told her, 'I would have gone with him . . . next time perhaps.' Now, looking at her Maggie wondered if there would be a next time. Panic that she might be having some sort of collapse was alleviated by the sound of footsteps approaching from round the house. Lorne came in, his shadow blocking the light from the open doorway. Maggie was leaning over the couch and he came quickly, his long strides covering the room in an instant.

She asked worriedly, 'Is she all right? We were talking . . .'

He leaned over, examining his wife's face. He didn't touch her. Then he said, 'She's asleep, that's all. She does that, quite suddenly. It's as if the last ounce of strength drains away.' He looked perturbed none the less. 'Don't worry, Maggie. I expect it was having you here that tired her, but I'm grateful.'

He looked strained himself, exhausted.

'Would you like some tea?' she asked.

'If you'll join me.'

She made a point of hesitating then said, 'Well, if you're sure Chloe won't mind. I mean, if I've worn her out already.'

'Don't take it so personally. It wasn't you, it would have been anybody. Even me.' Sorrow emanated like a fog. She wanted to touch him and say, 'I'm so sorry, Lorne. If only there was something I could do . . .' Instead she said, 'It's dreadful. I don't know how you bear it.' Then, briskly, 'Now, let me put the kettle on. Tea – the universal panacea!

Where do you get the Earl Grey? Do you have it sent from England? I see you have some more digestives! I really must remind Cassie to send me some.'

'Yours were so good I wrote to Fortnum's for a supply. I had forgotten the pleasure of them. Memories of milk and biscuits by the fire, all that sort of thing. They regularly send us tea. And Marmite. Chloe's very partial to Marmite. It's funny the things you miss.'

She looked across at Chloe. She was sleeping deeply, her mouth fallen slightly open, the darkened pockets of her eyes accentuated by the shadowy room and the plaster-cast pallor of her face. Marmite didn't seem too much to ask. To think Maggie had been frightened of her. She poured tea. It was impossible not to notice his long supple fingers as he handled his cup. Guilt smote her for the desire she felt. She stared hard at Chloe, willing her presence into the unconscious form, offering an apology. She stared at the table, at the biscuit in her hand, at the seascapes on the rough plaster of the wall. She stared at anything and everything, except at Lorne.

Chloe recovered as suddenly as she had collapsed and, to Maggie's surprise, invited her to stay to supper. When Lorne said he would prepare it, there seemed no very good reason for refusing.

'How are the exhibition plans working out?' Maggie asked him as they sat round the table.

He picked up a chicken leg, turned it over and over before biting into it energetically.

'Very well,' he answered eventually. 'It's such a splendid setting. Have you been inside the parador?'

'Not at Santiago, no. But I shall make a point of coming to the exhibition. As one of your most dedicated students!'

Chloe was picking wanly at some succulent breast. 'Is it still to be in November?' she asked. There was a bleakness in her face. Maggie met Lorne's eyes and looked away. November seemed impossibly out of reach.

'As far as I know,' he said. 'They seem to be involved in major renovation works there. It just depends on the room being ready.'

Maggie asked, 'And have you chosen the work you'll exhibit? I hope you'll include some portraits. They are still your best, I think.'

'I haven't many though. Usually, of course, they were commissioned.'

'Oh – I almost have a commission myself! Little Madrilena. Her mother seems to want to buy her picture. And I haven't even started it yet.'

'What did I tell you?' Lorne looked pleased.

'I hope you'll help me. I told her the first one would be for me. If she likes it, I shall do another.'

'Naturally I will. And we must think about your sitting for me.' His hand took Chloe's. 'I told you, darling, remember? I've asked Maggie to sit for me. It's a long time since I've done a portrait.'

'I don't remember.' Chloe looked confused. 'I suppose if you say you did, you must have done.' The old resentment flashed briefly.

'Perhaps you can exhibit me!' Maggie said brightly.

'Why not indeed?'

She gave him a brilliant smile of pleasure which she pulled into composure as Chloe's eyes burned into her like the dying embers of a fire.

Sheila walked off the plane wearing a neat wool suit and flat, comfortable shoes, carrying a large handbag and a raincoat over her arm. Her short hair was freshly permed and she looked with alarm at the girls in front of her in the line. From their frayed and patched jeans to their bleached and jagged hair they exuded a casual nonchalance which threw her sensible solidity into sharp relief. Maggie knew again the exasperated sorrow which so often afflicted her when seeing Sheila against the backdrop of other young women. Two months' absence had trapped her into unwittingly hoping that something might have changed. But nothing had.

She pushed at her own loose hair defiantly as she walked to greet her daughter. It was below her shoulders now, and while feeling she was too old for such a style she reassured herself that nobody seemed to think it strange. Indeed Nigel seemed to positively admire it, and he was over sixty.

She forced a welcome into her voice, her smile. The girl looked tired. She had been having a bad time, after all. Sheila said, 'What on earth have you done with your hair? Aren't there any hairdressers in Spain?'

Maggie said defensively, 'I'm sure there are when I feel I need one.' She felt resentful. She had never criticised Sheila's tight, middle-aged perm nor her unstylish clothes. Ever aware of her sensibilities, she had tried to allow her to simply be, even if now she looked almost older than herself, wearing as Maggie was a deep indigenous tan and bare legs brushed only by a calf-length cotton skirt. Sheila would certainly be wearing tights. She had never as far as Maggie knew embraced the new reversal to stockings and suspender belts.

'It's good to see you,' she lied sadly, wrapping her arms round the girl's stiff shoulders.

'And you. You look well.'

Maggie reached for her case. Sheila clung on to it. 'Where's the car?' She glanced round dismissively. 'What a small airport. I was expecting something like Gatwick.'

'Hardly, dear. And thank goodness for that. Shall I take your bag?'

'There's no need. I'm not an invalid. You really must stop fussing.'

'Do I fuss? I try not to. The last thing I want to be is fussed.'

There was a warning there but Sheila exclaimed, 'Oh dear, it's hot! And so humid.'

They had left the building. Maggie allowed herself, 'Well, you are hardly dressed for the Spanish summer.'

'But I left the English summer, remember. Manchester was obliterated with rain, Heathrow not much better. It's been a ghastly month so far.'

'It's only the second of July!'

'I mean the last month generally.'

Maggie opened the back of the car. Sheila lifted in the case and Maggie saw the Lunn Poly labels from her package tour to Rome and Florence. She had gone in October, when the crowds and the sun had waned. Sheila didn't like the sun, or swimming or lying on the beach. 'I hope you won't find the heat too wearing. I'm just about getting used to it but it is exceptionally hot this year from all accounts.'

Sheila wound down her window. 'It's like an oven in here certainly. Let's just get moving, for goodness' sake. By the look of the sky there's going to be a storm. It's very threatening.'

Glancing at the sky and with a smothered sigh of resignation Maggie agreed that it was probably so.

# TEN

The storm had broken overnight, relieving the pressure but not easing the tension. Sheila had slept badly on the makeshift bed Maggie had made by buying a thick foam mattress for the rickety sunbed, which she had installed in the dining room. It was cheerless enough with the heavy unused furniture and tiled floor, but she felt her daughter should be grateful. Despite her vague intimations of hospitality before she left, Maggie had not been expecting visitors.

'You're in the coolest place,' she said encouragingly as she took in a breakfast tray. She was determined to play her part.

'I'm glad you think so.' Sheila had never been good in the mornings, Maggie reminded herself, stooping to pull up the trailing blanket. Sheila growled, 'I don't need that, for heaven's sake. What time is it anyway?'

'Eight o'clock. It's late for me, but I thought you'd like a lie-in. I expect the storm disturbed you.'

She saw that Sheila was wearing long-sleeved cotton pyjamas. 'Perhaps a nightdress would be cooler?' she couldn't resist. She herself had slept naked. She pulled up the blind and opened the door into the garden which was steaming dry in the morning sun. Each leaf and bloom was vibrant and sparkling. She breathed in, deeply and desperately. 'The air has cleared wonderfully. I usually have my breakfast out here. Will you join me?'

'If you like.'

Maggie stepped outside with relief, setting the tray on a low wall and opening two folding chairs. Water streamed from their canvas seats. 'I'll get a towel for these,' she said, but Sheila had disappeared up to the bathroom.

'I thought we'd go into Vigo today. I need some things,' said Maggie when breakfast was eventually under way. She passed a plate of cherry cakes. Despite herself she had become quite fond of the decadent Spanish breakfast. Sheila looked askance, spreading a piece of toast. 'You'll get fat.' Then, 'I thought you only liked salted butter,' she commented. 'We always had it at home.'

'Yes well, when in Rome, as Nigel would say . . .'

'Nigel is the admirer, I suppose. The one who brings you flowers?'

'Sometimes, yes.' She was cautious. 'He has a certain old-world charm. And he's lonely.'

Sheila chewed disagreeably. 'And aren't you?' she asked at length.

'Not really. It's easier out here, where nobody knew your father. And I have friends now. There's Lorne and Chloe. And Lilli. She's amazing.' For Lilli had indeed become a friend. She had called in once or twice, uninvited but with a casual assumption of a welcome that Maggie could never have dared herself. Maggie had tentatively returned the compliment but found Lilli out, confirming that to call unexpectedly was never a good idea.

'Hasn't Chloe some ghastly disease? That must be cheerful for you.'

'It's not much fun certainly. But Lorne is charming and they are both so brave. And, of course, there's my painting. I find that a tremendous pleasure.'

'I was looking at them last night.' Maggie had arranged her watercolours along the top of the bare oak sideboard. 'I was impressed.'

'Thank you.' Was the compliment grudging? 'You'll meet little Madrilena Vara too. She's an absolute delight. I'm going to paint her. I'm quite excited about it.'

'That's good. I'm glad you're so contented.'

The girl looked bleak. Maggie reached out and took her hand. 'Oh darling, it does seem unfair, I know. When you've been having such a bad time. Why not have a nice cool shower now? And wear something light, won't you. But you'd better cover up at first. The sun is fierce.'

Sheila sighed. 'You're fussing, Mother.'

Washing up, Maggie thought grimly, 'Oh dear. Here we go again.'

Steamy mist hung round the lower slopes of the hills, sucked up like vapour from a kettle between the tall trunks. The eucalyptuses were damply pungent, a huge inhalation which stung the nostrils. 'That's nice,' said Sheila, breathing deeply, but she made no comment about the view which opened up as the mist cleared. Maggie was annoyed. Fortuitously, as if for Sheila's benefit, the countryside was freshly washed, bright, and lush with summer plenitude. The cluster of red-tiled roofs, the grey bulk of a church with its three bells clearly visible in the crumbling façade, the apple orchards and fields of sweetcorn already bursting out of its husks and the distant bluey hills, all were laid out for inspection and applause. But Sheila merely said, 'It doesn't look a bit like Spain.'

'If you mean it's not an arid desert, all dust, cacti and donkeys, you're right. But this is what Spain meant to me and your father. I couldn't have lived anywhere else.'

'Lived?'

'Yes. I live here. For now, anyway.' Maggie spoke firmly, feeling she had to make the point.

There was silence. Sheila stared out of the window, feeling curiously bereft. Her mother really had gone. It was a cold feeling, which manifested itself in a sullen expression. Noticing this, Maggie's heart sank.

105

'We're nearly there,' she said encouragingly. She knew of no other way to reach her.

White villas began, walls bright with bougainvillaea, ornamental cacti and tumbling roses. As they neared the town centre the streets became shabbier with peeling façades and tall, faded doors topped with iron grilles.

'It's a bit of a dump,' Sheila observed.

'Oh I don't know, it has its charm.' Perhaps, Maggie speculated, it was rather a busman's holiday for the girl – her work took her into slums and squats, with shared toilets and blocked drains, weeping children and battered wives. A holiday should be different.

'It gets better further in,' she said reassuringly. 'It's always a job to park, but with any luck – yes . . .' Maggie swung the wheel and sidled the car into a narrow spot beneath a dusty plane tree. 'Well, that saves a parking fee anyway.' She turned to smile at her daughter, willing a response.

'Are we far from the shops?'

'Just a step.' Maggie shouldered her bag and locked the car. She felt it was going to be a long day.

'I need some sheets,' she told Sheila as they picked their way over broken paving stones. 'Having visitors makes me realise how short I am. And maybe you'd like to look at some clothes. I'd like to buy you a present.'

'I've brought plenty of clothes,' said Sheila ungraciously.

'But just a blouse? For a treat?' Maggie was ashamed to hear herself wheedling her daughter, as if she were trying to buy her favour.

Sheila shrugged. 'Well, it's up to you.'

In the centre the streets were smarter, with shiny shop fronts displaying stylish clothes in a subtly non-English way. 'What I really need is a department store but I don't think there is one. But there's a linen shop in the next street.'

There wasn't a vast selection, but, desperate for some participation, Maggie engaged Sheila in making a choice

106

between some pink and blue striped sheets with matching pillowcases, and a blue and white set sprigged with flowers.

Sheila reluctantly joined in. 'I suppose the floral is the nicest. But you must please yourself.'

Maggie fingered the floral linen dubiously. 'I don't really know. I think perhaps I need them both.'

'Then get them both. I can't think why you asked me.'

Maggie sighed as she paid. To her surprise, Sheila held out her hand for the carrier bag, as if belatedly deciding to be friends.

Maggie didn't mention the blouse again and decided against choosing some new sandals for herself. The shopping trip was not turning out to be the convivial occasion she had hoped for. Walking back to their parking space she remarked that the sooner they got home the better, as the heat was building up. They had almost reached the car when she was surprised to hear her name called from the other side of the road, and turning she saw Nigel Tyson, with Finn bounding beside him. She paused, putting a hand on Sheila's arm, as Nigel grabbed the dog's collar, dodged the traffic and strode across the road to meet them.

'Maggie, this is a pleasure.' He was beaming and looked enquiringly at Sheila, who was staring at him in astonishment. Who, she asked herself, was Maggie? To confound her confusion, she saw the bumptious little man lean and give her mother a light kiss on the forehead. Now Maggie was startled too. He had never done so before: some curious compulsion to display his right to her company must have driven him.

'This is my daughter Sheila. I told you she was coming to stay.'

He held out his hand. 'Charmed, I'm sure. And have you had a successful shop?' He glanced at the bag in Sheila's hand. 'Women's treats, I expect.'

107

'Sheets, actually.' Sheila took his hand reluctantly. 'And you are?'

Maggie was flustered. 'I'm sorry. This is Nigel. I've spoken about him.'

'Have you indeed?' Nigel beamed again. 'Nothing untoward, I hope.'

Sheila said nothing. Just then Finn nosed at her skirt, and she pushed him away. 'Sit,' Nigel instructed briskly, and the dog sat obediently, gazing up at him in adoration.

'Perhaps you would join me for lunch?' he said now. 'I was on my way to a curry.'

Maggie hesitated. Did Sheila like curry? Maggie had never cooked it herself. Perhaps, in multiracial Liverpool . . . But it was difficult to imagine Sheila being ethnic. Curry would be something that smelled, annoyed neighbours and reduced the value of their property. Curry was something that Sheila's problem families ate.

She smiled regretfully. 'I don't think, so, Nigel, thank you. Another time.'

She sensed Sheila's relief, and the girl even mustered a smile as they said goodbye. Walking to the car, Sheila asked curiously, 'Would you have gone if it hadn't been for me? If you were on your own?'

Maggie wasn't sure. 'I don't know. Possibly. He's quite harmless and it's somebody to talk to. Even I like people to talk to.' She was conscious that her tone was propitiatory and gave an embarrassed smile as she opened the car door. 'Get in – and thanks for carrying the bag.'

There was silence until they had left the town behind. Then Sheila burst out as if she could restrain herself no longer, 'Well, I think he's a dreadful little man! I wonder you bother with him at all.'

Maggie was shocked, and angry. She gripped the steering wheel wishing wildly that it was Sheila's throat. She had rarely lost her temper with her, barely had the courage to stand up to her sometimes. But that had been before.

Now she snapped, 'He's not a dreadful little man, he's very kind, and you don't even know him.'

'Well, what's all this Maggie business? Bit of a cheek, don't you think?'

'He calls me that because I told him it was my name. Everyone here calls me Maggie. I like it. I'm tired of being Margaret. Tired of being the same old me. Can you try and understand that?'

The girl was looking at her in astonishment. Her mother was a stranger and once more she felt the coldness of exclusion.

'Okay, okay. No need to get steamed up.'

But Maggie found she liked being steamed up. It was liberating. The car bowled recklessly downhill as she stormed, 'I have every right. It's my life. Just because you . . .'

'Because what?'

Maggie had braked suddenly. There was a cart ahead, laden with hay which drooped to the ground like a grey-green head of hair. Hidden from view was the worn-out horse that pulled it, the gnarled farmer who would lovingly craft it into its pear-shaped stack. His wife, following on foot, black-skirted and beaming, waved them on with a sweep of her pitchfork. Maggie beamed back lovingly.

Now she spoke more gently. 'I love these people. I love this place. I'm happy here. I don't want you to spoil it, just because you're unhappy.'

The road ahead was straight and empty. She risked a glance at her daughter. 'You are unhappy, aren't you? It's more than just the job.'

Sheila bit her lip sternly in a way she had done as a child when she fell and was trying not to cry. She had always been brave and fierce. If only she had cried sometimes . . . Maggie could have warmed to her then, comforted her as a mother should instead of being left standing timidly on the edge of the battlefield. Cassie had always cried, extravagantly; at least that enabled one to offer a token comfort, irritating as it had become as she grew older. Now, Sheila sat rigid in her frumpy sundress, her feet encased in heavy plastic sandals, unshaven calves white, toenails unpainted. A terrible pain of pity turned Maggie's stomach to water. She parked the car untidily outside the house. They sat for a moment, not speaking. Then Maggie said, 'Let's go in. And perhaps you can tell me all about it.'

Cake was on the terrace crying to come in. Maggie opened the door and was surprised to see Sheila intercept his onward flight to the kitchen.

'We have a cat in the office. Everyone fights for his attention. Or did, rather . . . It's funny how flattered one is when a cat responds. Oh dear . . .' For Cake had let her down, jumping out of her arms with a swift rebuff and galloping down the stairs to be fed.

'Never mind,' consoled Maggie. 'He's hungry that's all. Sit down, and I'll feed him.'

They had bought a copy of the *Telegraph*. Sheila scanned the pages, eventually folding back page five. 'Here it is,' she said when Maggie returned. 'We seem to have been relegated. There's to be an interim inquiry. But not until August or September! Leonard is still suspended and the rest of us are "holding firm".' She pushed the paper aside onto the sofa. 'Poor Leonard. How it must be hanging over him.'

Maggie remembered the newspaper pictures of Leonard, a plump man with greying hair receding at the sides, though always described as 'Leonard Hawkins, 42'. She said carefully, 'And you are sure that this Leonard is innocent? Well – that's not quite the right word. I mean, he did do everything possible, he might not have been negligent after all? The rest of you have sacrificed everything for him. It can't be much fun for family men, living on the pittance you get from Income Support.'

Sheila said snappily, 'Of course I'm sure. And even if I wasn't – well, you wouldn't understand, everyone can make a mistake. You don't know the pressures. And there was such a furore, last time, about children being taken away unnecessarily. All those horror stories about families breaking up and children being scarred for life. Naturally, one thinks twice before unleashing that sort of a storm.'

'Yes, I do see. Is this Leonard a family man? How is he managing, I wonder. And what a terrible strain on his wife.'

'No. Well, he has a family but he's divorced.' Unexpectedly her cheeks began to glow and as Maggie watched, the flush turned to a violent, patchy red. Sheila began to scratch irritably at a mosquito bite on her arm.

So here's the crux of the matter, thought Maggie. 'Do you . . . are you . . . ?' She hesitated. This was new ground. There had never, as far as Maggie knew, been a man. She had wished, fervently, that there might be.

'What are you trying to say, Mother?' Sheila's gaze was direct and brave, the blush had paled.

'It's not my business but I did wonder whether perhaps, you and Leonard . . . Well, you do seem to be more than merely concerned for him.'

'He's a good man. We've worked together for a long time. I don't like to see him made a scapegoat for the shortcomings of the Department.'

'And do you think he'd do the same for you?'

'For me – for anyone!'

'But you're not someone special to him?'

'No, Mother. I'm sorry to say it, but no.'

'Nor he to you?'

Sheila stood up. 'What is this, the Spanish Inquisition?' She flung outside and leaned over the railings, her navy-blue skirt crushed against the vine. Then she turned and

111

said, 'There's somebody arriving to see you. In a shabby old estate car. I think I'll take a shower.'

'But that will be Lilli. Do stay and meet her. She's such fun.'

'Maybe, but I'm not, am I?'

'Sheila, dear . . .'

But she had gone.

At least the water was hot, thought Sheila. It could so easily have been a tepid brown trickle. Yet, perversely, while she had been prepared to tolerate flaws in her mother's adventure, to be understanding and sympathetic at signs of dissatisfaction or disappointment, what she hadn't reckoned on was the complete surrender to a life which seemed entirely dissolute and, moreover, which didn't seem to include her.

She soaped viciously, seeing her skin redden under the lash of water. She had come to Spain in the foolish hope that her mother would somehow sort everything out for her. Realistically, she realised that wasn't possible but, pathetically, she told herself that her father would have done so. She missed him, and to her horror she felt scalding tears mingle with the water which flowed down her face. On top of it all, Leonard, despite her loyalty, quite obviously didn't love her. Something like a sob escaped her and she grabbed at a towel and buried her face.

As if that wasn't humiliating enough, it appeard that her mother had a suitor! Nigel Tyson seemed to claim an intimacy which surely their acquaintance didn't deserve, and what's more he apparently had a villa with a swimming pool. The very real possibility of losing her mother completely to Spain knotted her into panic. It wasn't what she had expected to find. As she dried and dressed, she was wishing she hadn't come.

\*     \*     \*

'Come on up,' Maggie called to Lilli from the top of the stairs.

Lilli took the steps two at a time. 'Has your daughter arrived? I don't want to intrude.'

'Yes, but she's feeling the heat. Please excuse her, she's having a shower. We've been to Vigo.'

Lilli dropped into a chair, her legs sprawled carelessly wide. She pushed at her hair, which was sticking out like a bottle brush. 'I've come to tell you about the Sunday market tomorrow. There is one every month in a big field outside Vigo. I thought maybe you and your daughter . . . perhaps you will find some jugs for your collection?'

'I'd love it. I'm not sure about Sheila.'

'Oh, daughters! One has to just let them get on with it.' The bony fingers went to her throat, fingering the scar. 'Miriam is coming soon, with Pepe. They need the sun. In London it is hot, but all the time grey.'

'That will be lovely. Perhaps she and Sheila . . .' But that would surely be a silly idea. What would they have in common, after all? Sheila would regard Miriam as a 'case', and Miriam, if she was anything like her mother, could only regard Sheila as a tiresome bore.

Maggie was not sorry that her daughter didn't put in an appearance. She found Lilli both stimulating and refreshing. She would have liked to be like Lilli, but found that Lilli clearly thought she was.

'Oh the concert is a disaster,' Lilli said suddenly, leaning forward and scraping her fingers through her hair. 'Nothing will be ready in time I think and that child from the garage is beautiful but has no memory for the steps.'

'Madrilena? She's one of your pupils?' Maggie had a sudden stunning idea for her portrait.

'Why do you sound so surprised? She has been dancing with me for nearly a year.'

'I don't know. She never mentioned it, but why should

she? Perhaps I'm surprised because of her parents. I can't imagine them bothering to help her.'

'Oh, the Varas! They do not have much charisma! But the mother is full of ambition. Madrilena will not be ending up in a petrol station!'

'I hope not! At least not with a man like her father!'

'I must go. We are practising this evening.' She stood up, muscular and graceful. 'I'm so looking forward to seeing you dance,' exclaimed Maggie, enviously. 'Perhaps it's not too late for me to try?'

'Perhaps. But after the concert, please?'

They went downstairs. Maggie could hear Sheila moving about in the dining room. She decided not to call her out. To her surprise when she opened the door she found Madrilena on the step. She was wearing her pink Sunday satin with a bow in a hair. From her ears hung gilded hoops.

Behind her was the dark young man who had helped Maggie with her trunk.

'Marcos is back,' said Madrilena proudly. 'And my mother has sent me to have my picture painted.'

'And I was to make sure she came,' said Marcos. 'I am pleased to meet you again.' His hand was proffered, taken, dropped. Lilli slipped past with a smile and started her old car with a puff of exhaust.

'Come in,' invited Maggie. Sheila would have to stay in her room a little longer. 'Would you like a drink while I talk to Madrilena about her portrait?'

He accepted a beer. She made orange juice for Madrilena, carried the glasses up to the terrace where they were leaning over playing with Cake, who was following a twitching length of vine which Marcos trailed across the tiles. All dainty curiosity, the cat reached out, and sprang, reached out again, then turned his back, bored. Maggie put the glasses on the table. She turned at a movement behind her and saw Sheila, in shapeless white trousers and a black blouse, her hair a damp squiggle about her head. She was looking at Marcos and seemed poised for a retreat.

'Sheila, come and meet Madrilena. And this is Marcos, he helps her father at the garage. But he's really a student, I believe. This is my daughter Sheila.'

Marcos offered a hand and greeted Sheila in Spanish. She looked blank, but offered her own hand readily enough in return. 'I'm afraid she doesn't speak Spanish,' Maggie told him.

She was horrified to see that the patchy blush was once more staining Sheila's face. Marcos was smiling, white-toothed and confident, greeting her in stumbling English. Sheila returned the greeting awkwardly. The blush was still in place. Maggie felt uncomfortable. Then Madrilena shot out a hand and Sheila took it and smiled and Maggie heaved a sigh of relief.

# ELEVEN

To say the Sunday market was held on a field had been less than accurate on the part of Lilli, who had presumably forgotten that to the English a field meant a stretch of grass surrounded by trees, banks or hedges. The dusty wasteland of sharp shale and prickly scrub looked unappealing and far from welcoming when Maggie parked the car, squeezing it between a shabby white van and a purple monstrosity which appeared to have escaped from a 1950s movie. The wind which tore between the sprawl of stalls, vans and tents was armed with litter and was far from warm. Sheila thrust her white arms into a baggy hand-knitted cardigan and Maggie wished she had brought one herself.

Madrilena had come with them, and she skipped to the entrance eagerly, incongruous in shabby espadrilles and a white Sunday dress, apparently oblivious to the cold. Once inside, the crush was inconvenient if not actually uncomfortable. Maggie grasped Madrilena by the hand and went with the flow, Sheila tutting and complaining behind her. Thank goodness, thought Maggie, Sheila, at least, wore sensible shoes. She herself stopped repeatedly to shake the grit from the toe of her flimsy open sandals.

They reached a long run of trestle tables covered in old curtains which whipped in the wind, threatening to dislodge the muddle of curios, memorabilia and downright junk which weighed them down. The accumulation of tat and possible treasure looked inviting. Maggie glanced at Sheila and shrugged. 'Well, here goes,' she said apologetically. Madrilena was already diving into the mêlée like a pig foraging for truffles. Sheila leaned disconsolately against the bonnet of the rusty Bedford van which had presumably transported all the paraphernalia. Pointedly, she buttoned her cardigan.

There was a lot of china of uncertain age and quality. Mildly knowledgeable as she had now become on Mason's Ironstone and Chelsea, underglaze printing, bisque and Clarice Cliff, the various chipped and painted pots and cups, plates and saucers meant nothing to Maggie. But the squat fat jug with a curly handle and decided protruding lip was appealing if, in actual fact, valueless. It was definitely hand-painted, blue on white with touches of a satisfying crimson lake. Slightly crazed, which indicated age, it was none the less undamaged. For thirty pesetas it was hers. Extraordinarily pleased she handed it to Sheila, whose capacious bag could best protect it. 'Be careful,' she warned, for Sheila, expressing amazement, was pushing the loosely wrapped jug roughly into a confusion of purse and wallet, sunglasses and her passport, which she seemed to think it best to carry with her. With barely concealed impatience, as if the jug were a stone picked up from the beach by an irritating child, Sheila buried it deep.

'Will you be long?' she asked. 'It's bloody cold standing here.'

'Then come and help me look.' Maggie didn't like her tone or her language. Once, she would have reprimanded, but then once, she wouldn't have needed to. Neither of the girls had ever sworn. They had been polite, amenable. And dull!

Madrilena tugged at her arm. Eyes shining, she held out a china chicken, brightly coloured, its beak slightly chipped. *'Por mi madre,'* she explained.

Maggie was touched, but wondered what the severe señora would make of it. 'Well done,' she said, touching

117

the child's shiny hair. 'Have you paid for it?' Madrilena patted the pocket of her dress. 'Yes. I have money from Papa.'

Maggie shook her head wonderingly. Perhaps she had misjudged the greasy Vara.

Suddenly Sheila said, 'Give me the key. I'm going back to the car.'

Maggie was disappointed. She had wanted it to be a day out. Too late, she realised her mistake in bringing Madrilena, but she had been eager for the child's company. 'Can you wait just a moment?' she said persuasively. 'There's a pretty shawl . . .' She pulled from a pile a fragile square of silver and petunia pink, and paid quickly. 'Take it back to the car for me.'

'Surely you'll never wear it?'

'I just like it.' Playfully, she draped the flimsy stuff round Shelia's shoulder where it shone out, a bright contradiction against her brown wool cardigan and sturdy cotton skirt. Sheila snatched it off irritably.

Suppressing a sigh Maggie said, 'Give me half an hour, that should do it.' She watched her daughter trudging off across the unaccommodating ground, then turned to Madrilena, bright-eyed and eager beside her. She gave her a wide smile and took her brown hand. 'Let's see what other treasures we can find, shall we?'

They looked round, and Madrilena's arm shot out. 'Cherries!' She was pointing to a fruit stall covered in a windswept awning. Obviously, she fancied some. Indulgently, Maggie allowed herself to be led to the stall. The stallholder seemed to know at once that she was English.

'Delicious cherries,' he boasted. 'For you, fifty pesetas a kilo.'

Maggie smiled, allowing herself to be flattered. He weighed out two kilos, tipping them into a crumpled plastic carrier. They ate them as they wandered, dangling them unwashed into their mouths, casting stalks and stones carelessly onto the dirty ground.

They came on a white car draped, like a bride, from top to toe, from bonnet to boot, with lengths of lace; curtains, bedspreads, tablecloths, pillowcases and ragged scraps. It was presided over by a toothless old woman dressed in black, who sat bolt upright on a wooden chair. Madrilena was entranced, running her fingers through the crumpled piles. Maggie hunted more methodically and at length found a handkerchief with a white lace corner. She paid and it was pushed unceremoniously into a brown paper bag. She held it out to Madrilena, longing for her pleasure.

'For you,' she said. The child gasped as she pulled out the flimsy fragment. She stared at it wide-eyed for a moment, then stood on tiptoe and kissed Maggie's cheek. Something in Maggie dissolved into a clean, uncomplicated rush of love.

But Madrilena had seen something else. Standing beside a table laden with old radios and long-playing records, gleaming white in the sunshine, there was a twin-tub washing machine. They wandered over. To Maggie's surprise, it was a Hoover, its enamel spotless and unchipped, the tub radiant, and pipes neatly coiled and clean. It hardly looked used. She recognised the model from years ago, before she had gone automatic in Godalming.

'For you?' queried Madrilena. 'Then you needn't put the sheets in the bath.'

Maggie was doubtful. 'Well, I suppose so. If it works. You never know, with machines . . .'

'It will work,' said Madrilena firmly. 'Franco is a friend of my father.' She gave a winning smile to the swarthy man seated on a folding chair drinking beer out of a bottle.

'But how would we get it home?' protested Maggie, feeling cautious and English.

Madrilena tilted her head thoughtfully, staring into the

119

distance. Then her eyes focused and her hand shot out. 'There. There is Marcos. He will help.'

And sure enough, coming towards them, his hair black as the proverbial raven's wing, gleaming as a piece of coal, was Marcos.

Madrilena gabbled something at him. He flashed his teeth, his eyes glinted. He picked up one end of the machine easily and said something to Franco, who had put down his bottle and was eyeing them suspiciously. 'But I haven't paid. How much is it?' cried Maggie helplessly, crossly, feeling herself manipulated as surely as was the dubious Hoover.

Marcos let down the machine. 'See Franco. Haggle a bit.'

But Maggie had never haggled in her life. Feeling rather foolish she paid over what she feared might be an exorbitant sum, then looked helplessly at Marcos. 'I can't carry it,' she said. 'And it won't go in my car.'

He shrugged dismissively. 'I have my van. And Franco will help me.'

Thus enlisted, Franco hitched up his jeans over his flabby stomach and lifted his end of the machine. Madrilena skipped delightedly after them and Maggie followed, wondering it she had been made a fool of and for the first time irritated by the intrusive grit between her toes. To her surprise, Marcos's van proved to be the one beside which she had parked. Everything seemed to have been meant. She watched while he and Franco redistributed some of the rubbish in the back, and eased in the machine. From Maggie's car, Sheila was watching them, a paperback still open in her hand. She was wearing a look of resigned astonishment as well as her cardigan, still buttoned firmly to the neck.

Maggie thanked them. Her resentment was surely ungracious. Marcos was looking pleased, Madrilena delighted, even Franco now had a smile. They were certain

120

they were being a help. She opened the car and helped Madrilena strap into the back seat, then got in herself, grateful to be out of the wind.

Marcos watched as she pulled away, guiding her out of a tight corner, hemmed in as she now was by later arrivals. He had lit a cigarette, one hand hung at his side, the smoke coiling upwards, with the other he waved and checked as she manoeuvred. Watching him, Maggie knew that Sheila was watching too. With painful clarity she saw him as her daughter was seeing him: lean, muscular and tanned; arrogant, confident yet with undoubted charm. And how did he see Sheila? There was not so much difference in their ages. She remembered thinking how she would have liked him for a son. Yet it was horribly true that to Marcos, Sheila could only appear as an older sister. Maggie saw her wave, a hand lifted in a little fluttering movement, saw his answering wide grin which encompassed them all. The tyres complained on the stones as she swung the wheel, tightly, one more time, and then they were away, springing forward, spitting dust which was caught up by the wind, half-hiding him from view.

She drove a while in silence. Madrilena was eating cherries, humming to herself. She leaned forward and offered the bag to Sheila, who refused.

'They haven't been washed, I'd rather not.'

She looked appalled as Maggie took a handful. Defiantly eating, Maggie asked, 'What are you reading?' She was relieved to see that Sheila had indeed been apparently absorbed in her book, not gazing moodily out of the window.

'Margaret Atwood.' Sheila held out the paperback, showing the cover. '*Lady Oracle*. It's quite heavy going. She goes into her dreadful relationship with her mother in such depth, I'm wondering when, if ever, she will get on with the story.'

121

It seemed appropriate. Maggie said uncomfortably, 'I can never get on with her. I find her too fierce and introspective,' then added, 'but you might leave it for me to try. I'm running out of things to read.'

'I don't really think you'd like it,' said Sheila dismissively. 'Too serious for you, I'd have thought.' She dropped her eyes to the page.

Maggie seethed. What did Sheila know about it? Did she think that Mills & Boon romances were her limit? Her arrogance was insufferable. Just as her vulnerability was pathetic. Maggie's heart wrenched with both pity and anger and she stared silently ahead until they were home, the cherries untouched and forgotten in her lap.

She displayed the little jug on a shelf in the living room.

'Haven't you enough jugs already?' asked Sheila.

'Maybe, but not here.'

'But at home?'

Maggie didn't know how to reply. She had never actually envisaged the cheerful sturdy little piece on her shelves at Heathercote. The house in Godalming seemed so far away; Ralph and Doreen next door and their sedate bridge evenings were of another life, though she had received a letter from Doreen only the other day. Janet was getting married it seemed. To an architect. He was designing a house for them; very 'high tech' and experimental. Janet was to have triple glazing, solar heating, conduited electric cables, electronically controlled switches. There would be no Janet to partner her at bridge any more.

'I'm not sure I really see it at home. It seems to belong here, don't you think?' she answered noncommittally.

Madrilena was to come that afternoon for her first sitting. Maggie would have preferred to work in the dining room where the light was even and cool but Sheila had taken over the room, spreading her clothing and books and sparse toiletries untidily about the furniture. Besides, it would be unfair to intrude on her privacy. She set up her easel instead at the back of the living room away from the sun.

'What will you do?' she asked Sheila. 'Sit in the sun and read your book? It's sheltered on the terrace.'

'I prefer the garden, it's shady.'

'But you were cold this morning.'

'If I'm cold I'll come inside. I take it you'd prefer not to have me in here with you?'

Maggie was arranging her paints lovingly. This time, she was going to work in oils. The tubes were new, smooth and promising, unsullied as fresh snow. The camel brushes were silky and pointed, ranging from fine to thick and chunky. With them, she hoped to capture Madrilena, bring her to life on the canvas. Or rather, the special textured hardboard that Lorne had advised. And Lorne was coming too. He would help her make a start, guide her tentative hand. She was not entirely sure she needed his help. It might be better to dive in alone, follow her own nose, as Nigel would have put it. But he had offered and the temptation was too great. No, she didn't want Sheila there, a critical and demanding presence casting shadows of guilt, suggestions of impropriety.

'It might be best. If you don't mind?' she apologised. 'Now, let's see about some lunch. Will an omelette do? There's veal tonight, a recipe from a magazine. I hope I've understood it correctly!'

'Your Spanish is very good,' Sheila said surprisingly. 'All those classes you and Father took certainly paid off.'

'Yes, well it's using it all the time that does it. That was one of the things I wanted to do. Become fluent. I don't think I manage too badly. It certainly impresses Nigel anyway! For a travelled man, he's remarkably chauvinistic. If they don't understand, shout! Probably due to being an officer.' She got out eggs, began to beat them. There were some cold new potatoes. 'We'll have tortilla,' she said. Sheila had followed her down to the kitchen. 'You slice these. Do you miss him? Your father?'

'Of course. Especially now. He would have taken it all so calmly. Nothing ever ruffled him.'

'No. He was a very even man. I'm sorry he's not here for you.' She spread the potatoes into the hot oil. 'I'm sorry I'm not there for you either,' she said with an effort, 'but we didn't expect this, did we?'

But Sheila was not to be won; Maggie's defection was to be neither acknowledged nor forgiven. Was she guilty, or was she not? Resignedly, she pushed the potatoes round the pan, turned them, poured in the beaten eggs and watched the mixture rise and bubble while Sheila washed some lettuce, dried it and turned it in oil and vinegar, silently.

Lorne took her hand, guiding the pencil lightly over the board. She flushed deep inside with a painful pleasure. 'You see,' he said. 'Now the proportions are better.' He took the pencil, held it in his outstretched hand and focused on Madrilena, screwing up his eyes, his thumb marking the length of her head, moving it down over her seated body. He looked at the board. 'Yes. Now you try.' She took the pencil obediently, ignoring the warmth from his hand, studying the proportions of the seated figure, the respective measurements of her flat torso, erect head, and the tall comb holding the mantilla. The girl's eyes were solemn, deep shining pools as dark as the lace which fell in folds behind her gleaming hair. A suggestion of a slight, proud sneer held her mouth in an uncharacteristic yet entirely proper arrogance. Her olive skin was flawless, her face, throat and shoulders a graceful series of curves and shadows which plunged into the scarlet shiny petals of the dress which hid her latent breasts. Still a child, she yet looked both erotic and dignified. It had been an inspiration, Maggie thought, to dress her in her flamenco costume. It would surpass all her ambitions if she could do her justice.

'Do you have to watch me?' she asked Lorne as she sketched in, tentatively, the still features, the neckline of the dress, the balletic posture of the arms. 'It makes me nervous.'

'You're doing fine.' But he went out onto the terrace and stood looking down into the quiet street. The Spanish were still at their siesta. Only mad dogs and Englishmen, it seemed, were about their business.

After half an hour Maggie asked Madrilena if she was tired. The child had sat professionally still for all that time. Lilli had told her that the muscular control required by the dancing would enable her to do so, but still Maggie was surprised. She was only seven after all. She had the outline now to her satisfaction; it would be safe to let her move. Released, she ran outside to Lorne, the red layers of her skirt swinging round her legs, the lace dancing from the tall ivory comb. The Varas' daughter in all her glory, her potential womanhood glowing satin red and poised, explosive and warm. Once more Maggie asked herself how such a pair . . .

'She's been marvellous,' she told Lorne, who had come in to have a look. 'I only hope I can be half as professional.'

'That's not at all bad. And you'll be fine, I promise. And you will still come tomorrow? Despite your daughter being here?'

'Of course.' She didn't say that Sheila's reaction to her sitting for Lorne had been scornful, almost accusatory. 'She won't come with me, of course. That would hardly be fair to Chloe, even if she is feeling better.'

'Why not? You'll ask her anyway? It might cheer Chloe up, to have another visitor.'

'Yes but Sheila's hardly – well, comforting, I suppose.

125

And she has problems of her own. She's depressed. And touchy. That's the last thing Chloe wants.'

Neither did she herself want to be upset or embarrassed, to apologise for her daughter's behaviour. She wanted to concentrate, to do her best for Lorne.

It was shameful. It was embarrassing and humiliating. But she just wanted to be with Lorne.

In the event Sheila professed herself to be happy to stay at home.

'It's quite pleasant out here in the garden, and I'm getting into my book,' she said. 'Good heavens, what have you done to your hair now?'

'Lorne wanted it put up. It's all right, isn't it? I couldn't quite get all the ends in.'

'It makes you look fat about the face. It's all the breakfast you eat.'

Maggie clenched her hands furiously. 'That's really rather rude,' she rebuked, more gently than she felt. At least Sheila was making herself at home and was willing to find something, at least, that she enjoyed. She had dragged her bed and mattress outside and certainly looked comfortably installed but that didn't stop Maggie bringing out a jug of fruit juice and standing it in the shade and saying, 'There's some garlic sausage in the fridge. And fresh rolls – I went out early.' She fetched a dish of olives, a bowl of fruit. After all, she supposed that it was a holiday. Alone she might be, but her daughter would have every comfort. As a hostess, at least, Maggie would not be found wanting. Almost furtively, as if their positions were reversed and she herself was an errant daughter, a teenager escaping to the pub or a disco, she finally closed the door and turned her face and her anticipation to Serenidad.

She was surprised to find Chloe outside in the garden. She had parked her wheelchair alongside a raised bed of roses and was pulling out weeds from among their prickly stems.

'This has all gone rather wild,' she said by way of greeting. The weeds and grasses were indeed thick and high, tangling with the lower branches.

'But the roses don't seem to mind,' Maggie pointed out. 'They are blooming like crazy.'

'A last-ditch attempt at survival perhaps. Plants all bloom best when threatened, didn't you know? It's an attempt to reproduce, to keep the species going.'

Maggie didn't know. 'Is that so,' she said thoughtfully. 'I suppose there's some sense in that. Do human beings do the same, do you suppose?'

'Think of the war. All that frantic coupling and copulation.'

'But I think reproduction was the last thing on their minds. Rather, the opposite, I imagine. The intention would have been *not* to bring children into a troubled and dangerous world. At least, that's how I would have felt about it.'

'I expect so.' It was not clear what Chloe meant by that but she smiled at Maggie none the less and said, 'Lorne's waiting for you upstairs. He hasn't been so excited for a long time.'

Nor me, thought Maggie. But I can't admit to that. 'It's good to see you so much better,' she said instead, agreeably. 'You must be enjoying the sun, and the wind has dropped today.'

'I've been reading. Emily Dickinson. Do you like her poetry?'

'Well . . .'

'You must try it sometime. You can borrow this.' She pulled a slim volume from the folds of the rug across her knees. 'Oh, and I've put out a couple of my own books. They're on the table, if you still want to see them.' There was an uncharacteristic reticence in her offer.

Touched, Maggie, said 'I'd love to. I'll take them with me. Thank you, Chloe.' She turned, Lorne was coming round the corner of the house. He was wearing a blue smock, much besmeared, and his thick grey hair was wild. 'My – here comes the master!' Maggie said lightly, concealing her admiration, the lust which claimed her body.

'Come on, Maggie,' he called. 'I can't wait any longer.' Her heart lurched a foolish, desperate response. He smiled. It was a joke. 'The muse is on me. I am in the grip of inspiration!' He took the handles of Chloe's chair. 'I'll wheel you in, darling, we can't leave you out here on your own'

'Why not? I shall be inside on my own. At least here, I can see the sun.'

'Very well.' He leaned to kiss her, to smooth her hair with the remembered gesture.

She smiled up at him wanly. 'Anyway, I'm doing some weeding. Making myself useful.' There was pathos in her words, in the weak plucking of her hands at the virulent weeds. Above, the roses bloomed bravely on, their lavish fragrant transient flowers perhaps also a last-ditch grasp at survival.

# TWELVE

'This is what I want you to wear.' Lorne handed her a dress of pale smooth powder-blue silk. 'It will bring out the colour of your eyes.'

'Is it Chloe's?' she asked, appalled at the thought. She held the flimsy garment nervously, with revulsion. Dead men's shoes. Besides, she had no right.

But, 'Of course not. I bought it specially. It should fit, the style is very easy.'

She opened it out, dandled it in her hands. The style was indeed easy; vaguely Grecian with a draped wrap-over bodice and low neckline. The sleeves were short and flared, the skirt loosely pleated. 'And please wear this with it.' He handed her a necklace, of tiny seed pearls with a large blue stone suspended. 'It was my mother's,' he answered her unspoken question. 'The stone's not precious. Do you mind changing in here or do you want to go downstairs?'

It seemed absurd to make an issue of it, to imply that he might be the least bit interested in her undressing. He had retreated into an impersonal absorption that she recognised, that she wished to emulate, the inward exclusivity of the creative urge. Swiftly and without fuss she unwrapped her skirt and unbuttoned her blouse. The blue silk shivered her skin, the pearls tingled against her throat.

'It suits you very well,' said Lorne, turning from the window from which he had been tactfully staring out at the tree-covered hillside. 'I thought it would. Are you sure you're comfortable?'

'Quite comfortable.'

'Then sit here.' There was a hard chair with low carved wooden arms set in front of a draped blue curtain. 'It's not made for relaxing, I'm afraid, but I don't want you to relax. We won't make it too long at first. About twenty minutes? Tell me if you can't stand it any longer but please, don't move until I say so. Okay?'

'All right. I'll do my best.'

She felt nervously certain that she would let him down, painfully exposed under his scrutiny as he measured her up with his outstretched pencil as he had done with Madrilena. Unconsciously, she adopted the girl's rapt and haughty expression. 'Relax your mouth a bit. That's better – more like you.' She sensed his pencil moving over the outline of her lips. Her skin pricked; she longed to move, to smudge the sensation with her hand. She followed his hand on the paper, guessing which part of her body was passing under the sure and fluid movements. He would look up, eyes screwed with concentration, seeing all yet quite unseeing in his absorption. When he stared into her face she could not intercept his gaze. She yearned to look at her watch. Twenty minutes stretched like hours. She fixed her eyes on his hand, the long supple fingers holding the pencil so delicately, etching the contours of her breasts and throat, trailing fire. Her skin crawled; in disgust she recognised that she was as aroused and hungry for him as if he had touched her naked body with his own. Panic manifested itself in waves of heat and almost an inability to breathe.

Lorne said suddenly, 'You've had enough. I forgot the time, I'm sorry. That was nearly half an hour. But it was useful, very useful. You were excellent. I've got the outline all complete.'

The ferris wheel had stopped, leaving her hanging in the topmost seat way above the stars. Slowly, it lowered her to the ground. She moved her limbs stiffly, turned her head, got up off the unforgiving chair. Yes, she had had enough.

The question was, would she ever be able to do any more?

She changed out of the silken dress, grateful for the commonplace brush of cotton, the reassuring persona that she saw in the mirror. Gone was the Hellenic wanton; there was Maggie, Margaret even, as shockable as she was shocking, ashamed and revolted but trembling still. She allowed herself a few moments before following Lorne downstairs, where she found him talking to Chloe who sat by the door in her wheelchair, her lap full of roses.

'Can I arrange those for you?' Maggie asked. Surprisingly her offer was accepted and in the gentle placing of the blooms the aberration seemed somehow to be annulled.

She told them about the fair, the struggles the three of them had had to instal the washing machine in the kitchen. And Madrilena's picture. Lorne told Chloe, 'It looks very promising. Maggie has a sure touch,' and Chloe said, 'Indeed? And how about yours of her?'

'Oh mine looks promising too. I have an excellent model, of course.'

'Indeed,' said Chloe again. 'Maggie is a positive paragon of talent.'

'Oh no,' cried Maggie. 'He's exaggerating.'

'But I'm sure he's not. Lorne is always generous, but very honest with his praise. He was my best critic, when I was writing.'

'And will be again,' put in Lorne. 'I see you've been reading Emily. That usually means you're about to write.'

Maggie was unbearably touched. 'I think I had better go. See how Sheila's getting on. I'm afraid I have got dreadfully used to having only myself to think about.'

Did she detect a flash of fear in their eyes as they looked at each other, Chloe from her chair, Lorne from the door which he had not hesitated to open? Did they see, in all its terrifying clarity, the future, or was it just a wish that she be gone, that they could be alone together in the fastness of Serenidad?

She drove fast down the hill, Sheila's solitude weighing on her conscience where she let it lie, comfortably cancelling her other more inadmissable shame. To her surprise, she found her not impatient, moody and indignant, but settled comfortably on the terrace in the late afternoon sunshine. And she was not alone. Marcos was there, his long legs sprawled and looking quite at home.

He got up, gallantly offering Maggie his chair.

'Sheila tells me you are being painted too. I came to see if you are pleased with your washing machine.' He spoke in Spanish.

'I'm afraid I haven't got a plug for it yet.'

'A pity. But I am sure it will work.'

'I hope you're right.' She glanced at the table. 'I see Sheila offered you a drink.'

'She offered me tea, but I had beer. Sheila had been telling me she has problems with her job. My English is not good enough to understand the details, unfortunately. But I have told her to forget them and enjoy her holiday in our Spanish sunshine. Was I right?'

Maggie smiled. 'Quite right.'

Sheila snapped, 'It's very frustrating, you know. I was managing fine until you got back. Marcos has more English than he lets on.' She gave him a smile that was almost conspiratorial, smoothing her skirt over her legs then tucking her hands beneath her thighs. Maggie was pleased to see that her arms were bare, and beginning to pick up a tan. Her cheeks too looked rosy, her eyes bright. 'Marco is studying physics,' Sheila told her. 'He wants to be a nuclear scientist. Or something like that!'

'Really?' Maggie glanced at Marcos, standing tall and arrogant between their chairs.

'Chloe is much better today,' she told Sheila, who nodded a feigned interest. 'Lorne seems to think she'll start writing again. I've brought two of her books to read. You may like to look at them too.'

'Maybe. I'm not very keen on poetry.'

'Chloe thinks I haven't read Emily Dickinson. Like you she obviously thinks my reading tastes are puerile.'

'I didn't say that.'

'Well, it's how I took it. I didn't disillusion her. I could hardly tell her my favourite is "I heard a fly buzz when I died; The stillness in the room Was like the stillness in the air Between the heaves of storm."'

Sheila looked unimpressed. Marcos said, 'May I?', taking out a packet of Ducados. He lit up at Maggie's nod of agreement then said, 'But I must leave anyway. Thank you for the beer. Let me know if you have any problem with the machine.' He shook Maggie's hand, then Sheila's and the bright blush flared again. To Maggie's shame, Sheila went and leaned over the railing amid the tangling vine watching him go, doe-eyed and yearning, a matronly Juliet who should know better.

But then, thought Maggie, who am I to talk? What a pair we are and how sad and disagreeable it is.

To Maggie's relief, the washing machine worked. It gave her a surprising nostalgic domestic pleasure to push their dirty linen into the turning foam and to see it whisked away, down into the steaming depths. Automatic washing was so distant, so impersonal, like a flight in a modern airliner. You knew something was happening, but were at the same time unaware of it. It was soothing, as she had in the early days of her marriage, once again to heave the steaming bundles into the dryer with wooden tongs and

133

watch the suds and presumably also the dirt spinning away down the sink. And it was infinitely preferable to washing everything by hand.

Lilli had invited them to lunch; stuffed peppers with avocado salad and garlicky saffron rice. Maggie was pleased to see that Sheila ate the food with apparent enjoyment, even took an interest in Lilli's extraordinary house. She had been with her nearly a week and was marginally easier to please, less aggressively critical. She would spend long hours stretched on her bed in the garden reading. Maggie had taken her on drives into the hills, and to the coast at Baiona; the girl had been quiet but not actually disparaging. They had been going to walk the battlements but a thick sea mist had swept in, followed by driving rain which washed them back home in the teeth of a gale. Maggie had persuaded her to get up earlier, to walk with her to the bakers where she had introduced her to her neighbours who greeted her generously. They understood about daughters, even grown-up ones with neat permed hair and unfashionable clothes. For the most part, they were unstylish themselves, the older ones in rusty black, the younger ones, from the few new houses grouped at one end of the village, dressed usually in simple summer frocks. There was no need to apologise for Sheila in the village.

She used Sheila's continuing presence as an excuse to Lorne. 'Would you mind if we postponed any more sittings until she's gone? I would like to spend the time with her.'

His voice over the phone was regretful but compliant. 'I quite understand. But I hope it won't be too long. We've got off to such a good start.'

Maggie's feelings were more ambivalent but on the whole she hoped it wouldn't be too long, also. Sheila had made no mention of when she was to leave and, in her sensitive and touchy mood, Maggie had not liked to ask.

Sheila often took herself off for walks on her own. She

didn't invite Maggie along and, glad of some solitude, Maggie didn't suggest she joined her. Sheila was noncommittal as to where she went: 'Oh just round and about. Down towards Lilli's,' or 'I had a look at the new houses. They do seem rather out of place.' Maggie was not entirely surprised when Lilli said to her after giving them lunch, when Sheila had gone to the bathroom, 'She is looking well. I think she is a little in love, yes? I have seen her with Marcos, making the eyes, you know!'

'I think maybe she is in love, but not with Marcos. I think we would call that a crush. But where have you seen them together?'

Marcos had called at the house several times, it was true. Each time, Sheila had leaped up, offered him beer or coffee, the painful blush spoiling everything. Maggie had left them to it, noticing that, alone, Sheila managed some sort of conversation with him, bridging the gap of noncomprehension with her own need to communicate with him. Wildly, Maggie hoped that he might find Sheila attractive in return, though beyond such an unlikely possibility she couldn't imagine. Had they in fact been meeting, unbeknown to her?

Lilli said, 'I have seen them at the garage. Three times this week, the car is being repaired. Marcos is supposed to be doing it but I think he doesn't do a lot of work. And each time, Sheila is there watching him. I wonder, why doesn't greasy Vara send her away?'

'You think she's stopping Marcos working?'

'No. I think he doesn't work much. She is just content to look, and he is happy for the chance to talk. He is very charming. I think he is practising his English.'

'But nothing more than that?'

'No, Maggie. I think not. Sadly, no.'

So Maggie's feelings were confirmed, and with them came the dread of another hurt, another failure, and

Sheila's consequent unhappiness. It seemed foolish to let it go on.

An extra worry began to niggle as the days went by. The Major had brought them in a couple of newspapers but there was nothing, now, about the case. Water pollution in the south-west and a horrific fire in a cinema had stolen the thunder from the recalcitrant social workers of Liverpool. The situation would seem to have reached a stalemate. But what was Sheila doing about it? Shouldn't she be there, ready to take appropriate action when the time arrived? What the appropriate action would be Maggie could only wonder. Presumably, she could have her job back. There was an acute shortage of social workers. Maggie had wondered if any of her colleagues, maybe even Leonard, would write to her to put her in the picture, but no letters came, only one from Cassie, when Sheila had been there for ten days and gave no indication of ever going home.

'Anthony didn't get his promotion. Poor Cassie.' Maggie laid the letter in her lap with a sigh.

'Poor Anthony! It's *his* job. Why is it that Cassie always seems to demand such sympathy?'

Maggie shook her head. 'Don't ask me. She's just made that way, I suppose. I've tried to make her more self-sufficient.'

'It isn't even as if she's on her own. She has Anthony, for heaven's sake. I don't know what he sees in her.'

'Sheila! Don't talk like that.' She smothered her own doubts. 'They're a very happy couple.'

'Lucky them. She should be grateful then.'

Was it jealousy? Or loneliness? Maggie had to offer something.

'I know it must be hard for you, dear. I'm sure you'd like a husband, a home of your own. Somebody to look after you for a change. One day, I'm sure . . .' But was she sure? 'Of course you've had your work. Cassie doesn't have that,

136

remember. It's a great thing to have a career of your own. Especially one as worthwhile as yours.'

'Huh.' She looked fierce, defiant, seemed about to speak then changed her mind and said instead, 'But I'm not jealous of Cassie, I can promise you. Anthony's really weird, I think, always dashing about in that hideous car. Cassie's welcome to all that. She'd far prefer someone who stayed at home and did the decorating and dug the garden.'

'Is that what you'd like?' Maggie's heart sank. It sounded so predictable, so stultifyingly dull.

'I don't know what I'd like, and anyway it seems I haven't the choice,' returned Sheila tartly. 'And hadn't you better get ready for your sitter? Isn't Madrilena due this morning?'

The portrait was going well. Maggie was longing to show it to Lorne but equally reluctant to see him. She felt degraded and self-contemptuous. She resented the inconvenient and uncomfortable demands of her body. It was humiliating that she, who hated to be needed, must acknowledge such a need. Was this what her freedom had become: subjection to this new tyranny, of secret and forbidden lust, a hectic excitement and longing she had abandoned with her teenage years? It brought her little pleasure. Essentially she was a moral woman, constrained by both upbringing and custom. But she had never been tempted before, never put to the test. It had always been easy to live by her own rules. The new life she was constructing for herself didn't include adultery, especially with the husband of someone like Chloe. It wasn't just Chloe's dependence, her diminishing lease on life. It was her strength too. Chloe was daunting, self-certain, to cross her was unthinkable. Even should the occasion arise, which it surely wouldn't. Lorne was in Chloe's thrall, as tied to her by tenderness and responsibility as by passion. For this, Maggie was tempted to love him as well as hanker after his body

137

even though it put him out of reach, as tantalisingly unattainable as a jewel in a crown.

So what was she to do about it? Sublimation in her work was one answer. She laid on the paint of Madrilena's dress, thick and living like fresh blood, and vowed to forget the nonsense once and for all. She was a grown woman, in charge of her own life. Not lost in a hopeless morass like Sheila and getting nowhere. She was independent, she was happy . . . she was free.

A young woman from one of the new houses always called early on Fridays pulling a trolley on which was displayed fresh fish, garlanded with melting ice and little sprigs of parsley, dark green and curling against the white and silvery flesh. Maggie marvelled at the strangeness of the sight. She could not imagine such a thing in Godalming. There, the young mothers worked in banks and building societies, sold Avon cosmetics or made commission on sales from catalogues from Great Universal Stores. The young woman had a crisp haircut, made-up eyes and wore simple cotton dresses and skirts. She had told Maggie she had two children. Her mother looked after them on Fridays. Her mother lived nearby, she was always happy to have them. When they went to school, she would take a proper job, maybe in Vigo. She was learning to drive her husband's car. He worked in the market gardens, he went there on his bicycle so he didn't need the car. The money she made from the fish she spent on driving lessons, any over went on the children. And she paid her mother something too. She had it all worked out, and Maggie was impressed.

She commented as such to Sheila as she skinned a thick piece of white fish whose name she had forgotten but which, she was assured by her latest issue of *Telva*, would be delicious simmered with tomatoes, garlic and basil. Chloe had given her a bunch of basil from her herb bed and it stood fragrantly in a small glass on the window-ledge.

'I can't imagine such initiative at home. But then people here are so much more energetic. And less proud, perhaps. They don't mind what they do. Though I can't see there's much pride in just drawing the dole, or whatever they call it now.'

There was a pregnancy in the ensuing pause. 'Will you chop some basil?' Maggie asked. 'And skin the tomatoes, perhaps?' She waited; Sheila seemed to be winding herself up to something but, in the end, she only said, 'It's not much fun, being unemployed.'

Maggie's heart thudded. 'Is that how you see yourself? But surely it was of your doing? I mean, technically, you are still on the payroll? Aren't you?' She crushed a clove of garlic violently, squirting it out in translucent pungent squiggles. She scraped them into a saucepan, added water and a glass of wine. She really didn't want to have this conversation, somehow knew that she had opened a can of worms.

'Actually,' Sheila said at last, 'I'm not. I've finished with it all. Good and proper.' She stripped the skin off a tomato viciously, dropping its gory nakedness into the saucepan, plunged her fingers back into the hot water for another. 'I'm sorry to say so, but I'm not a social worker any more.'

Maggie's heart sank; she could actually feel it dropping into the pit of her stomach which caught it in a tight constricting knot. It was worse than she had expected.

'What do you mean?' she asked rather pointlessly. It seemed obvious what Sheila meant. 'Do you mean you have resigned permanently?'

'Yes. It was an impossible situation, neither one thing nor another. It was difficult to make any claim for benefit, for one thing. And for another it gave me time to think. Despite the particular pressures of the situation, reading about it in the paper, seeing Leonard going through the mill on the

139

television news, all the arguing and infighting among ourselves about the pros and cons of everything, there was still
a most extraordinary feeling of release. Not to be exposed,
every day, to all those ills I couldn't cure. All that misery.
I don't expect you to understand, you can't possibly know
what that side of life is all about.'

'I think I can dear,' objected Maggie mildly. 'You've told
me about it often enough. And I do read the papers. I do
know there's misery and deprivation and degradation. I was
always so proud that you were trying to do something about
it. I can't believe that you've just thrown in the towel. I
thought you were made of sterner stuff.'

Sheila threw the final tomato into the pan angrily. 'I
knew exactly the line you'd take. That's why I didn't tell
you before.'

'That's not very fair. How could you possibly know? And
I'm not saying I don't understand how stressful the job is.
Rather, the opposite. And if you feel you've had enough
well, it's not up to me to comment, I suppose. I'm sorry.'

Sheila said nothing, just stared moodily into the sanguine
mess in the saucepan.

'So what are you going to do now? Am I allowed to ask?'

'I've given up the flat. If you give up your job voluntarily,
you have to be out of work for six months before you can
draw full benefit. I obviously can't manage on the little bit
I'm entitled to at present.'

'So?' Maggie had sat down at the table, a horrible pre-
monition weighting her limbs.

Sheila looked at her crossly. 'So I was thinking perhaps
I could stay out here with you.'

Maggie didn't believe it. 'I don't believe it,' she said.
'What ever gave you that idea?'

'Well, you are my mother! And it would be company for
you, I thought . . .'

'I see.' Maggie didn't have to think; all of a sudden the

words were there. 'And that's what mothers are for, is that it? And this mother in particular can't manage alone. Well, as you can see, I can. Much to my surprise perhaps. I'm sorry if that's bad news for you. And besides all that, how long were you proposing to sit about out here? With no income to speak of? There is the little matter of getting another job. And what are you qualified to do? Have you thought about that at all?'

'Of course I have. I'd wondered about doing a year's teaching diploma. I'm used to children. They're crying out for teachers in some areas, and I've got my degree.'

That was better. 'Well, that seems a sensible idea. But you can't arrange that from over here. Can you?'

'I thought I probably could. That at least I could spend a month or so here. I wouldn't be starting until October.'

October! Maggie shook her head. 'Well, I really am amazed. I'm sorry, but I'm astonished that you should assume anything at all. Maybe you are my daughter, but you are nearly twenty-eight, for heaven's sake. And I am entitled to make a few choices of my own, I should have thought. I have chosen to come to Spain, to live alone. You made it quite plain that you thought it a stupid idea, reckless, childish, tilting at windmills. Now you seem to have decided to come along for the ride! You don't even much like it here so far as I can see. And you never stop hectoring, criticising my hair, telling me I'm putting on weight, disparaging my friends. Well, believe it or not, Sheila, I've grown up now! I don't need you to tell me what to do. I'm not one of your battered wives.' She took a deep trembling breath. 'I'm sorry your life is such a mess, but I don't think the answer is for you to take refuge out here with me.'

She had never spoken to her like this before. Sheila looked up from the saucepan which was beginning to bubble odorously. She looked shocked, her face white, eyes wide and startled. Her mother had always been there for

141

her. Now she had drifted wilfully off into a life of her own, and had become a stranger, who answered back, who made Sheila herself feel small and unwanted.

Her mouth clenched into denial of what she didn't want to understand. Now, Maggie was riven by guilt, by the conflicting clamours of pity and a wish to have her gone. She almost surrendered to the pathos of the situation – then, fighting back, she thought of a solution.

With relief she said, 'You can stay at Heathercote. That's the obvious answer. It will save Cassie having to pop in all the time. And I can help you with money, until you find something. There must be plenty of work during the summer.' She cast desperately about her mind. Students, she knew, did waitressing, served behind bars, stacked supermarket shelves. But Sheila had never done any of that even when she was a student. It was unlikely that she could contemplate it now. 'You do really need to earn some money. Will you get a student grant, do you suppose?'

'I'm not sure. That all has to be looked into.'

'Well,' said Maggie triumphantly. 'As I say, you need to be at home. On the spot. There's obviously heaps to be sorted out.'

Sheila looked deflated. 'I'll go tomorrow,' she said sullenly.

'Darling. Don't be ridiculous. I'm not throwing you out on your ear.' Wasn't she? She became conciliatory, placating. 'Stay a few more days at least. You seem to be enjoying it more now, and the rest has done you good. I've asked Nigel to lunch tomorrow. I feel perhaps we snubbed him the day we met in Vigo. Stay and be nice to him, there's a good girl.'

Sheila winced visibly, at her tone and at the mention of the Major. 'Why you bother with him I don't know, but I'll be all sweetness and light if you think it will make any difference.'

'I'm sure he would be delighted to see you.' Maggie chose to ignore the further insult. 'I've seen how friendly and lively you can be. With Marcos, for instance, you're quite a different person.' She hadn't meant to say it, made matters worse by adding 'Of course, he's younger than you. About twenty-three, would you say?'

'Actually, he's twenty-nine. And at least he has interesting things to say.'

'But can you understand them?'

'Mostly. His English is improving. I'd rather hoped . . .'

'Oh Sheila. You can't just hang around here, in the hope that . . . well, I mean, we know so little about him. He has his own life, in Santiago . . .'

'I know.' She seemed to pull herself together, visibly stiffening and bracing. 'This fish is cooked already,' she said, giving the saucepan a stir. 'I thought we were going to boil some rice?'

The drains had blocked at Nigel's villa. He telephoned just as Maggie was preparing the paella for their lunch.

'Sorry, my dear. Won't be able to make it, I'm afraid. I'm waiting for the plumber.'

'Nigel. Can't you clear a drain yourself?'

'I've got all these rods, but either they've stuck, or they're not long enough. Best to get the experts in. But I don't know when they'll be here.'

Maggie sighed, but reflected that at least Sheila would be pleased. When she told her he wasn't coming, Sheila commented, 'I suppose what he really wanted was for you to drop everything and go and help him clear his sewage!'

'No, of course not. Anyway, a fat lot of good I would be. Your father always dealt with things like that.'

Sheila looked at her thoughtfully. 'Don't you miss him dreadfully?'

Maggie thought long and hard. The girl was so vulner-

143

able, and obviously missed her father so much herself. Finally she said, 'Sometimes, yes. Of course, after all those years. But –' she paused then continued carefully, 'it's not insurmountable. I can find consolations.'

Oh yes, thought Sheila. She threw her a bitter glance. 'Like Nigel Tyson, I suppose.'

Maggie swallowed hard on her anger and managed calmly, 'No, not like Nigel, though I value his friendship as I value Lilli's, and Lorne and Chloe's. I mean like my painting, and learning to speak Spanish properly. And finding I can be independent.' She gave her daughter a defiant look. 'I'm sorry if you don't like it.'

To her huge surprise, Sheila looked at her with something like distress on her face. It's just, she was thinking, that where does that leave me?

After lunch, which was eaten largely in silence, Sheila went out, presumably to hang about the garage with Marcos. Maggie washed up, feeling depressed. Now that Sheila's ticket was booked for three days' time, she felt pathetically anxious to please her. But it was very difficult to think of anything she would like. She had suggested a visit to the beach but Sheila didn't like beaches. She complained it was too hot to walk far. She showed no interest in Maggie's friends. All in all, Maggie reflected, it was quite a relief when she went out. She decided to take advantage of it and go and see Lilli.

'I think,' she told her friend, 'that Sheila thinks Nigel has designs on me. She is always warning me off, and in a way that is most offensive to poor Nigel.'

Lilli was hemming the lace edge of a mantilla, the flimsy red fabric bunched in her hands, her eyes screwed. Without looking at Maggie she said, 'I think you will be happy to see your daughter go?' It was a question rather than a statement but Maggie was ashamed at how obvious she must have been.

'Oh Lilli, does it show? I've tried so hard to enjoy her. But she does make it hard work.'

Lilli bit through the thread and stuck her needle carelessly into the arm of the sofa. She looked at Maggie sympathetically. 'Ah daughters! Why do we have them, I wonder? But then, we were daughters ourselves, once.'

'And it never occurs to you, when you are young, that you are giving a moment's anxiety.'

'That is because you think you are always right. And that you are in control. Be calm, Maggie, and tell yourself that Sheila knows what she is doing, it is her life.'

'But am I right to just let her get on with it?'

'If that is the best you can do, yes,' said Lilli fatalistically. 'You are hard on yourself, Maggie, always punishing yourself with guilt.'

Maggie looked at her gratefully. 'Thank you Lilli. You're a good friend. You make it all sound very simple. None the less, I am determined to make her last two days happy.' Getting up to go she smoothed her skirt and said suddenly, 'Sheila accuses me of not needing anybody. I don't think it's entirely true – but I can see why she'd think that.'

# THIRTEEN

The telephone rang early, as Sheila was finishing her packing. Her flight was at noon. Maggie didn't want to be delayed and picked the receiver up impatiently.

Much to her amazement it was Harriet.

'My dear, what a surprise. You're the last person I expected it to be. Not that I get that many calls, of course, but it has been known.'

'I can imagine. You seem to have made quite a little circle. You wouldn't want me out there, I suppose?'

'You? Why – can you come? Aren't you back at work?'

'Not until August, and this was supposed to be my holiday. My partners are adamant that I take it. So I wondered, if you're not too busy . . . Cassie tells me Sheila has been with you. Is she still?'

'She leaves today. Tell me, how are you really?'

'There's not much to say. It's slow . . . perhaps a week in the sun is what I need. It's been dreary here, no question of water rationing this year. Can I come for the last week of the month?'

'Of course you can. That's wonderful. It's rather a makeshift bedroom, I'm afraid, but Sheila seems to have managed. But will you get a flight?'

'I've checked all that. I thought it best.'

She wrote down the details on the calendar. 'It's a pity you won't be here for Lilli's concert,' she said inconsequentially, seeing it entered in for 7 August. 'But you'll be here for my birthday! What luck. Oh Harriet, it's wonderful. I can't believe it.'

'Neither can I, quite,' said Harriet rather doubtfully. When Maggie turned she saw Sheila standing in the doorway clasping her bag and raincoat. 'I'm ready,' she said, and there was reproach in her eyes, an indictment of all that her mother had failed to be.

At the airport Maggie kissed her warmly. 'Do you want me to wave you off? I can, it's not like Heathrow or Gatwick, as you've observed already.'

'There's no point really.'

'Anthony will be there to meet you and Cassie will see you into the house. She sounded quite excited on the phone.'

'I don't really need that. I know my way around by now, I hope.'

'Yes, but I did sort of leave her in charge.'

'And we don't want to upset her. I know the rules!'

'Sheila! Do try and get on together. You used to play so beautifully when you were little girls.'

'But we're big girls now, Mother! That's what you've been telling me. I just don't want all Cassie's problems dumped on me on a daily basis. I've quite enough of my own. If she needs a social worker she'll find she's come to the wrong place.'

'It will all sort out. You'll see.' She gave an encouraging hug, was not repelled. 'And Marcos will write, perhaps. Did you give him the address?'

'Mother!' she warned.

Maggie tried again. 'I hope Leonard manages to clear himself. Or perhaps that doesn't matter any more?'

'Of course it does. He was a colleague.' Her face was shuttered, her eyes averted to the departure gate through which straggled a desultory line of travellers.

Maggie sighed. 'Well, you'd best be off. Take care. And keep in touch . . .' she called in a sudden panic as the stiff-shouldered navy suit was absorbed by the departing crowd.

*　　*　　*

147

I need something to cheer me up, she thought, driving out of the airport towards the main road south. Some reassurance that I am not just an unmitigated selfish cow. She smiled rather grimly; she was not used to thinking of herself in such evocative terms. Sheila's influence perhaps. On an impulse, she turned the other way, into Santiago de Compostela.

The city was eight miles away. She remembered the approach from her two visits with Robert, the climb of buildings up the surrounding hills, the medieval centre at its heart with the huge confection of the Baroque and Romanesque cathedral clasped in a protective tangle of narrow colonnaded streets. They had walked those streets late one evening and come across the student singers in their period costume, singing their madrigals and Renaissance love songs under a stone archway. Further on, somebody had been playing a grand piano to a rapt audience on plastic chairs under the navy summer sky while others watched and listened from fragile balconies embroidered onto stone façades. Now, she approached under a fierce sun, threading her way with difficulty through the busy outskirts, then getting lost and flustered in the central maze of one-way streets and traffic-free zones. At last she found a parking space. She had two hours, to recapture the magic of the place, to find some refreshment, to mourn for Robert . . .

She wished she had him now. He would have known what to do about Sheila, confirmed that she hadn't been entirely wrong. But then, if Robert had been alive she wouldn't be here. Maggie wouldn't exist and Margaret would be at home where she belonged, placidly answering to them all. She ordered a brandy and an omelette, crumbling bread while she waited, watching the milling crowds of tourists pushing past the café tables, peering down at guidebooks, up at stone mullions and in at the deep-set shop windows displaying the silver scallops of St James,

148

cheap miniature cathedrals and jewellery, the paraphernalia of the modern pilgrim. She decided to go to the
cathedral.

Inside, like everybody else, she touched the shiny stone
of the Pórtico de la Gloria with its myriad angels, apostles
and saints, before walking the body of the nave. The soaring
roof reduced them all to ants, the hushed voices to an incon-
sequentiality against the distant background roar and hum
which seemed to come from the stones themselves.
Although she had done it before, she joined the queue
descending beneath the altar to gaze at the silver casket
which purported to hold the remains of the Apostle James.
Belief that this was so had brought the pilgrims here for
centuries, on foot, sometimes crawling on their knees, from
all over Europe. Now they came by car and coach and plane
and on package tours, to worship sun and sea and drink
the wine and call in, briefly, as they passed. Dutifully, they
mounted the steps behind the altar and peered down at the
body of the church from behind the kissed-smooth silver
mantle of the seated saint. A little card of blessing was
handed out to each by a hunched man in a corner. Maggie
took hers gratefully, feeling undeservedly forgiven, and
pushed it into her bag.

The pilgrims had once been housed in a hostelry at right
angles to the cathedral, forming a second side to an open,
traffic-free square. This square was criss-crossed by tourists
with their cameras, civil servants in suits heading for the
Town Hall, students in their beribboned gowns selling tapes
of their music, charming all the women. She evaded one
with a smile. There was just time for a cup of tea. The
hostelry was now a five-star parador, catering for the needs
of very different travellers. She had never been inside, now
passed with awe through the tall glass doors and looked up
at the vaulted ceilings, to the left along a vast lounge set
with chairs and sofas like a furniture showroom. She

wondered where tea would be served, turned to the reception desk, and felt a hand on her arm checking her purposeful step.

'Maggie? What on earth are you doing here?'

'Lorne!' She had been careless of his touch until she saw his face, now it burned. 'I could say the same to you.'

'I've been making arrangements about my exhibition. This is where it's to be held, remember? If they ever get their act together that is. And you?'

'I've just seen Sheila off. I felt like a brief respite. I was hoping for some tea . . .'

'Splendid. And so was I.'

And he ushered her through to a small room set with white cloths and silver knives and spoons and ordered tea and luscious cakes as if they were back in England taking tea in a timbered teashop, and Maggie was both relaxed and wound up like a spring and talked and laughed as if she had been released from solitary confinement.

'You sound very cheerful, I must say,' he commented at last. 'I thought you would be missing your daughter.'

She had a sudden longing to confide in him. 'Enough is enough,' she said at last. 'And she has things to sort out. She's changing her job.' It would be pointless to explain. She would feel too revealed, too vulnerable, too susceptible to the comfort he would undoubtedly offer. And he had problems enough of his own. 'How's Chloe? She's obviously well enough to be left.'

'She came with me. To see her doctor. I'm collecting her at five.' He didn't say how she was. Maggie didn't ask again.

'So – we can resume the portrait, I hope?'

She flattened her fork onto the last delicious crumbs of lemon sponge. 'I suppose so. Yes – why not?'

'You don't sound very keen. Did you find it such a trial?'

'No. If Madrilena can do it, I'm sure I can. Mine's going very well. At least, I think so. I can't wait for you to see it.'

'I was waiting to be asked,' he said accusingly but with a redeeming smile.

Suddenly remembering, Maggie told him, 'My friend Harriet is coming in a few days. For a week. The solicitor friend who has had the operation, I'm sure I told you.' His face expressed disappointment. 'But that needn't matter. I'm sure she would love to meet Chloe. And she'd like to see your paintings.'

'Well then, that's all right.' He called for the bill which Maggie thought must be exorbitant.

'You must come to lunch,' she offered by way of return. 'Would Chloe manage, do you think?'

'I don't see why not, the way things are at present.' He bestowed on her a wide-lipped hopeful smile. 'I must leave you now. You'll let me know when you can come? I'll wait to hear?' He leaned over her, brushed her forehead with the briefest of kisses as any man would do after all, having taken tea with a neighbour, and turned and strode away.

With the utmost foreboding, and feeling more doubtful and agitated than before, Maggie brushed the crumbs from her skirt and looked around for the ladies' room.

There was another letter from Cassie awaiting her return. 'So soon?' Maggie asked herself, fearing the worst. She tore the letter open standing in the kitchen, the car keys still in her hand.

'I gather Harriet is planning a trip to see you. She called in for the key; apparently she had left something in one of the bedroom drawers. She didn't look at all well – I just thought I'd warn you. Maybe she just needs a holiday, but then what's she been having since May? But she seemed depressed. I hope she manages to come. I like her, she's very understanding . . .'

Maggie lowered the letter thoughtfully. It was unlike

151

Cassie to concern herself overmuch with other people's problems, being usually far too absorbed in her own. A nudge of worry pushed at her anticipation of Harriet's visit. She had unconsciously been planning to unburden herself; envisaged in her old friend's presence a chance to get some things off her chest. Harriet saw things so clearly. It was her legal mind. And she was so blissfully uncluttered herself. She had time and energy to plough through the morasses of other people's complicated lives and feelings. But if Harriet wasn't well . . . ? If Cassie thought so, then Harriet must badly need a holiday. She bit her lip. Once more it seemed calls were being made on her. This time she hoped she wouldn't fail.

Cassie meandered on about Robert's first days at nursery school. 'He cried a bit when I left, but was apparently fine as soon as I'd gone. I feel better about next week now.' So she was learning already. Feeling the pull on the rope, the relief when it loosened. 'Anthony is more cheerful, he says there's always a next time. But it means we can't afford a holiday after all. He's off to a rally next weekend – but I don't want to go. He says it would be a sort of holiday but I don't find it so.

'I've had dreadful sinus trouble all week, or maybe it's hayfever. The doctor has given me antihistamine, which makes me sleepy. And my nails are splitting. Why is that, do you think? Perhaps I should wear rubber gloves.'

Why indeed? thought Maggie. And perhaps you should. And she put the letter away to answer later.

She switched the television on. It was hard to admit it but the place seemed quiet and empty. There was bullfighting, which she had always claimed to find disgusting and immoral. She could never see herself joining the clamorous mob to watch innocent animals being bloodied and bowed. But she found it surprisingly compulsive on the small screen, the movements of the toreadors and matador graceful and balletic, the kill almost secondary to the dance, swift and subtle and immediate. The tense, compelling commentary which she could mostly comprehend threw light onto the subtleties of a sport which could hardly be called that, she felt, yet which had its undoubted moments of beauty. There was a majesty in the bulls, doomed as they were, and a vengeful triumph when one of them broke loose sending a toreador running for his life behind a barrier. She sat glued to the screen, picking at some corned beef sandwiches without realising the irony of it until the end.

She went on staring at the set, watching a news bulletin about a train crash outside Madrid with bodies, seats and suitcases thrown about an arid slope, rescuers burrowing like moles into tunnels of bent metal. At first she thought it was a plane crash and sensed fearful retribution. She had sent her daughter to her death. When she heard a masculine call from the street outside she thought, stupidly, Lorne? Even as she crossed the terrace she knew not. It was Marcos.

'Can I come in?' He was gleaming as ever, gaily confident of welcome. He waved a bottle of wine. She was going to say, 'But Sheila's gone,' instead found herself hurrying downstairs to open the door. 'But Sheila's gone, surely she told you?' she said when they were both inside.

'Yes. She told me. So I have come to see you.' He spoke slowly, in English.

'How kind. You thought I'd be lonely. Well, I suppose I was, a little . . .'

'Maggie!' She heard rebuke in his voice. 'I came to see you.'

And he moved forward, pressing her backwards against the wall. She felt his teeth click against her own, the intrusion of his tongue, tasted tobacco and garlic, wine and desire.

Reluctantly, she pulled her mouth away.

'Marcos?'

'I came to see *you*, Maggie,' he murmured in Spanish. 'Only you.'

Incredulously, with an infinite relief, she felt herself sag towards him, letting her thwarted desire grow and expand towards fulfilment. Tentatively she put his hand on her breast. His eyes, so close, glittered down at her and he nodded, triggering a wild abandoned joy. In the face of more tangible possibilities, her desire for Lorne expired in a long trembling sigh. She kissed him again, hungrily, and heard him groan. She pressed against him with an upward motion of invitation and then, because by then nothing else would do, she took him upstairs and into her bed.

# FOURTEEN

Maggie woke to a sensation of blissful ease, stretched slow and long in the crumpled empty bed and looked at the drained bottle of wine, the two glasses that bore witness to an abandoned debauchery of which she hadn't known she was capable. A slow indulgent self-satisfied smile spread itself across her face like thick butter. She felt released, reckless, accomplished.

Her self-satisfaction was not to last for long. The wetness between her thighs which she had taken to be the inevitable outcome of their passion, of Marcos's explosive climax which had startled her into gratitude and an exquisite drawn-out pleasure of her own, turned out instead to be blood. Her fingers when she touched herself came away stained, a long smear trailed across the sheet as she slid out of bed, her thighs were bright with it as she walked to the bathroom. At the same time she became aware of a familiar forgotten discomfort, the low ache of menstruation. Shock and disgust were pushed aside by the implications that thundered in on her. She had come completely unprepared, so sure was she that she had done with all that, it was Sunday and the chemist would be closed and more horrifying still there was the possibility now, remote as it may be, that she could become pregnant.

She stood under the shower washing away the lingering smell of his sweat, the gory unwelcome visitation between her legs. She was fervently glad that he had gone. He had left her bed with the dawn, saying, 'I have to go back to Santiago. I will see you in a very little time.' She had murmured, 'What

155

about the garage?' and he had told her, kissing her eyelids shut, 'I am bored with the garage. But I will be back.'

She had been astonished at his vigour, astonished at her power to match him. When he came he had called out something incomprehensible; she suspected it was crude but she didn't care. Drowning, she had clung to his undulant shoulders, drawing blood with her nails. When he left she had let him go, wanting no more from him, wishing only to fall back into oblivion.

She dressed quickly, stuffing her pants with toilet tissue. The tedious inconvenience depressed her, dulling the memories of the night which she had thought to savour. She drove to Lilli's house, found her sitting idle in the spiky shadow of a spiteful cactus on her patch of unmown grass. Lilli nodded and offered female comfort in the shape of pads and packages, hot coffee and aspirin. Maggie refused the aspirin but gulped three cups of the black unsweetened coffee. Tidied up and restored, she felt her spirits revive. Like a virgin fresh from defloweration she hugged her secret to herself, at the same time wishing to broadcast it from the hills. But Lilli might think her promiscuous; worse still, pathetic and ridiculous, as indeed it seemed she must be yet, strangely, she didn't feel so at all.

Eventually, she noticed that Lilli herself was depressed, her usual ebullience held down by some anxiety. Pressed a little, she said it was because her daughter, Miriam, and little Pepe weren't expected after all. They had been due that week, Lilli had prepared their room, made up the bed and a second-hand cot she had bought from an advertisement. Now, Miriam had a man friend. She didn't want to leave him.

'Well, it is up to her,' Lilli sighed, fingers busy at her throat. 'But I should have liked to see Pepe. He grows so fast.'

Maggie thought of Robert, who'd started nursery school. 'Can't you go to England?' she asked.

'Perhaps. After the concert. Little Madrilena's performance is much improved. She thinks her picture is wonderful. Be careful, all the little girls will be wanting one.'

As Maggie left, Lilli said, 'Poor Sheila will be missing Marcos. But I don't think he'll be missing her. Do you?'

She telephoned Lorne, 'I can come tomorrow, will that suit?' hearing with equanimity his pleased affirmative. She spent the day cleaning, stripping her bed and plunging the redolent linen into the twin-tub though she would have liked to sleep awhile in Marcos's essence. Smooth and crisp once more, the high bed was innocent of association. She removed the bottle and glasses, replaced Sheila's *Lady Oracle* beside the clock and dusted the few, uncluttered surfaces.

She made up the spare bed for Harriet, finding crumpled tissues underneath in balls of fluff on the red and brown tiled floor. Guiltily, for she had not done so for Sheila, she brought down a woven rug from the living room, and spread a lace tablecloth she had bought on the beach at Baiona across her trunk for a dressing table.

In the afternoon it began to rain. Relieved of the necessity of watering she lay instead on the couch with Cake, listening to music on her Sony tape machine. She fell asleep, awakening to lowering skies and a premature dusk. For a moment, she thought herself in England.

It was still raining next day when she went up to Serenidad. Lorne had asked her to bring some shopping. Chloe was not well, the trip to Santiago had exhausted her, he didn't wish to leave her. She added grapes to the list and some oozing sticky buns which leaked a yellow custard into their cardboard box. The grapes were for Chloe, who would scorn the effusive shop-bought confectionery. Just in case, however, she had purchased three.

To her dismay, she found that Chloe was in bed.

'Will she mind if I go in?' she asked Lorne, thinking to pre-

157

serve for Chloe some vestige of her dignity. But he took her none the less into the yawning room at the front of the house which looked out over the rainy plain and the distant hills of the Cordillera Cantabrica, a bruised uneven line beneath the livid clouds. Despite two high windows the room was dark, its ambience cheered neither by the heavy carved provincial furniture which echoed the scale of the room, nor by Chloe's face, her eyes dark craters in a waning moon sunk into huge square pillows of creamy satin. Her thin mousy hair was drawn back, exposing the bones of her cheeks and forehead. Her dark eyes were dull, the fierceness softened into apathy.

Yet opposite the bed, hung between the two windows on a panelled wall, was another Chloe, vibrant and challenging, looking out between curtains of silky hair with a book in one hand, pen in the other. It was Chloe as she had been, as Maggie had never seen her. She turned to Lorne admiringly.

'Yours, of course. It's magnificent. You must be so glad . . .'

'I am. Do give her the grapes – she'll love them.'

'Yes, I'll love them. Do give them to me.' Chloe's tone was petulant, abrasive as ever. Maggie sat on the bed and handed her the tissue-wrapped bundle.

Lorne switched on the bedside lamp which cast a deceptive roseate glow over Chloe's cheeks. 'I'll get a dish,' he said.

'Poor Lorne,' murmured Chloe when he had gone. 'He hates to see me like this.'

'And so do I.' She was tempted to smooth the pale forehead but it seemed irrelevant, would be a redundant gesture smacking of sentimentality. 'It's a dreadful day,' she said instead, with nannyish briskness. 'You're in the best place.' She could remember it being said to her as a child when confined to bed with a cold, had said it herself to Cassie and Sheila.

158

Less compliant, Chloe said, 'I'd rather be out there any day. Wouldn't you?'

Lorne arranged the grapes on a dark green plate and persuaded her to eat a few. 'Now we have to go and work, darling,' he said eventually when Maggie thought she could bear to watch the wan nibbling not a moment longer. Chloe made no protest, closing her eyes. A swathe of rain was flung across the window by a rising wind.

Maggie said suddenly, as they left the room, 'I've been reading your poems, Chloe. They are wonderful.' In fact, she had found them largely incomprehensible, otherwise disturbing. But it seemed important, at that moment, to tell her otherwise.

This time the blue silk left her calm and untroubled. Even Lorne's fingers at the clasp of the necklace failed to excite her; she could watch his hands moving over her body on the canvas with equanimity, as far removed from him as he was from her. The fire which had consumed her had been doused; when it flared again, Marcos would be there to both fan and quench it. Of that she felt absolutely, complacently sure. This time there was no treachery in the silent room. Chloe could sleep sure and peaceful in her silken marital bed. The twenty minutes passed in no time at all and this time she thought she could sit there, if necessary, for ever.

But after a while Lorne put down his brush, cleaning it with turpentine and placing it carefully at the bottom of the easel. 'That's enough for now. I'm afraid I feel like talking and I can't do both at once.'

Maggie shifted in the chair, realising that after all she was getting stiff and was in fact quite chilly about her shoulders.

'Shall I dress first?' she asked. 'It's rather cold.'

'I'll light a fire,' he said. 'And lunch perhaps? Is it rather early?'

It was noon, though the sky outside suggested evening. 'It's not for me. Will Chloe mind?'

'Why should she? I don't expect she'll want anything, but I can take her some soup later. I'm rather good at soup.' He spoke without complaint, carrying his load lightly, with love. Maggie felt ashamed. What had she ever done but fulfil the normal duties of wife, mother and fellow citizen? Worse, she had recently made it only too plain that she didn't intend it to be otherwise. She wondered about Sheila as she shed the silk, pulled on a floral shirt and tailored linen trousers. Alone at Heathercote she was yet surely in the best place. Maggie had done her best for her, offered her shelter, subsistence, time.

The fact that it suited Maggie was surely neither here nor there.

She smelled the soup, rich and fragrant, a thick broth of vegetables and bacon heavily tinged with garlic. They sat by the fire breaking bread together onto wooden platters. Lorne, as usual, ate exuberantly, rather desperately, slurping slightly as he drew in the soup.

After a while, when his bowl was empty, he said, 'Do you feel very lonely sometimes, Maggie? I mean inside? A deep, cold loneliness which has nothing to do with whether people are there or not?'

She considered the question. It was the first time such an answer had been required of her. After the first shock of bereavement, the initial rallying round, she had found that people withdrew again, assuming that as you were still on your feet, going through the motions, you were coping, you were in control. You were 'getting over it'. Now reluctantly, as if admitting some real and basic failing, she said, 'In all honestly, I don't think I do. Is that very dreadful?'

'Lucky, I should say, rather.' He stared into the fire, crumbled the last of his bread, then leaned forward and threw it into the flames which flared greedily for a moment, devouring. 'I have this awful feeling, which I find hard to put into words. I know that, soon, Chloe will be gone. Until then, I can only do my best for her. I can't prepare myself for afterwards, although I've tried. You didn't even have the chance to do that, of course. I just have this terrible feeling, which comes over me worst at night when I lie beside her, listening to her breathing. That having helped her as best I can, hopefully right to the end, and sent her on her way in the knowledge that I love her, that I'm with her – I shall then be left alone. And there'll be nobody to help me die.'

She was silent, glad of the dimness of the room. Unwelcome tears struggled at her eyelids. Then she said quietly, 'I should have thought it was the living without her that would be difficult. That's what takes the adjustment. I confess I hadn't looked that far ahead. Not to my own dying.'

'Perhaps because it was different for you.' He was turning the platter round and round in his hands, staring at its scratched and crumby surface as if seeing his future in a crystal ball. 'That's bad enough, of course. The living bit. But then another feeling comes over me, so strong I can hardly bear it. The thought that while I'm alive, and remembering her, she's still here, we can still be together even if only in my memory. But when I'm gone, then I've lost her completely. I don't believe in an afterlife. Do you? As far as I can see, when we're dead, we're gone. Chloe will go one way, I another. It will be as if we had never been. We'll leave no children, no grandchildren. What will it all have been about? As Andrew Marvell said – "The grave's a fine and private place, But none, I think, do there embrace." I do keep on thinking of that lonely grave.' He looked at her then for the first time with haunted eyes. 'Is this dreadful of me? Do you understand what I'm saying? I had to tell somebody. And I wondered, somehow, if you might have felt the same.'

She shook her head. 'I'm sorry. Maybe I just don't have your imagination. Or maybe I just can't love enough.' That

161

must be true, she thought sadly. But she could understand. 'But now you put it to me I can see, quite clearly, what you mean. I can feel your pain, and your terror. I wish I could help you, Lorne. Could you speak to the priest perhaps?'

'We're not of his "flock" and anyway, he would only offer an afterlife as some sort of consolation prize. I don't find that reassuring. I don't expect to see Chloe somewhere on the other side, skipping about in Elysian fields of daisies, restored to her former self, any more than I expect to see my parents.

'And just think of the problems that would create for some people. All of life's conflicts carried on in perpetuity, with no escape at the end.'

She took the platter gently from his hands then enclosed them with her own. She found herself rubbing vigorously at his thumbs, feeling them rough, the skin around the nails ragged. She hadn't noticed it before. What is required of me? she asked herself. Why don't I have the words? She said, 'I'm not strong or wise, Lorne. I don't know any answers. I can only say I understand what you are saying, and I can see that it is dreadful.'

'And that's enough. Just to know that someone knows. Thank you, Maggie.' He withdrew his hands. 'I'm glad you'll be around,' he said, 'when it happens.'

She felt angry as she drove home, taking the hill fast as she had done with Sheila, though her anger now was at herself. 'Why am I so useless?' she cried out loud. 'And why does everyone expect me to be otherwise?'

She felt distraught for Lorne, touched that he should have confided in her and more than anything grateful that her physical longing had been assuaged. If not, who knew where the afternoon's encounter may have led her. Given his obvious devotion to Chloe, she was both ashamed and

162

embarrassed by the desire she had entertained, the response she had hoped to arouse and which he would quite clearly have been unable to invoke. Sensing an escape from humiliation, her gratitude to Marcos knew no bounds.

She found herself dreaming idly as she negotiated the village street, overtaking a buzzing scooter with two youngsters on the back, a treacherous wasp with long hair blowing free unprotected by either helmet or scarf. The driver was as dark as Marcos, his girl's arms tight about his waist. The rain had stopped; they wore tee shirts and jeans, their arms were brown and smooth. She was thinking of Marcos's skin as she parked the car, and of the red branding of her nails across his back, marking him as hers.

Cassie had been right. Harriet didn't look at all well. Seeing her walk into the airport building carrying one small bag and peering diffidently through her tinted glasses Maggie thought, That's never her. Harriet always strode purposefully into concourses, foyers and lobbies, she smiled at porters, waiters and receptionists with a calm authority. Harriet had presence. Now she seemed as insubstantial as Sheila had seemed awkward. For the first time she realised she had been remiss in letting Harriet invite herself. She had become too absorbed in her new life, and belatedly she blamed herself. She found herself running, taking Harriet's arm protectively, hugging her and thinking how tall she seemed, or was it just because she was so thin?

'Silly of me but I felt quite overwhelmed,' apologised Harriet. 'And it's only a tinpot little place!' From Harriet it didn't sound derogatory, or if it did, Maggie didn't mind.

'It's small, but it's my own,' she declared. 'For the moment, anyway. Are you as exhausted as you look? You're going to feel the heat, I'm afraid. Maybe a cup of tea or something, before we go?' But the little cafeteria was a crush of potential travellers wolfing beer and *bocadillos*.

Excited children ran hither and thither among a drift of crisp and chocolate packets. The English school holidays had started and the babble of familiar accents sounded strange to Maggie's ears. She looked with some distaste at the pale faces of new arrivals, the raffish tans of departing holidaymakers in their travel-weary shirts and shorts and trainers, and felt sure most of the litter was due to them.

'Come on,' she said. 'I'll take you home.'

Disconcertingly, Harriet fell asleep as soon as the car began to move. Maggie had hoped to display the scenery to her in a way she had been unable to do to Sheila. Instead she drove fast and in silence, hearing Harriet's light snoring as her mouth fell open, and worrying about her.

However when they arrived, Harriet seemed refreshed. She exclaimed with satisfactory enthusiasm over the whole house, professing herself delighted with her bedroom and the fact that it opened onto the garden. 'I shall sleep with the door open,' she said. 'Maybe even outside, do you think? At least there's no flight path overhead!'

'Just the mosquitoes,' warned Maggie. 'I think I've become immune by now. Why don't you unpack? I'll start the supper. You are hungry, I hope?'

Harriet was so thin it looked as if she hadn't eaten for weeks. Maggie looked at her worriedly, was relieved when she said, 'For your cooking yes, Maggie. I suppose I must get used to calling you that. It seemed so strange at first, when you wrote, but now I think I can see it. You're looking astonishingly well. You've put on weight, it suits you. And the tan. And I like your hair like that, it looks positively Grecian.'

'That's how I always thought of you,' laughed Maggie. 'Well, not so much Grecian as artistic, both sophisticated and interestingly tousled all at once!' She saw that Harriet's hair was much greyer than she remembered and the heavy bun accentuated the thinness of her face. She was horribly reminded of Chloe.

164

Harriet had turned to the watercolours which were still displayed along the sideboard. She removed her glasses which hung down on a black cord round her neck, picked up one and peered at it. 'You know these are very good. I'm so pleased you've taken it up again.'

Maggie laughed again. 'I think you're flattering me. But I am enjoying it. You wait till you see my *pièce de résistance*, it's upstairs. No one's seen it yet, but you're different.' She suddenly crossed to Harriet, hugged her impulsively, feeling her like a brittle bird in her own strong arms. 'It's so good to see you. I didn't realise how much I missed you. Have I been dreadfully selfish, abandoning you all like this?'

'Maybe. But then again, why not?' Harriet replaced her glasses. 'Do you have a bottle of wine? Let's open it, and drink to Maggie. I'm glad I've met her at last; she's obviously alive and well!'

Next morning they met Lilli in the bread queue.

'Come back for a drink,' she invited them gaily. 'I've been longing to meet you, Harriet.'

Maggie could see that Harriet was charmed, the more so as Lilli, galloping them along the road at a fair pace, kept up a ceaseless questioning about her work. Eventually Harriet stopped, her hand apologetically on her side. 'Please – can we slow down? I'm not up to this yet.'

Lilli was swift contrition. 'Oh Harriet, your operation. Forgive me. I am always too hasty. Here – take my arm. We're nearly there – you shall put your feet up and I shall bring you a long cold beer.'

To Maggie's relief Harriet responded to Lilli's ministrations and was soon chatting amiably, seated in Lilli's overcrowded living room which probably, Maggie reflected, reminded her of her own cluttered childhood home. When they left they sauntered slowly up the lane to the road and Harriet said, 'She's delightful. I'm so glad you have a friend.'

'Two friends,' said Maggie firmly. 'I have you.'

They turned into the main road to be greeted by a joyous barking. Finn and Nigel were striding towards them from the direction of Vara's garage.

'Maggie! Good to see you. And this must be Harriet – delighted I'm sure.' He held out his hand to Harriet and gave a little bow. Maggie saw her smile, which she turned into a beam of greeting.

'Allow me,' Nigel said, taking from Maggie's hand the bag of bread. 'I have just taken the car in for a service so am walking back. It's hot,' he added pointedly, so that Maggie felt constrained to ask him in for a beer.

When he had gone, Harriet said smilingly, 'I do see what you mean. But he's kind.'

'Indeed. I suppose I'm lucky to have him. But I'm afraid I'm not asking him to my birthday lunch. Lilli unfortunately can't come – a concert rehearsal which she can't miss. But Lorne and Chloe are coming.

'Ah – Lorne. I thought it wouldn't be long before I met him. Dare I say it, but he seems to have become quite important to you?'

Now it was Maggie's face that flared. 'Lorne? He's helped me with my painting, certainly.'

'And?'

'And nothing.' Maggie acknowledged with relief that this was so. 'Anyway,' she said after a moment. 'I want to measure the width of the hallway to make sure it will take the wheelchair. Will you mind very much if we use your room as a dining room? Chloe obviously can't get upstairs.'

Fetching a tape measure she marvelled at Harriet's perspicacity. She hadn't realised she was so transparent, resolved not to be so again. She wasn't sure if she would mention Marcos. The remembered ecstasy and trembling anticipation seemed too trivial and self-indulgent in the face of the realities of Chloe and Lorne, and Harriet's obvious distress,

166

the measure of which she hadn't yet divulged. No doubt, in her own good time . . .

She drove her to Baiona. It was a bluff and breezy day, white clouds scudding on a rain-washed sky. It was easier to talk in the car while Harriet's eyes were on the green countryside, its tumbled deep-tiled roofs and ripening apples, the bulging golden corn cobs and musing cows. Maggie's own eyes were on the road, on the donkey she could see ahead laden with sweet grasses and followed by a sprightly dog and a languid young man with a stick.

She said, 'Sheila's visit wasn't an unmitigated success, I feel. I don't think she was very impressed with Spain. And I think she disapproves of me completely.'

'I don't see why. Everything here is beautiful, I can see why you and Robert always loved it. I'm not sure about the other. Why should Sheila disapprove?'

'I think she thought at first that I'd just gone off my rocker. What would someone like me be thinking of, doing something like this? And anyway, I obviously couldn't cope. Then, when she saw I could, I think she felt cheated. She seems to resent the fact that things have worked out well, that I don't need her. I felt mean, sometimes, because I was happy while she's so miserable. And, of course, I've failed her. Her whole world has fallen apart and I'm not prepared to help her pick up the pieces. Or I dare say that's how she sees it.'

'But she's living in your house, on your money, by all accounts. What more does she want?'

'Oh – something I can't give her, I suppose. Commitment perhaps. Somebody to carry the burden for her. She's so inconsistent; fragile and dependent and rather pathetic in some ways, so prickly and critical and bossy in others. I just don't want it any more. I suppose I just wish she'd find someone else to look after her. To take her off my back. Is that dreadful? It is dreadful. I feel so riddled with guilt . . .'

They had reached the coast road. Harriet drew in her breath. 'I haven't seen the sea for two years. You do miss it. That feeling of being on the edge, being able to breathe ... You mustn't, you know. Blame yourself so much. You've been a marvellous mother. I always envied your little family – both when you were a girl, at home, and afterwards, with Robert. It was all so civilised, so predictable and safe. Neither of the girls has ever been any problem. If you were so very dreadful they'd have gone off the rails, dropped out, rebelled in some way. I see it all the time.'

The battlemented walls of Monte Real had risen on their right. Maggie pulled off into the car park at the bottom. Skateboarders were weaving in and out of the cars and olive-skinned youths were tossing a basketball into a net watched by an attendent group of glossy girls.

'Could you manage the climb up there, and perhaps a walk on the battlements?'

'Why not?' But their progress up the hill was painfully slow. Maggie stopped frequently to look back at the view, giving Harriet time to rest. 'I just don't want to be bothered any more,' she said at one such moment. 'There's Cassie, bringing home every little hiccup, involving me in every decision, expecting me to take Robert off her hands when-ever she chooses. Is there no limit, do you think? Can a parent ever say "no", and not feel they're in the wrong?'

'Not being a parent, it's easy for me to say that they certainly can. I can see exactly what you mean about Cassie. She's a dear girl, but demanding. One has to be involved in everything. I'm not even her mother, but I could feel the way she drains.'

'Oh Harriet! Was she a nuisance?'

'No. Because I was able to leave. As you have done. And it doesn't seem to have done her any harm.'

'But it's there, none the less. Like a barnacle, clinging to my skin.' They moved on, slowly, and reached the top.

'Coffee, I think,' said Maggie. 'And a slice of almond tart.'

'I learned a little bit about Cassie while I was at your house.' Harriet took a mouthful of tart, pushed the rest away. A fountain in the centre of the little courtyard drifted towards them in the breeze, misting her glasses, spotting their summery skirts and bare arms. 'I think a lot of her uncertainty is because she feels she has failed you in some way. Could that be so?'

Maggie was appalled. She raised her cup, lowered it untouched. 'Can she really tell? That's dreadful . . .' She clenched her hands. 'I wanted so much for her, I must confess. I've never told a living soul, not even Robert. But it was obvious from the start that Sheila was always going to conform. Not surprisingly, of course. I had never exactly broken out. The one rebellious thing I ever did was to insist on leaving school and in retrospect I know that to have been a mistake. I thought, With the next one it will be different. She will be the one that shines, who will break the mould, push out the boundaries a bit. So I called her Cassandra. I know you all thought me mad, but it seemed that it would give her a head start. After all, what could a Sheila be, but ordinary?'

'Poor Cassie – an *enfant terrible manqué*!' murmured Harriet.

'Pathetic, isn't it? As if it could make a scrap of difference. Genes will out, whatever you happen to call them by. And they just didn't have the genes. Neither of them. They took after me, and Robert. It's not their fault. The fault is that I have never been able to accept it. Just as I have, latterly, not been able to accept myself. I abhor ordinariness. I don't want to be ordinary. I don't want *them* to be . . .' She gulped coffee. 'I saw poor Sheila, all set to break her heart over Marcos who never in a million years . . .'

'Who's Marcos?'

Maggie's heart tripped, stumbled on again clumsily. 'You

might meet him. He helps out at the garage sometimes, but he's away at present.' Did Harriet read her like a book? 'She had quite a crush on him, she called it helping him with his English. But I think her heart's elsewhere, and that's equally hopeless. I feel such pain for her, and such impatience. And then again, she frightens me. No wonder I couldn't wait for her to be gone . . .'

'Poor Maggie!'

'Hmm. I'm sure you're really thinking what a selfish cow. What a feeble weak-kneed creature, who should be grateful for what she's got. I had all those years with Robert. You had – what? Do you know, I even envied you all that ghastly business with Jake? There was something different about it, a vicarious glamour in the sheer horror of it all. It was at least original! Everything that happened to me was entirely unoriginal, unremarkable. Even your family, that lovely shambolic house with all your brothers and sisters, going their own ways doing interesting things. We were so staid, so tidy. No wonder I'm how I am. Now, at the eleventh hour, I've decided to try and be different. If it means tossing aside my responsibilities, whatever they may correctly be considered to be, then so be it.' She drained the cold dregs from her cup. 'So now you know it all. And am I still your friend?'

'Of course. As ever, and more.'

'Thank you. I don't deserve it.' She felt ashamed but released, as if a noxious boil had been opened in public. 'And now, what about you? Quite frankly, you look ghastly. Here am I, droning on, when you obviously have problems of your own.'

'But I'm all right.' Harriet smiled brightly. 'Mending nicely and all the better for being here. Now, how about those battlements? Three kilometres you say? I'll manage that, if it kills me!'

# FIFTEEN

One night, when Harriet was sure Maggie must be asleep, she sat at the dining-room table and inserted a tape into the personal stereo she played each night to help herself to sleep. Her hands were damp and her voice husky as, quite calmly, as if she were drafting a legal document, she began to dictate.

'Maggie dear, I was going to tell you, but now I know I shan't. I shall leave this tape, addressed to you, among my things. Forgive me for taking the easy way out.

'But what could you say, after all? What can anyone say, when you tell them that you're dying? It's not fair to ask it of you. You would only feel you'd failed, and resent me for causing your failure.

'In a way, it's a relief, having decided. Now I can enjoy the rest of my stay, like the holiday that it pretends to be. Too many ghoulish revelations, morbid reflections, too much sentimental nostalgia would turn what time we have into something that you would prefer not to remember. I want you to remember it – to remember me – happily. I want to remember it happily myself, for as long as there is to remember.

'Jake had this theory that if, after every period of suffering, every experience of pain, we could have it blotted out, surgically removed from our memory – then we would go through life thinking we were happy. I believe he may have been right.

'I think, by now, I could almost have said that I never wanted children. If I didn't remember how it felt to hold

171

little Cassie on my knee in her warm nightclothes, how it hurt to see babies in prams outside the supermarket, children running to school – then I could assume that I had been immune, inviolate – content. Now I can even be grateful. I am not leaving anybody behind, not anyone who needs me, that I shall miss unduly. Wherever it is that I am going.

'I would like to be able to forget sitting in Dr Patelski's surgery and hearing him tell me the truth. But that wouldn't make any difference. The truth would still be there, as I knew it was all along.

'I just wish I knew how it is going to end. Whether to warn the family, or not. Whether it is easier, in the long run, to face it alone, not to have to take their own grief as well as mine. I'm too frightened to be able to offer the merest crumb of comfort, I could not be brave for them.

'You, Maggie, are radiant now. You seem to have found what you are seeking, discovered your Holy Grail in this unexpected place with these unlikely people. Lilli I love. She is so robust, so colourful, gay and honest. I am glad you have her. Major Tyson is exactly as you described. But well meaning – how that does damn with faint praise! He seems very keen on you – be warned. Tomorrow I shall be meeting Lorne and Chloe. I am curious about Lorne. The thought of Chloe frightens me. I recoil from the presence of death. But maybe we can talk about her poetry. I can understand that, it is angry and questioning, the way I feel.

'Tomorrow is your birthday, Maggie. I wonder if I shall see mine, but it's useless to speculate. "A few months," he said. What's a few months?

'I can't say any more Maggie. I'm sorry to leave you. Be happy.'

She snapped off the machine, wiping angrily at the bitter tears.

# SIXTEEN

'We've got cider for a change,' Maggie announced. 'I hope you like it.'

She and Harriet had finally been unable to resist the roadside notices of '*Sidra*' for sale, had gone into an orchard already heavy with the next year's crop, seen the wooden crusher in the shade of the *hórreo*, bought several bottles and a stone flagon from a bent and wizened creature who toiled laboriously up the steps to the verandahed first floor of the ramshackle building to fetch them.

'I wish we could go inside,' Harriet had whispered. 'They're such fascinating buildings.'

'Yes, I love them,' Maggie whispered back, then laughed. 'But why are we whispering, I wonder?'

The bottles were dusty with chaff and seed, the cider clear and gold and lambent as they carried it into the sun. Now it gleamed dully in her cool dining room as Maggie served noisettes of pork with apple, thin courgettes in tomato and garlic sauce and tiny potatoes bathed in butter and herbs. She felt nervous; similar occasions at Heathercote seemed a long time ago. And Chloe made her nervous; she was unused to seeing her away from the farmhouse. Outside the familiar setting she looked frailer yet at the same time more uncompromising. Maggie had felt her eyes on the carefully set table, the texture of the fish pâté, now the cider in her glass. 'Is that all right?' she found herself asking as Chloe's vaguely trembling hands cut into the pale flesh of the pork. 'I thought it would be easy . . .'

173

'Thanks.' Chloe's tone was caustic, not welcoming the concession.

'We should have a toast, I think.' Lorne raised his glass. 'A very happy birthday to Maggie. And may she never look a day older.' His eyes appraised her approvingly but no longer had the power to disturb.

Chloe went through the motions, Harriet repeated them and Maggie met Lorne's eyes gratefully. 'Fifty-four,' she said brightly, not believing it. 'It hardly seems possible.'

'No,' said Chloe.

'No, I won't be able to believe it either,' added Harriet. Maggie glanced at her, thinking she looked, sadly, every day of her age and more. She herself, she knew, looked smooth and glowing, like a peach removed from cold storage and belatedly ripening in a hothouse. Chloe seemed frozen in time; she would never, as they said, 'make old bones'. It was unjust and insupportable. Maggie tore at her meat in anger.

Harriet began to talk about Chloe's poetry and elicited an animated response. Chloe's eyes lit up and her cheeks flushed with every appearance of vivacity. Maggie had never seen her so, was ashamed that she had not made more effort, at least pretended to understand if she could not. She could perhaps have asked her to explain the loose unstructured verse with its searching and painful messages. To Maggie most of it hadn't even seemed to be poetry. She liked Emily Dickinson, Thomas Hardy; she was used to meter and scansion and rhyme. Conscious of the naïvety of this she had been reluctant to admit it, found it difficult to think of anything positive or constructive to say. But Harriet seemed to have grasped it admirably. Grateful to her friend for finding a point of contact which allowed her to relax and Lorne to enjoy his food with his customary rapacity, she was yet chastened at her own multiple failure

174

of incomprehension, intellectual laxity and lack of consideration. Chloe had little enough left but her poetry. Harriet had demonstrated a compassion that Maggie lacked. Once again she felt the pain of her inadequacy.

She took coffee into the garden. There had been rain the previous day and the little lawn was damp, tall and tangled. 'I have no mower,' apologised Maggie, dragging chairs across the hummocks.

'But the flowers are lovely,' said Lorne, helping her. 'Such colours. A proper English garden.' The petunias were blazing purple, pink and white behind the orange and yellow border of marigolds. They looked, thought Maggie suddenly, rather crude.

'I miss an English garden,' said Chloe, surprisingly. 'The dappled shade and the swing beneath the tree. Birdbaths, croquet – and cabbages all in a row.'

'And statues, you must have statues,' added Harriet.

'And rows of runner beans.' How prosaic, Maggie thought, but then I am. 'Perhaps a summerhouse?'

'And a swing seat, rampant with Sanderson flowers but always covered in plastic against the rain,' said Lorne, realistically, and they laughed.

He and Chloe had brought Maggie a present, a small framed watercolour of the view from the terrace at Serenidad. It was wintertime; the rose beds were clipped and low, the hydrangea bank hung with muted mops of dusky browny-blue. Gondomar huddled in a hazy middle distance, the far mountains describing parabolas against a pale-washed sky.

'I shall treasure this,' Maggie told them, knowing that she would. 'Look, Harriet.' She turned, holding out the picture for inspection. To her horror and embarrassment, Harriet seemed to have fallen asleep, quite suddenly, in the way that Chloe sometimes did. Her unsupported head lolled on her shoulders which stood tanned but bony above a

175

light dress, her empty cup resting in her lap, fingers slipped limply aside.

'Oh,' said Maggie, startled and upset. 'I'm sorry. She's still not well.'

'Don't wake her,' said Chloe sharply, and looked at Maggie with a gaze both warning, meaningful and disturbing.

'I suppose I should really ask Cassie and Anthony for a holiday. Since they're so hard up. They could have my room.'

'Do you want to?'

'I'd like to see Robert, certainly.' They were sitting on the terrace in the last of the light. Chloe and Lorne had long since left; Maggie had cleared up while Harriet slept. When she had woken, abruptly and apologetic, they had persuaded her to lie down on Maggie's bed. Now, with the fading of the heat and light, she seemed refreshed and relaxed. She was fondling Cake who had adopted her during the week, choosing her lap in preference to Maggie's. It was their last evening. Maggie felt suddenly, desperately, sad.

'Have you enjoyed your holiday? I wish you could stay longer.'

'Me too. But I need to get back to work. I've lolled round for long enough, it's bad for my self-esteem.'

'Are you really well enough?' Maggie looked at her doubtfully. 'Don't rush things.'

'I'll see the doc. But it's been three months now.'

'I suppose so, but if you don't feel ready . . .'

'Maggie. Don't fuss. It's not your role, remember?'

She was about to reply with compunction that nonsense, with Harriet it was different, when she heard her name called from the street below.

'That's Marcos,' she cried, half rising, then forcing herself back into the chair. Harriet's eyes were on her, questioning. Slowly, she got up and went to the railing, leaning over into the dusk as she had done before. This time she gave both warning and instruction, 'Harriet's here, it's her last night.'

She couldn't see him clearly, whether his face expressed disappointment or irritation. 'Perhaps tomorrow?' she called quietly and saw him wave in compliance, consent, agreement? 'That was Sheila's Marcos,' she proffered unnecessarily, returning to her chair. 'Perhaps he's missing her after all.'

Her sorrow at their parting was ameliorated only by the thought that he would be coming to her that night.

Harriet was quiet and withdrawn on the drive north, anxious to go through quickly when they arrived at the airport although they were early for her flight.

'Why don't we have some lunch first?'

'But wouldn't you rather get back?' Harriet asked, as if she knew.

'Not at all. And I'd like to eat.'

So they crowded into the cafeteria and pushed a space among the cans and empty packets on the table and Maggie got them beer and sandwiches while Harriet guarded her bag. Sitting in the scrum there suddenly didn't seem to be much to say.

'I don't know when I'll be coming back,' said Maggie at last. 'So goodness knows when I shall see you again. It's dreadful.'

'It is indeed.'

Maggie allowed herself to feel hurt. She had expected, she required, a little more regret. 'You've not been bored, I hope? By my dissolute life? By my friends? Well, acquaintances really. They're not friends like you, you know that, don't you?'

But Harriet seemed distant, as if peering distractedly over a high wall over which scrambled confusing impenetrable foliage. Maggie couldn't breach the leaves and prickles of her defences. When Harriet professed to loving her friends, being charmed and enchanted by Spain, by the house, by Maggie's new image, and feeling nothing but delight at her happiness, Maggie felt she was being deluded, bought off by words she wanted to hear but which weren't, in the end, the whole and nothing but the truth. And if she had wanted tears and effusiveness, she was to be disappointed. Harriet simply embraced her once, firmly and quickly, at the barrier leading to the electronic scanner. 'I'll write, of course. Thank you, Maggie. For everything. And don't worry about the girls. We're none of us perfect.'

'Thank you. You will take care.'

'And you. I'll write. Goodbye. Dear Maggie . . .'

'Dear Harriet.' And she was gone.

Maggie drove home to wait for Marcos, but he didn't come.

Which was probably just as well, she told herself, because there was a problem which needed addressing and which she hadn't quite got round to; the problem of contraception. While it was tedious and ludicrous at her age to be worried about such a thing, her cautious nature dictated that discretion would be the better part of valour. The thought of Sheila's reaction to a sudden announcement that she was pregnant was enough to bring a chilly smile to her lips; the idea of announcing it to Marcos, Lilli and the Major held an element of farce.

There was also another threat that she had complacently assumed herself to have escaped, that of Aids. With a shock she had realised that Marcos was of exactly the age and circumstance to be carrying the sinister antibodies, even if he were not, himself, a homosexual, which she knew to be true, or a drug addict which she acknowledged she could not be sure about. Hardly able to recognise herself as she pondered, for the first time in her life, the risks and practicalities of promiscuity and passion, she was equally unable to see herself producing the necessary equipment and asking Marcos, politely, to oblige. She had actually been beginning to wonder if the whole thing was worth the bother, whether once was enough and from now on a sensible abstinence should be her chosen course, when his voice from the street had kindled the ashes of her desire. His failure to arrive when she was ready and waiting, with wine in the fridge and her body already on fire, was as bellows to an already-consuming blaze. She resolved to visit a chemist, not in the village but in Vigo. In the meantime, ashamed but shameless, she found herself driven to enquire of Madrilena as to the whereabouts of her lover.

'I think he is in Santiago. He has an apartment there.'

'But he was here the other night. I saw him passing by.'

'There was something he wanted in his room. He bought me ice cream and some ribbons.'

'Did he? You lucky girl.' Carefully, with controlled considered strokes, Maggie painted in the innocent curve of the olive cheek, the jut of the chin which was paled by the light. The flesh tones she had found difficult to match; in the end Lorne had helped her, showing her how white and ochre, balanced with a little burnt sienna, produced the desired effect. In just such tones he had painted in her own arms and brow, burned as she was now like a native. Studying the child's smouldering but innocent eyes Maggie was conscious of a humiliating envy of that ice cream, those ribbons. Her questioning of the girl for such base ends was sullying to Madrilena's purity, diminishing her own self-respect. Still she asked, 'Do you know if he's coming back to work in the garage?'

Madrilena shrugged, tipping a fold of her mantilla from

the peak of a shoulder. 'Perhaps. My father hasn't said.'

'Keep still,' snapped Maggie, 'you're spoiling everything,' meaning everything was spoiled and she was now as surely entrapped and accountable as ever.

The days went by, hot, bright and drier than she had expected. The coast roads were crowded with tourist buses and cars though not, as Maggie was grateful to acknowledge, the more unruly element of the package tour industry. On their particular stretch of the coast there were no huge modern hotels, no villa and apartment complexes. The British tourists were for the most part older, as she and Robert had been, staying for a night or two in one of the more discreet hotels and moving on, or families camping or caravanning on one of the sites further north and east. Most of the holidaymakers were Spanish, escaping north from the grill pan of the south in August, and she could look on them indulgently.

Lorne finished her portrait and professed it good enough to go into his exhibition. Maggie was absurdly proud, though a little surprised at the way he had portrayed her. She didn't look as young as she had expected despite the softness of the dress, the sparkle of the blue stone against her throat. Perhaps it was the hair; perhaps after all the Grecian goddess look was not for her. She remembered Harriet's heavy greying coils, always so elegant, but resolved to wear hers loose in future.

Harriet wrote to say she would be going back to work in a week, there was lots to be sorted out, she had been away too long. Maggie wrote to Sheila asking her to ring Harriet sometime and ask her down to supper. 'And give me a full report,' she added. 'I confess I'm worried about her. And about you too, of course. I'm sorry you are having difficulty getting into a teaching course. Perhaps you'll have to think

180

again?' She wrote also to Cassie, but she didn't ask them to come for a holiday.

She went to Vigo one day in a thunderstorm which raged in from the sea. It blotted out the road and the shore so that she had to stop in a lay-by along with tourists with luggage on the roof, and a bus full of restless children drawing faces on the windows, till the worst of it had passed. Meanwhile, lorries thundered past, careless of the havoc they caused, the havoc they risked, shooting waves of water and a mist of spray across the road. Maggie's Vauxhall steamed up inside, she opened the window a crack but the rain poured in. She sat, fretting, wiping the windows with tissues and listening to news from Madrid on the storm-crackled radio.

When she reached the city the streets were already steaming dry but she felt damp and crumpled, had the beginning of a headache. Depressed, she bought herself lunch, homesick for the first time for a simple English café, for poached egg on toast and a pot of tea. She swallowed aspirin, acknowledging the power of her hormones. Mid-cycle, she had always developed a headache and a ravenous appetite, always felt tense and depressed. The unwelcome evidence of her renewed, her continued, fertility, made her feel worse. The obvious necessity of some precautionary measure was outweighed now by the dreary certainty that Marcos would not come again. He was back in Santiago with his friends. His young friends. Soon the university term would start again. It was just as well. The risks were too great, the whole thing was a nonsense, she was old enough to be his mother. Hadn't she even coveted him for a son? She went shopping, bought herself a dress and some lipstick, some pretty pillowcases for Cassie in a sale. She didn't go to the chemist.

A week later, on the night of the flamenco concert, it was too late.

*    *    *

181

She went to ask Nigel Tyson if he would like to go with her and he accepted with alacrity. 'I've missed you,' he told her. 'Don't see nearly enough of you.'

'Well, I've had my visitors. And the portrait. I've only just finished that.'

'Splendid. Are they pleased with it? The Varas?'

'I haven't shown them. This one's mine. And I'm not sure that I want to do another.'

He looked at her shrewdly. 'Not your cup of tea after all?' When she didn't answer he added, 'I was in the kitchen clearing up a bit.'

With a little sigh, not knowing quite why she did it, she followed him into the kitchen, automatically reaching for the tap, sweeping crockery into the sink, rubbish into a black bag, abandoned purchases into cupboards and drawers.

As she worked she said, 'I think maybe you're right. It's the man-made objects I enjoy. Waves and trees are all very well, Madrilena was a challenge and I shall treasure it because it's her, but none of it really excites me.'

As usual he accepted her uninvited efforts without question or gratitude. It was as if Edna had been reinstated in her kitchen, doing only what was due. As always she asked herself why she did it; decided it was because she couldn't bear the muddle, nothing more. She certainly wasn't doing it for Nigel. She wrung out the dishcloth and dried her hands.

'I suppose I have never been especially awestruck by nature,' she resumed as they sat down on the terrace. Faced with the spectacular view stretched out in the afternoon light the statement seemed contrary. 'It's man's achievements that impress me, and man in conjunction with nature which satisfies. And woman, of course.' She laughed. 'Do you understand what I'm saying?'

'Of course, Maggie. Of course. Did I tell you the postmaster's daughter will be giving me an hour or so each week?

She's finished school and is waiting to be a nurse. Little slip of a girl she looks, but beggars can't be choosers. And she'll be cheap.'

'Nigel, I hope you aren't exploiting her.'

'Of course not. She's glad of the job.'

'Well, there'll certainly be plenty for her to do. And what will *you* do? Have a kit inspection before she starts, issue orders in triplicate and make spot checks under the rugs?'

It was meant to be a joke but he looked hurt. 'I'll be fair, of course. I don't want to lose her. A bird in the hand and all that . . . Now tell me about this concert. Do I know this Lilli of yours?'

'She runs a little school at home, for the children. I have told you all about it. They learn flamenco and classical dance. Lilli plays the guitar beautifully. She also takes an adult class in Vigo. I think most of her students are taking part. I want to support her, of course, but really I'm going because of Madrilena.'

'I think I've seen her. Lilli. At the bakery. Tall, athletic sort of woman. Fair untidy hair, like a bush. Will you drive or shall I? I know you're not awfully keen on the Citroën.'

'I'm sorry, Nigel. I always feel that I arrive so battered and untidy.'

'Quite. Quite. Edna was always on at me to change it but it's cheap to run. And it would seem disloyal, somehow, to change it now, when she's not here to get the benefit.'

'Oh Nigel. That's very sad. I'm sure she wouldn't mind at all. After all you're not as young as you were.'

'Neither does my pension go as far. Now, you'll have some tea?'

But she declined, thinking she might very well find herself making it.

The school hall in Vigo was almost empty when they arrived.

'I do hope there'll be more people than this, Lilli will be terribly disappointed.'

The Major looked glumly round the vacant rows of chairs.

'It is early, of course.'

They sat in silence for a while. Maggie skipped through the duplicated sheet which passed for a programme, seeing Madrilena's name among the juniors. She felt an almost parental pride and nervousness. She wished she could have been behind the scenes, giving the shining hair a last-minute brush, adjusting the comb, applying rouge to the high cheekbones. She doubted whether the Varas would come, but she was wrong.

'Somebody is waving at you,' said Nigel, who had been watching with relief as the seats filled up. She turned, and with a hammering of the heart saw the Varas waiting for a programme and, standing with them, Marcos, fluttering an almost peremptory hand.

She raised her own, casually; was quite unprepared when he left the Varas and made his way between the seats to the vacant one at her side.

'Maggie. It is very good to see you,' he said in English, his eyes speaking volumes.

'Do you know Major Tyson?' She introduced them and they shook hands across her body. Nigel, she thought, looked ever so slightly put out.

'Marcos is Madrilena's cousin, that's why he has come, like me,' she explained, unnecessarily, as if the child were some jointly prized possession. 'I'm glad her parents have come,' she said to Marcos. 'I didn't expect it somehow.'

'But they dote on her, she is their youngest and their treasure,' he said, in Spanish now, caressing her with his eyes so that her body melted achingly into the hard plastic chair.

The rest of the evening was a confusion; a heady draught of sound and movement, rhythm and twisting stamping bodies. Now she could understand the deft, birdlike movements of Madrilena, her grace and dignity, the banked-down fire in her eyes. The black and red waterfalls of the skirts, the black flashing boots and tossed heads, the stiff yet graceful arms and the click-clack-click of the castanets combined with the haunt and throb of Lilli's guitar in a turgid inflammatory stream which entered her blood and made her own heart race in time. On another level, one of anticipation and physical intoxication, she was aware only of Marcos by her side, beating out the rhythm on his knees with lean brown fingers then sliding one hand under her elbow against her breast so that she could hardly breathe. She could not turn her eyes from the gyrating dancers, dared not acknowledge the tacit suggestion in his eyes. She clasped her own hands wetly in her lap, turned to say something trivial to Nigel whose attention seemed to have wandered, to be focusing on the shabby curtains of the stage, the flickering faulty Exit sign, the straight absorbed back of the child kneeling on the chair in front.

The evening drew to a climax; a passionate excitement of cascading sound, singing and shouting and clapping, of twirling stamping bodies and a wild final frenzy of delight. The audience exploded into its own ecstasy of appreciation and Marcos murmured, 'Later. I will come at midnight,' leaving her to stumble out of the hall behind Nigel in an imbecilic trance of excitement.

# SEVENTEEN

This time he stayed two nights and in between they cooked pasta in cream and garlic, brought grapes and wine into the bedroom where they sprawled together carelessly on crumpled sheets while the burning day turned outside. The morning lorries shook the house unheeded; the silence of siesta was broken only by their cries; the night fell on their sated sleep. She woke to the cock's crow at dawn and turned to him, straining once more towards pleasure, digging deep into her hunger, taking him with her into realms she had only ever imagined. When she woke again the sun was high on the front of the house and he was gone.

She stood inside the terrace doors, naked, hidden from the street, feeling the sun on her belly and thighs. She looked down at herself, flattening her belling stomach with wide fingers, unconsciously stiffening her breasts. The smell of the sun on hot tiles, of geraniums wilting in dry soil, of Marcos's juices on her skin, seared her nostrils in an intoxicating bouquet which she knew she would remember for ever. The whole moment, one of release and fulfilment, fecklessness, daring and exultation, was imprinted for ever on her senses, with the realisation that she would never be the same. Whatever happened, she had finally buried Margaret. Laughing out loud with joy, swooping the cat up into her arms so that his fur caressed her breasts, Maggie skipped, naked, long hair flying, across the bare tiles and slippery hand-woven rugs of her house in Spain as if she had been doing so for ever, as if Godalming had never existed, as if there was no past, no future, and only the delicious, careless and self-indulgent present.

By nightfall, reality had intruded again and with it the realisation of folly and irresponsibility. She slept restlessly, disturbed by memories of his presence, counting with an awestruck amazement the numbers of the risks she had taken, and next day, early, she drove to Vigo and the chemists. Once there, both her courage and her dictionary failed her. Unlike Boots at home in Surrey there was no reassuring and humdrum display on the counter among the throat pastilles and lipsticks. A starched and thin-lipped spinster was hovering behind the glass counter; Maggie purchased some tissues and sun lotion and hurried out. Her face burning, she recollected films of the fifties where pimply youths did much the same, emerging eventually with Lucozade and hairnets and, inevitably, got their teenage girlfriends pregnant on uncut-moquette sofas in terraced Midlands houses. She glanced curiously into the window of a hair salon where several young men sat on pink velvet chairs awaiting the stylist. 'And anything for the weekend, sir?' the barber had been wont to say, in the reliable old days when men went to barbers and women had sat in private cubicles at Evelyn's and Andrea's. Now, everyone sat together on white carpets at marble sinks and the only things for the weekend were mousse and hair spray and glossy wigs displayed on faceless heads.

There was clearly going to be no alternative but to speak to Marcos about the problem. He was coming again, he had said, in three weeks' time. He was going to take her to Portugal. In the meantime there was nothing for it but to wait. And pray.

Her face, she noticed, began to assume the haunted look of those more wayward girls in her fifth- and sixth-form years in the non permissive fifties. For the first time since her two painless and carefree pregnancies she had the sense that her body was holding her in thrall; whatever it would or wouldn't do, it would decide in its own good time. Sensibly, considerate as ever, Robert had had a vasectomy when he was forty. She had discarded the horrible Dutch cap, been relieved of the necessity of risking her life with the contraceptive pill. Relieved also of the monthly question mark which now filled her days and nights with a hideous dread. Angrily, she blamed herself for her recklessness; bitterly, she reflected that the freewheeling life did have its drawbacks. As Robert's wife she had had few concerns more pressing than getting Robert's suit from the cleaners, as his widow the choosing of suitable large print books for her housebound library customers. Now here she was, alone and friendless; for after all in whom could she confide a problem of such ludicrous and humiliating proportions at her age, in her circumstances? She longed inexpressibly for familiar Dr Gibson, while knowing that to reveal herself to him would have been almost as impossible. Restlessly she lived out a week of threatening stormy weather, and then another, keeping herself to herself, neither reading nor painting nor tending her plants which alternately wilted then were flattened by the rain.

She met Nigel one morning in the queue for bread.

'Long time no see,' he said.

'Two weeks,' she said with a sickening accuracy.

'The night of the concert. Great stuff, what? Most invigorating. Don't know where they get the energy. The Valeta was more my line and Edna's! And the gay Gordons. Wonderful dances we used to have. Every Saturday night, in Cyprus. Edna made all her dresses herself. Marvellous with the needle. Are you all right? Look a bit peaky, Maggie.'

'I'm fine. It's this weather. It gives me a headache.'

'Then let me carry your bag. I thought I'd take a run to

the sea this afternoon. It won't be quite so airless. Can I persuade you to come? Perhaps it would blow your head away?'

'Oh it would do that all right.' She summoned up a laugh, thinking, oh well, why not? There'll be no more invitations when he knows. When everybody knows. But of course I couldn't risk that. I'd just have to go home, sort things out. Like those erring daughters of old, sent off to fictitious relatives and returning six months later subdued and wan and desolate. Like every other silly girl before me; but I'm not a girl, for goodness' sake. I'm a grandmother, little Robert's grandmother!'

'I'd like to come,' she told Nigel. 'I think I'm missing Harriet.'

Sheila wrote, 'I telephoned Harriet at the weekend but there was no reply. Perhaps she's gone away again? Cassie is keeping me busy; nothing but problems – with the house (they need a new hot water tank), the car (the clutch is going, while Anthony has just spent a hundred and twenty pounds on new seat covers for the Capri), her fingernails, which are splitting – you know the sort of thing. If she could see some of the problems I've seen, she'd just be grateful . . .' Maggie sighed, and sank back into the pulpy depths of her own despair.

When she was ten days overdue, Lilli asked her to supper.

'Well?' she asked impatiently, when she had sat Maggie on the sofa among the fans and feathers, handed her a glass of wine. 'You haven't told me what you thought of the concert. It's over two weeks now. Where have you been, Maggie? I have called by, several times. Your car was there. Perhaps you were in the garden?'

'Perhaps. I've been preoccupied, I'm sorry. Oh Lilli, do forgive me. *Lo siento* – I am sorry. I did want to tell you, at

189

the time, how wonderful it was. Just magic! And Madrilena was a delight. She never missed a step as far as we could tell.'

'You and Marcos? I saw you there with him.'

'No – I was with Nigel actually. Marcos just arrived. Obviously preferred us to the Varas.'

'Obviously . . . Have an olive.' She pushed across the glass dish, taking one herself with her bony fingers. 'I'm going to England next month. To see Miriam.'

'Oh I am glad!'

'I shall meet Joseph. It's an unexpected name.' She popped the olive into her mouth, fingered her scar with oily fingers.

'Oh I don't know. No more so than Miriam. A positively biblical pair.'

'I wonder.' Lilli looked thoughtful.

Maggie said, 'You'd be happy if she were to marry surely? Especially with young Pepe? It must be hard, on her own.'

'If he is the right man, yes. But I wonder. Anyway – I think it is time for me to go and see. I have left her to her own devices long enough. Now . . .' she seemed to shake herself, said quite gaily, 'come and see what I've made us to eat!'

Maggie stood up. She said quickly, 'I must just go to the bathroom,' and fled along the hallway to discover that she had been reprieved. Incredulous, yet thinking immediately, Of course, I knew it would be all right, she fumbled in her bag with trembling fingers and put herself to rights. Despite a drag of discomfort her face in the mirror seemed to have shed a decade in an instant.

Having concealed her terror, she couldn't conceal her relief.

'Lilli,' she cried, returning to the kitchen, beaming hugely, 'I've just been granted a reprieve!'

190

Lilli was dishing out veal which steamed in a rich wine sauce. 'From what? Help yourself to rice and salad.'

It was too late to go back.

'I thought I'd been silly enough to get myself pregnant.' The statement sounded bald, unlikely enough and infinitely foolish. 'I know,' she added. 'I must be mad. But there it is. Or was . . .'

But Lilli was grinning with delight. There was neither surprise nor condemnation. 'But, Maggie, you dirty horse! Who was it then?'

'Dark horse.' Maggie didn't care for the alternative. 'And it really doesn't matter. Nobody you know.' She stabbed a piece of veal, feeling the sharpness of appetite for the first time for days. Gratefully she let the pungent sauce slide down her throat, chewed the tender meat sensuously in relief that life could hold such simple innocent pleasure.

After a while, perhaps just a little disappointed that Lilli didn't probe further, she said, 'Do you realise – in six years' time I'll be collecting my pension? And my free bus pass! And here I've been, worrying like a teenager about ruining my life! Can you believe it?'

Lilli shook her head. 'No, because I have not been so lucky.'

'Lucky? You think so? It's just got to stop. To stop, do you hear?' And she began to laugh, and the laughter got wilder and higher in the hysteria of relief and she rocked in her chair and choked until Lilli brought her water and Lilli was laughing too, and when they stopped Lilli said seriously, 'But can you stop, Maggie? Can it be stopped? These things are like buses, rolling down a hill. They do not always have any brakes.'

Maggie considered while she wiped her eyes on her hand-kerchief, her hands on her paper napkin. 'I don't know,' she said at last, truthfully.

'Then you must do something about it.'

'I tried. I did try, Lilli. But it's difficult, over here. And I never had to bother, before . . .'

'Then I'll do it for you. Get you something. Oh Maggie, haven't you heard of Aids?'

'Of course . . .'

'Well then, it is settled. You are a lucky old lady, Maggie, and I envy you.'

And they began to laugh again and Maggie clutched at the possibility of a future while the veal cooled on her plate and she knew herself once more to be free.

The next day Lilli arrived looking mischievous and conspiratorial and handed her a paper bag.

'You didn't get them in the village?'

'Why not? It will do my reputation the world of good. Old Alvarez the chemist looked at me with new eyes, I think. I may even have him knocking on my door.'

'But is there no one knocking, Lilli? I find that hard to understand.'

'There has been, in the past. But it is all too much trouble. They are either young, or old, or married. Usually married. Perhaps I will find myself a protector in England? Someone who wants to warm his chilly winter nights with some Spanish sun.'

'A sugar daddy. We call that sort of man a sugar daddy. But you deserve better than that.'

'Well, and so do you, but I think you haven't found it yet. Now put these beside your bed, Maggie, and don't forget them when you forget yourself. *Comprendo?*'

'I understand.' Maggie took the packages as warily as if she had been handed a gun. They were entirely foreign to her experience. She said, 'What am I doing, Lilli?'

'Only you know that. But it's a big dangerous world out there. I am not sure if you realise that.'

'I'm beginning to.' She dropped the packets into her

handbag, shutting it firmly. 'But this is ridiculous. I'm an old woman.'

'You certainly don't look it. And more ridiculous to take risks. Now, sit down and look at these, I have some pictures of Pepe. I can't believe I shall see him next week. Isn't he a treasure? Such a handsome boy, he takes after his grandfather.'

'Your husband? Are there any pictures of Joseph?'

'No, she is keeping him in cloths.'

'Wraps. Pepe is gorgeous, Lilli. I must get Cassie to send me some new ones of Robert. She never thinks of things like that . . .'

'Why don't you ask them all to come and see you?'

'Perhaps. I've had other things on my mind.'

Lilli swept the photographs into their paper wallet. 'Well, mind you behave yourself while I am away. I will send you a postcard of London – if you promise not to get too home-sick. I will tell you it is raining every day.'

'And it probably will be. Don't worry, you won't unsettle me now. I have too much to look forward to.' She patted her bag and they both burst into laughter. 'You know, I didn't talk like this when I was a girl,' exclaimed Maggie, waving her off at the door. 'You are a good friend, Lilli. Come back soon, I may need you!'

A letter arrived from Harriet. Seeing the envelope Maggie felt culpably contrite, belatedly conscious that she had almost forgotten her in her preoccupation. She had also been feeling ashamed: of her wanton behaviour, her stupid-ity and, now, of her good fortune. Remembering Harriet's strange defensiveness when they parted she wondered if there might be some censure there, some unspoken criti-cism. Maggie had talked very freely, used Harriet rather as one might a confessor, letting the blotting paper of her generous friendship, of their long acquaintance, soak up the stain of her guilt over the girls and leave her cleansed and purified.

Perhaps Harriet didn't really understand at all? Perhaps her envy of Maggie's family life, which it had never occurred to Maggie might exist, had spilled over into intolerance of Maggie's dissatisfaction? She tore open the envelope nervously, more concerned that it may contain a scolding than that the news of Harriet herself might not be good.

The letter was not as long as usual, and it was typed on Harriet's portable typewriter with the smudgy 'e' rather than hand-written. 'Forgive the typing,' Harriet said. 'I find it less effort than to write. I am enjoying being back at work, but it leaves me drained by five o'clock.'

Maggie bit her lip. She didn't like to think of Harriet going home exhausted to her empty house. She perched on a chair in the kitchen, anxiously scanning the lines.

I can't thank you enough for our time together. Not just the holiday, but all of it. I have had cause to be grateful for your friendship in so many ways, over the years. I hope that I have been as important to you. But not too important, that would never do. It makes me very happy to see that you have a new friend, in Lilli. Make use of her, Maggie – that is what friends are for.

Maggie was touched but uneasy. It wasn't like Harriet to be sentimental. What was she trying to say? She went on to describe a weekend spent at her brother's house, how she had been unable to relax and had been glad to get home. 'I found it impossible to talk to them,' she said. About what? wondered Maggie. Harriet had always been so close to her family. Except perhaps over Jake. They had never quite understood about Jake.

About Cassie and Sheila, [she finished] if you didn't care so much, you wouldn't have had to run away, perhaps.

You would have carried it all more lightly. Think about it. One cannot carry guilt for ever. We all do what we can, no more.

I hoped to have heard from you by now. Perhaps I shall. I love you. Harriet.

Then Maggie burst into tears.

When it was over, which wasn't for a while, she took her notepad out into the garden and sat on the bed which had been Harriet's and wrote to her. It was the first day of September.

A week later she woke to torrential rain, and Marcos beside her sleeping like a swarthy baby. She looked with possessive love, wonderingly, at the damp glossy curls on his forehead, with awe at the youthful muscled arm flung across his bare chest. His chest was almost devoid of hair but his arm was silky with it, dark and gleaming as his head. She wanted to stroke it, instead slid stealthily from the bed. She saw the torn-open packet on the bedside table and smiled in triumph. For he had understood, perfectly, when she had mentioned Aids, tentatively, not mentioning the other thing, not at her age, it would seem ridiculous, almost optimistic. She had been able to welcome him freely, into her bed and her body. She felt impossibly, ludicrously, happy. She would take a shower, make him breakfast. It would without a doubt stop raining later. She would make a picnic. Today, they were going to Portugal.

She put on her raincoat, took an umbrella and a plastic bag, and ran up the quiet shining road to the bakery. She greeted the other women radiantly, thinking, I am still warm from my lover's bed. Do any of you have lovers? I doubt it. They stood, dripping, in their black and their waterproofs, patiently awaiting the hot and fragrant loaves, the crispy rolls and sweet fruity cakes. Among them, she

195

felt blessed. Liberated, fortunate, beautiful, eternally young, moving in the mainstream at last.

'I'm going to Portugal today,' she told one woman who greeted her. 'Will it stop raining, do you think?'

The woman glanced outside, up at the sky. '*Yo creo*, I think so. Later,' and gave her a generous smile, permitting her good fortune without envy. Maggie took rolls for the picnic and an almond tart and a thin warm loaf for breakfast, covered in seeds and honey. She thrust them deep into the plastic bag but once outside found the rain had already stopped, rising up into a low misty cloud. She glanced up the hill, towards Serenidad, and could not see the church of San Miguel. Up there it would still be raining, dripping off the wide eaves of the farmhouse, making the cavernous rooms dark and dank. She shivered, thinking of Lorne and Chloe. She did not want to think, either, of Nigel Tyson, making tea in his messy kitchen, missing the efficient ministrations of Edna, with only the wispy daughter of the postmaster to smooth his path. While she was going to Portugal, with Marcos. But there was nothing she could do for any of them, nothing at all.

'Lilli is off to England today,' she said to Marcos as they drank their coffee, broke the fragrant bread and smiled at each other across the table. She wanted to confirm that somebody, besides herself, was happy.

# EIGHTEEN

Marcos collected the rusty white van that had been parked on the forecourt of the Varas' garage. Maggie looked at it dubiously.

'Should we take mine perhaps?' she asked. The inside looked scruffy; an old coat, a travel bag with a broken strap, a small, incongruously shiny leather document case and a thin tartan rug were scattered on the uncarpeted floor at the back; in front, the two seats looked sagging and none too comfortable. 'I could let you drive,' she added persuasively.

But he jutted his jaw arrogantly. 'I prefer to be the driver, and I prefer to drive my own.' He spoke carefully, in English, looking at her for approval not of his sentiments but of his grammar.

'Very good,' she had to smile, as if humouring a child, though proudly. He was making great strides in his English. She smothered the thought that Sheila would have been pleased; then again, she would certainly have not. Not if she knew the truth, which was inconceivable.

She decided to make the best of it. 'I have some cushions in mine, and another rug. We'll need them for the picnic.' But she spread the rug over the passenger seat with one of the cushions at her back. The sun was shining directly up the street, hot on her back as she put the picnic basket on the floor among the jumble. Marcos added to it two bottles of wine from Spar and another small bag which he had taken indoors overnight, in which she presumed he had personal toilet items. She took its removal to mean he would not be staying again, but she made no comment.

197

She had already resolved to take from Marcos only what he wanted to give. Emotional entanglement and dependency were far from what she sought; liberated, she would meet him on his own liberal terms. There were to be no claims, no questions, nothing to cast a gloom over the glitter of their unlikely passion. She would share his youth; through him live the one she now felt she had thrown away. When she tired of him, or he of her, they would cast their liaison aside like a used and outgrown plaything. Or so she assumed. But she rather hoped that she would be the one to tire.

She felt very exposed out there in the village street, especially when Marcos, helping her into her seat, patted her bottom playfully as she climbed in. She found herself glancing up and down the street even as she flushed with delight. A lorry roared by, rocking the van and splashing mud against Marcos's trousers. They were white, and very tight. He gave a fiery Spanish expletive as he glared down at the brown streaks and splashes.

'Never mind,' consoled Maggie. 'It will brush off.' She touched his hand on the door, anxious for his resumed good humour. 'And you still look very handsome.' She said it teasingly but there was doting in her eyes, she knew, and a greedy hunger as he met her gaze with his own.

She saw the anger vanish, replaced by a brilliant smile. He slammed the door shut. 'And you look beautiful, Maggie,' leaving her awash with pleasure as he jumped into the seat beside her and they roared noisily away.

Leaving the village, she saw Major Tyson's yellow Citroën coming the other way. She turned her head sideways and away, sitting very still. She didn't want him to see them. She remembered how she had complained about his little car, now she was sitting in an advanced state of bliss in the sort of conveyance she associated with greengrocers or perhaps a self-employed window-cleaner. She wondered if

198

there was any limit to the surprises she would serve herself. When Marcos took her hand and began to sing *'Viva España'* in a rich, lilting voice, she hoped not. She sang cheerfully with him as they bowled along the road to the coast.

Portugal was only thirty kilometres or so away by the rugged coastal road off which was the tiny shabby village and the abandoned glory of the monastery she had painted with Lorne, the picture she had given to Harriet. The monastery was now a private dwelling; its restored and elaborate frontage faced a bleak little beach. The village itself was a scramble of decaying houses with birdcages in the windows, motor scooters leaning against walls decorated with peeling posters and graffiti. She and Lorne had walked down a narrow alley towards the sea and found all the refuse of years pushed haphazardly down the cliff, open to the weather and the scavenging gulls and rodents. Out of sight, out of mind. She had been appalled; now as they sped past the turning to Oya she told Marcos about it but he only shrugged.

'It is expedient.'

'But so careless. There must be alternatives. Don't they value their environment?'

'There is plenty of environment. Plenty of sea and rocks and beach. Maybe they have other priorities.'

'Maybe. But how can the authorities allow it? Just a few miles away, Baiona, that lovely headland with the parador, all those quaint streets, the tourist beaches and the harbour.'

'There is rubbish there, too. Perhaps it is spread more thinly.'

She thought for a bit. Certainly, the sea sometimes had looked dirty; paper tissues, cardboard cartons, even more unsavoury items washing in and out on the turning waves. But it was hardly surprising with the open dump of Oya a few miles south. The whole thing made her sad.

Marcos said, 'I have heard that England is not so clean, either. Your beaches and your water. Perhaps it would be better not to criticise, eh, Maggie?' He half turned with a half-smile, but she felt rebuked.

She had expected him to follow the coast all the way. The sea was calm yet still managed to break quite noisily over the rocks, sending white sparkle up into the sunshine which glittered on the surface and on the white gulls riding the swell. She had settled back to enjoy it when Marcos swung left off the main road and began to climb into the inland hills. Soon they were submerged in a thick, clinging mist.

'Why have we come this way?' She spoke timidly, unwilling to annoy him again yet at the same time enjoying his chauvinism. Something in her wanted to be scolded, perhaps even struck. She had never been frightened of Robert. He had never lost his temper, never forced himself on her nor bullied her. But he had never excited her either. She sensed that Marcos, if crossed, could be very exciting indeed.

'I was enjoying the coastal scenery. Now I can't see anything at all,' she added, pushing her luck a little.

But, 'You'll see,' was all he said. 'It will be worth it.'

The mist blurred the woods through which they drove, smudging the road ahead beyond the windscreen across which the wipers swept uselessly with worn blades. The air felt damp and cooler as they climbed. There was a feeling of isolation in the silent van. Marcos was concentrating on the road, Maggie strained ahead for a sign that the mist might be thinning, that they might be breaking through into the light. All around huge eucalyptuses dripped the mist off their long drooping leaves. The peeling bark hung in golden strips like sunburned skin, and now and then they passed piles of felled and trimmed trunks, the wood stripped bare, the bark piled like coils of giant-sized pasta beside the road. Maggie shivered and reached behind her for her embroidered shawl. When she turned back, adjusting it round her shoulders, Marcos put a hand on her knee. The warmth was reassuring, persuasive, titillating. 'Soon,' he said in English and she clutched his hand, pressing it to her flesh.

And sure enough, the mist began to thin. As they climbed, so the vapour seemed to be dragged upwards, visibly rising between the shining trunks into a gilded steam above them. The gold paled, became white, then blue. Like divers rising to the surface of the sea, they broke suddenly through into the benediction of the sunlight. The sky was vivid blue above them, the trees glossy green and gold, the valley below a basin of white foaming steam fingering upwards and dispersing. She gasped, 'Oh! Please stop. It's so beautiful.'

'Do you want to take a picture?' he asked as she removed her camera from her bag.

'Yes please. Is there room?' The road was narrow, a continuous series of bends, but they had seen no other vehicle. He stopped without comment, watching with amusement as she climbed out, walked to the dropping edge and stared back towards the invisible sea, the damp and secret road up which they had climbed. Above the shining meringue of the clouds the brilliant world they now inhabited shone like a newly discovered planet, an unnamed place far removed from the life she knew, from the people she cared and worried about. She took two pictures, then turned the camera and took one of the van with Marcos's dark head staring out towards her. She took a quick gasping breath of rapture. The day stretched ahead, glistening and new, fingering her senses with a delicate promise of pleasure; out of time, out of place, she and Marcos in an old white van, going to Portugal. She wished she could have told someone, anyone, about it.

But there was no one, and it made their isolation the more complete.

The road straightened and flattened onto a sunny alp, winding away ahead of them across smooth-cropped grassland with the occasional clump of trees and a group of red-tiled roofs atop crumbling walls. Maggie was stunned by the beauty, by the unexpected contrast, by the total silence when Marcos parked the van and invited her to get out. The air was motionless, the sun burning towards its zenith. She held out bare arms, luxuriating. She slipped off her sandals, feeling the grass soft as velvet, the pebbles hot and as pleasurably sharp as an acupuncturist's needle.

To her surprise Marcos said, 'Will you wait here for a while? I have to see someone at the farm.'

He indicated a tumble of stones some two hundred yards down a stony track, which presumably was the farmhouse. It looked almost derelict.

'Can't I come too?' She would have loved to visit, to see inside the low huddled building, but he said, 'It's a rough walk, and I don't want to take the van. I won't be long.'

He opened the van, took out his overnight bag and began to walk down the track. Puzzled, she watched his tight white bottom covetously as he swung easily away from her without a backward glance. Then she settled down with her back against a warm stone to wait.

A lark sang far overhead, invisibly, reminding her of the Cornish moors. The distant donk of a cowbell and the gentle tear and crunch of some sheep grazing on the verge were the only other sounds. She wished she had brought a sketchpad. The cheerful scene was as neat and tidy, homely and comforting as a picture in a children's storybook. She could almost see Heidi bringing home her herd of leaping goats, or Maria in *The Sound of Music* herding the singing children. After a while she got up and wandered over to a pair of grey *hórreos* behind a dry-stone wall. Their stone legs with their mushroom caps stood knee-deep in grasses bending with the end of summer, the slatted sides support- ing a steeply ridged and corrugated red-tiled roof. On the gable end of one was a little cross, giving it the appearance of a shrine. In the shade beneath a dog was lying, watching her carefully over his brindled paws. She saw that he was chained. Then she heard Marcos returning, crunching over the stony track. He was talking to another man, older than he, who didn't wait to greet Maggie but got into a tractor parked on the track and bumped away, over the grass.

'Did you get impatient?' Marcos asked. 'I didn't keep you long.'

'No, not at all. It's been delightful.'

'Good.' He threw his bag into the back. 'Well, next stop Portugal.' They climbed in. He passed her a map and said, 'We're here, and we're heading for the ferry here, on the River Miño. It is quicker than going all the way to the bridge at Tui.'

'A ferry?' She was surprised, having pored over her own map marking out the supposed route. A ferry sounded much more fun. When they reached the river, dropping back down through the woods but this time in the full glare of the midday sun so that the shade was welcome, theirs was the only vehicle in the scorching shadeless car park. To her surprise, Marcos got out and collected her basket from the back. So they were to go on foot. She decided not to ask him why.

Across the slow broad river she could see the flat white ferry leaving the further shore. Marcos put the wine in his overnight bag. Maggie raised her eyebrows. 'Something to carry it in,' he explained. 'No problem.'

'But it could go in the basket.'

'This way we each carry something.' He didn't offer to take the basket. He bought their tickets and they wandered down to the water to watch the passengers disembark: a handful of pedestrians who made at once for a shady patch of grass and sat down, apparently waiting for something, two or three cars with Portuguese numberplates and a smart new van with a Vigo address on the side. They walked onto the flat deck and the vessel moved off. They were the only passengers. Midstream Marcos put his arms round her and kissed her. 'Have you ever been kissed between Spain and Portugal before, Maggie?' he asked gently and she murmured, 'No,' her knees melting weakly, offering up her mouth again. When he released her and she opened her eyes she saw the ferry-man looking at them in amazement; realised cruelly how it must seem to others. A young man with his mother, transmuted into a ridiculous woman well into middle age, swooning in the embrace of an over-sexed gigolo, all her libido showing in pathetic indiscretion. But Marcos seemed to think nothing of it. He took her hand arrogantly as they walked up the ramp, past some waiting cars, and a group of children wearing badges, following a teacher. She held her own head proudly, defying them to snigger.

They showed their passports at a kiosk with a formality out of keeping with the isolation of the little frontier, the two glittering car parks, the slow brown river and the plying white ferry stitching the two countries together.

'This is incredible,' Maggie told him. 'We're not used to frontiers in England. I can't imagine what it must be like having boundaries with other countries.'

'Oh, it has its uses.'

'I'm sure it does. It makes travel so much easier. The English Channel has a lot to answer for, even if it does protect us from rabies and invasion.'

'You have the tunnel, now.'

'Perhaps. But I wonder how many people will use it. We English get very set in our ways.'

He glanced at her knowingly. 'Not all of you, Maggie. Not you, I think.' She blushed like a girl. 'Would you like to see the town first, or have some lunch beside the water?'

'Lunch, I think. And there'll be less to carry if we do.'

'How sensible. Are you always sensible? I think not . . . I know not,' he whispered, leaning down towards her.

'Sensible enough to say, "Not here",' she said firmly, dizzily. It was like being drunk all the time, she thought, following him blindly along the deserted river bank under some spindly pines. And the more incredible because Marcos seemed to be intoxicated too. He led her over a narrow footbridge across a sluggish litter-filled channel of the river and into a patch of scrubby growth. A narrow path ran for a hundred yards towards the main stream, emerging suddenly onto a rocky platform set with silver birch and bracken. The river flowed towards them and past, on towards the sea, thick and slow and shining, sucking quietly at the rocks. To their right the ferry was docking on the Spanish shore where a line of cars was now waiting. The white van stood alone in the glare, the party of pedestrians was piling into a minibus. They were tiny. She and Marcos would be invisible on their island, sheltered by the bracken, protected by the relentless water. She put down the basket, slipped a package out of the pocket of her skirt and turned to him.

'Make love to me, Marcos,' she whispered urgently, in a way she had never asked before in all her life. 'I've never made love on an island in a river in Portugal.' She closed her eyes and opened her lips and sucked him into her, greedy and grateful and unabashed, wondering, even as she convulsed beneath him, where and how and if it would ever end.

He rolled off her, onto the stony ground. She had not thought to bring the blanket. He watched her through narrowed eyes as he regained his breath. 'You are a very sexy lady,' he told her in English. *'Muy salada.* We say "very salty". Did your husband ever tell you that?'

She shook her head, her hair full of dust and grass. Robert had never told her that. She supposed she had never been that, though they had been happy enough. She had thought that was all there was; discounted the naked urge of carnal desire as something either beneath contempt, or beyond her aspiration. Well, now she knew. She gave him a smile of pure triumph, their eyes glittering together, brown and blue, their breath slowing and the sweat drying on their skin.

At last she said, 'I'm hungry. And the wine will be getting hot.'

She sat up, buttoning her skirt and blouse, watching him arrange himself, go to the water's edge and splash his hands and face. The water looked cloudy and she resisted its invitation. She unpacked the rolls and cheese and salad, the peaches and the tart, waited for him to pour the warm red wine into glasses, and they drank companionably and ate in silence, watching the water passing remorselessly beneath their feet.

'Why?' she asked him suddenly. 'Why, Marcos, when I am old enough to be your mother?'

'Shall we say,' he answered, peeling a peach with a knife and biting into the warm flesh, 'that it is just because you aren't my mother? And that you are beautiful and warm and exciting. And because you want me.' He offered her a slice of peach dangerously, on the blade of the knife and, dangerously, she took it with her mouth, swallowing it whole.

'But many women must want you.' Sheila, she thought. Poor Sheila . . .

'And many women have me. Of course that is understood, *sí*?'

Of course. She had always understood. She hadn't

expected to mind. She didn't mind. It would be ridiculous if it were otherwise. 'Of course I understand. It is as it should be.'

'Then all is okay.' He jumped up. His white trousers were grimy and creased. He eyed them with displeasure. She packed the basket and reached for his bag. 'It's all right,' he said, almost snatching it from her hand. 'I'll do that.' Feeling put out, this time she led the way, without waiting for him, through the bushes, over the bridge, and back onto the bank.

He caught her up. 'We shall walk slowly up into the town, perhaps find a cup of tea? I know what you English ladies like, you see!'

His smile teased away the ruffle of annoyance at his abruptness.

'Surely everything will be closed. Don't the Portuguese have a siesta?'

She could see a shining metallic dome above the rooftops. 'I'd like to see the cathedral if we can get that far. I have no money so I don't need shops. Even if they were to be open.'

'They will take Spanish money here. It is a frontier town.'

'Unlikely as that may seem!'

The whole place seemed deserted, the streets inhabited only by panting dogs on shady steps, a few small children playing in the dust outside a sombre church and a police-man in a grey uniform staring into the dusty barred window of a shop selling televisions and hi-fi equipment. When they reached the cathedral – or was it really only a large church? – Maggie was panting and thirsty. She would have given anything for a drink, irritably brushed off the approaches of a beggar squatting on the steps and hurried irreverently into the cool interior.

Inside, Marcos put a coin into a slot and lit a candle, placing it among dozens of others flickering in wooden racks. He turned to the altar and crossed himself, muttering under his breath. Maggie gazed round at the ornate painted statues, the gilded saints and smoking votive offerings. The air smelled of incense and wax, the front pews were filled with black kneeling figures. There were no tourists, only herself and Marcos, walking silently beneath the dully glittering ceiling between the elaborately decorated walls. It was oppressive, stifling despite the cool, and she was glad to get outside. She thought of the stern grey walls and frayed banners, the brass plaques and recumbent stone figures of Salisbury and York, and felt herself far from home.

'I think I prefer Spain,' she said as they walked more easily down the hill towards the river. 'And I've always found Portuguese a very strange language, quite impossible to learn.'

'Yes, it is different from Spanish. I'm glad you like my country.' He looked at his watch. 'It's a little late for tea . . .'

'There's coffee in the van. I'd prefer that now, I think.'

He nodded. 'Wait here, I'll get rid of this bottle. I can't think why I have been carrying it.'

She sat on a low wall bordering the ferry car park and watched him walk to a rubbish bin. It seemed to be full, litter was overflowing onto the concrete and surrounding grass. She saw him fumble in his bag then set the empty bottle on the ground with the rest. He nodded to a shabby man who was sitting on the grass; Maggie thought he was going to give him money but he turned on his heel and walked briskly back. The ferry was just leaving and they had to run. Maggie, looking back at Portugal without regret, saw the man patiently going through the rubbish, picking up the bottle and upending it as if he hoped there may be a drop inside.

He drove her home along the coast, wild now in an increasing breeze and dazzling gold in the westerly sun. They sang

208

as they drove, '*Viva España*' and '*Arrivederci Roma*' and '*Volare*' and several Beatles numbers, he in Spanish she in English. Marcos was carefree, excited almost, more boyish and relaxed than she had seen him. It crossed her mind again that he would make a lovely son.

'Tell me about your parents, Marcos,' she said.

'They live in Barcelona and my father is a doctor. He wanted me to do the same. But I prefer research. That way I can help many, not a few.'

Maggie laughed. 'Sheila thought you were going to be a nuclear physicist.'

'There was a lot Sheila didn't understand,' he said, not unkindly.

'And what about your mother?'

'She is just a mother. There are five of us. She does not work outside the home. It is better that way. Did you work, Maggie?'

Normally she would have wished it were so but now said almost proudly, 'No, I was just a mother.'

'Until now.' His look crawled into her belly, plucking strings. She wished that he would stay. But when they reached her house, he carried the basket into the kitchen for her together with the unopened bottle of wine.

'I have to go to Santiago now,' he said. 'Drink the wine later, and think of me.'

'Maybe,' she said carelessly, keeping to the rules. She kissed him first, casually, on the cheek. 'It has been a beautiful day, Marcos. Thank you.'

'Perhaps you will come with me again. In a few weeks? Revisit our island?'

'Or we could take the car across, drive a little further?' she suggested.

'Perhaps,' he said noncommittally.

When he had gone she stood in the kitchen with Cake rubbing round her ankles yowling for food. She closed her hands round the bottle, feeling in it the heat of the day. She opened it. The wine was red and warm as blood. She drank a glassful, savouring its harsh bite. It had been a strange day, pointless, without form or purpose, yet she supposed that measured against all her other days, a happy one, harmless and happy. She fed Cake then took the bottle and glass upstairs, baring her feet and curling them under her on the cushions of the sofa. Soon, Cake joined her, purring his satisfaction. They were both of them nearly asleep when the telephone rang jarringly in the dusky room.

It was Sheila, sounding strange and harsh and distant, ringing from another world to tell her Harriet was dead.

# NINETEEN

Maggie had never expected to hate Sheila, but now she did. For Harriet wasn't only dead, she was already buried.

Her brother had telephoned Heathercote repeatedly. But Sheila hadn't been there.

'So where were you?' Maggie had yelled accusingly, unjustifiably, down the telephone.

'Liverpool,' said Sheila miserably.

'Speak up.'

'Liverpool,' Sheila bawled, bursting into tears.

'What for, for God's sake? You're supposed to be looking after the house,' shouted Maggie unfairly.

'It was Leonard's hearing, though I wouldn't expect you to remember. I just wanted to be there.'

'I see.' Maggie reached for the wine bottle, splashed some into her glass and drank it swiftly, in one gulp. It was cold now, and sour. The darkening empty room, the disembodied voice of her daughter, only served to make the news improbable, impossible, a figment of her imagination. Yet the hideous chasm in her stomach and the incontrollable shaking of her hands told her something very dreadful must have happened.

'Tell me again, Sheila. Slowly. And for heaven's sake stop crying.'

She heard her struggling to do just that. 'I just got back today. I've barely been gone a week. There was an envelope on the mat with the other mail, one with black edges. It was addressed to you. Of course, I had to open it. It was

211

an announcement of Harriet's death. And the funeral. Just like that! I felt sick. I was sick . . .'

'Then how do you think I'm feeling?'

'I know. Then the telephone rang. It was James. Harriet's brother from Maidenhead. He was sorry you hadn't made the funeral. Today. The funeral was today, at noon. He said he had tried to contact you but couldn't seem to find your Spanish address at Harriet's house. I couldn't believe that, but there we are. He had tried ringing here on the off chance, several times, assumed the house was empty but that somebody would be collecting your mail. He said he was sorry. I said I was sorry. And that was that.'

'I see.' So while she had lain beneath Marcos, palpitating on the warm soil, Harriet had been laid beneath it cold, alone. Without Maggie there to shed a tear, to say goodbye, to throw a flower into her grave.

'It was a burial I presume?'

'No, cremation, Harriet asked for it.'

So Harriet, too, had been consumed by fire.

She couldn't understand it, found herself blinking her eyes in bewilderment as when, a very little girl, her grandmother had tried to teach her to read. 'Don't blink, dear,' her grandmother had told her. 'You'll wear out your eyelids. Besides, it looks foolish.' She looked foolish now no doubt, but didn't care, didn't care about anything save that Harriet was unaccountably dead, that she hadn't been warned. That she didn't know why.

'She must have been much iller than I thought. I could tell something was very wrong. I wonder, did she know?'

Sheila was silent.

'Sheila? Did James say how it happened?'

'He left a number. I thought you'd like to ring him.'

'I would indeed.' She wrote it down on her calendar, beside the buoyant reminder that she and Marcos were going to Portugal, today, on the day that should have read

'Harriet's funeral'. When she had rung off she realised that she hadn't asked Sheila anything about Leonard and the hearing, nothing about her plans, or Cassie, nor offered her any consolation. She looked at her watch and decided it was too late to telephone James now. She went instead to bed and slept a deep sleep induced by wine and shock and a forgotten sexual gratification.

It was easier to blame Sheila than her own negligence. She asked James, 'Did you find a letter from me?' and he said that yes, one had arrived the day after he found Harriet. So she hadn't read it, hadn't been able to forgive Maggie for her tardiness, her self-absorption. And it had carried no address. Margaret and Robert had always used printed notepaper, the address discreetly printed in grey across the top. She was not accustomed to giving her address, had just written 'Spain' with a showy nonchalance she found hard now to excuse. Yet how could she have known?

There was very much worse to come. James had arrived at the house in Kew by invitation; Harriet had asked him to come to lunch, said there were things that he must know. He had found her strange and withdrawn on her recent visit and had been both worried and curious as to what she had to tell him. When there was no reply, he went round to the back of the house and broke in through the kitchen window. He had found Harriet on her bed, apparently still asleep. James was an accountant, not a doctor, but it was easy to see that her unconsciousness was too profound to be merely sleep. He telephoned for an ambulance and it was while he was waiting that he had found the empty bottles of pills.

'You're not trying to tell me that she killed herself?'

His voice was gentle, tactful. She hardly knew him, remembered him as a lean elder brother to Harriet, something to be envied. Now she found herself hanging onto

213

his words for comfort as if he were the sibling she had craved, the baby brother she had lost before she ever knew him. But he had little comfort to give.

'I'm afraid that's how it is. She died in the ambulance. She never woke up, appeared not to suffer at all.'

'You were with her?'

'Yes. Holding her hand.'

'That's good. I feel so bad . . . why did she do it? I simply can't believe . . .'

'Neither could we. But eventually we spoke to her doctor, and he told us what Harriet had never told any of us and, presumably, not told you. That she was dying. The tumour in her womb had been malignant, they were too late to stop it spreading. She had a few months at the most. She would have suffered great pain. Obviously, she couldn't face it. One can't blame her. Only be grateful, I suppose, that it's all over.'

'Yes.' Maggie pressed the receiver to her cheek, rocking backwards and forwards on the chair and staring at the sunny rug, at Cake sprawled on a patch of violent purple, at the dust motes in the still air shining across the innocent face of Madrilena's portrait. She let it all sink in; the implications of lonely suffering, the fear faced alone without comfort or consolation, the withholding from her family and from her, Maggie, of any possibility of trying to help. At the same time she realised what Harriet had spared her. 'I'm so ashamed,' she burst out into the empty air, into the blank telephone which carried her words to James.

'Of what? There was nothing you could do, my dear. Nothing any of us could do.'

'We could have helped, if we had only known.'

'If she had wanted that, she would have told us. Sometimes, problems are easier to bear alone. And she would have had little comfort to offer any of us.'

'That's true.' How wise Harriet had been. And generous.

She had given Maggie the gift of that last, happy week. And, at the very end, she had tried to absolve her too. 'You can't live with guilt for ever,' she had told her. And, 'Lean on Lilli.'

Only Lilli wasn't there to lean on. Lilli was in England, far away like everybody else she loved.

'There's one more thing,' James was saying. 'There's an envelope here marked "Maggie". Give me your address and I'll send it.'

Obediently Maggie did as she was asked. It was only after she had rung off that she wondered what the envelope might contain.

Cassie burst into tears when Maggie spoke of Harriet.

'Don't,' she sobbed. 'I'm terribly upset. I'm going to miss her so.'

'But you hardly knew her really.' Maggie was surprised. 'Not since you've grown up, anyway.'

'I got to know her when she was staying here. I liked talking to her. I can't believe she was so ill, and didn't say.'

'Not everybody broadcasts their problems, Cassie. Harriet wasn't like that. Even so, I wish she'd told me.'

Did she really? It sounded better to say so but Maggie doubted it. What could she have done but added to her grief?

'Don't take it to heart. Just remember that you helped to look after her for a while. She appreciated your visits, you know. And she loved seeing Robert. It reminded her of when you were little. She always adored you girls.'

Cassie was crying again.

'What's the matter, darling? This is more than Harriet, surely?'

'I'm sorry. I wasn't going to mention it, not now.'

Maggie thought that unlikely. 'Mention what?'

'I think I may be pregnant again.'

Maggie found herself smiling with relief. 'Nothing to cry about, surely? That's wonderful news. It's time Robert had a playmate.'

'I know it seems like that. But things aren't going well. I was wondering whether I shouldn't be going back to work . . .'

'That bad? I know Anthony didn't get promotion, but you've always managed . . .'

'Things aren't going well with me and Anthony either.'

'But he's pleased about the baby?'

'I haven't told him yet. Not till I'm sure. It's very early days.'

'Then maybe you're wrong. That can happen, especially if you're worried or upset.' Maggie smiled again at the irony of it. She wished she could share her recent predicament with Cassie, but their relationship had never been like that. Maggie herself had never been like that. Cassie would only be appalled, uncomprehending. It would hardly be fair.

'So what's wrong between you two?'

She found herself cringing back from Cassie's reply but she only said, 'Oh, nothing much I suppose. I just seem to hardly see him.'

'Well, it's always been like that. He does ask you to go to his rallies but you won't go.'

'It's difficult, with Robert.'

'I know. But maybe you should make an effort.'

'Don't nag. Harriet wouldn't have nagged.'

'Harriet?'

'I was going to ring her up and talk to her. She always seemed to understand . . .'

Startled and hurt Maggie said tartly, 'It's easy for outsiders to understand. They are not involved. They don't have to pick up the pieces . . .'

Cassie burst out, 'Harriet wasn't an outsider. How can

you say that? Now that she's dead as well . . .' She began to cry again, noisily and childishly.

Maggie felt an urge to slap her, instead said loudly above her sobs, 'This won't do, Cassie. It's upsetting for both of us. We're both upset, and shocked. Don't let's take it out on each other. I'm really sorry you feel so bereft. Just imagine how I feel. Harriet was my oldest friend. And I wasn't even able to be at her funeral. I shall never forgive Sheila for that . . .'.

'But it wasn't Sheila's fault. She's entitled to her life . . .'

'I know. But just at this moment it doesn't seem like that.'

'That's very unfair.'

'Life is unfair. Otherwise Harriet wouldn't be dead.'

There was a long silence, broken by a distant wailing. Then Cassie said, 'I'll have to go, Robert's pulled a whole shelf of books on top of him. I don't know however I'll manage two of them. I'm sorry about Harriet. Perhaps we could come out and see you, if you're lonely –'

'We'll see. I need some time to get over it.'

'Well – goodbye, Mum. I am sorry, really . . .'

'Goodbye, Cassie dear. Give Robert a kiss for me. And send me some photos of him, will you? And better give Anthony a kiss too, from yourself. That might be a start. And let me know about the other, when you know.'

Replacing the receiver she found she felt worse, not better. Desolate, depressed and anxious, she longed inconsolably for Robert. At length, and instead, she found herself drawn in her lonely misery up the hill towards Lorne and Chloe at Serenidad.

She found Chloe once more in the garden. She was absorbed in something she was writing in a notebook on her lap and didn't hear Maggie's approach across the crunchy gravel. Maggie was relieved to see that there was colour on her cheeks and that her hand on the pen was firm and sure. She did not think she could have borne more intimations of death. Today its cold hand seemed banished, held at bay by the warm glow of a September afternoon as yet untouched by autumn. The roses were heavy with a second flush of bloom, bees buzzing drunkenly in their fragrance. She stood still until, eventually, Chloe looked up with unseeing eyes then focused and smiled in greeting.

'This is a nice surprise. We were beginning to wonder what had become of you.'

'I'm sorry. I've been very remiss.'

'No matter. You have no obligation to visit us.'

'It's not a question of obligation . . .'

'How have you been? Lorne passed you in the car one day and said he thought you looked drawn and pale.'

'I was for a while. I had some sort of bug. I didn't want to bring it up here to you.' Maggie was as shocked at the fluidity of the lie as at the need for it.

'You look better now. And how about Harriet? I found her so delightful. I hope she's feeling better.'

Maggie sat down on a stone bench, clasping her hands tightly between her knees. She had come to tell them, but in her own good time. With relief she saw Lorne coming round the side of the house. At least she would only have to say it once. He greeted her with pleasure and sat beside her on the sun-warmed stone.

'I have something to tell you both,' she said quickly.

'You're not leaving?' His concern seemed genuine, surprising her.

'No. It's far worse than that. There's no easy way to say it.' She glanced at Chloe who was doodling on her pad with her eyes fixed on Maggie's face. 'I'm afraid Harriet . . . has died.' It seemed less brutal put that way. Though the result was still the same: Harriet was dead.

She heard Lorne give a little gasp beside her but a look

passed across Chloe's face that was almost one of confirmation. She seemed to give a little nod. 'I'm not surprised, now that you say it. I had a feeling, somehow. There were things she wasn't telling anyone.'

She felt Lorne reach for her hand. 'You must be shattered, Maggie, even if you had an inkling . . .'

'But I didn't. Well – that's not quite true. She didn't seem to be as recovered as I'd expected. But she never gave me a clue. I'm clearly not as perceptive as Chloe.'

'But even I didn't guess it would be so soon.'

'No, but –' Maggie stopped herself, just in time. What possible excuse could there be for telling Chloe that Harriet had chosen death in her own time, rather than await its coming. 'But even the doctors were surprised. She just went into a coma, sooner than they thought.'

'Was she in hospital?' asked Lorne, his eyes wide and wondering, staring ahead into the future.

'No. At home. But her brother was with her.' It was a harmless distortion of the truth, and comforting.

'Are you going to the funeral? Could I take you to the airport? You must be very shocked.'

'Thank you. That would have been kind, but it's too late for that, I'm afraid. They weren't able to get the news to me until it was all over. I shall regret that all my life I think.' Crossly, she found herself crying painfully with little dry jerky sobs. 'I can't bear the thought of my letting her go without saying goodbye,' she cried, 'even if it wasn't my fault.'

'But she wouldn't have been alone. She had a large family . . .'

'Yes. I always envied her that.' Brothers and sisters, nieces and nephews. What need did she have, at the end, of Maggie? Who would Maggie have, when the time came? Her daughters, grandchildren – everything that Harriet had wished for. Why was it that nobody seemed to get what they wanted? She let herself sob convulsively for a bit, unaware that Chloe had turned her wheelchair and gone away, inside the house.

'She was upset,' Lorne explained, helping her at last up from the bench. 'Do you feel better now? I think you needed to cry.'

Her eyes were dry, her chest and throat were hurting, but she said, 'Thank you. Yes. I'm sorry I had to inflict it on you.'

'Why? Don't you think we can take it?'

'Yes, but maybe it's a bit too close to home. I'm sure Chloe found it so.'

His face was tense as he walked her round to the kitchen door, a hand beneath her elbow. Chloe was there, making coffee, her eyes dark and round in cheeks now pale and drawn.

'I'm so sorry,' said Maggie.

'It's all right. I'm just tired. I'm very sorry about your friend. I was going to send her one of my books, but hadn't got round to it. I feel guilty now.'

'Ah, this guilt,' said Maggie. 'Is there any end to it?'

She sat down, gratefully, letting Chloe minister to her, bringing hot coffee and chocolate cake as if she herself were an invalid, and Chloe was as strong as she pretended to be.

After a few more days she realised that her fury at Sheila was unjustified, and that it did little to console her over her loss of Harriet. She wrote to her to tell her so, saying that her anger had been due to shock. She asked Sheila what had happened in Liverpool, expressing every hope that Leonard had been exonerated. Perhaps, after all, Sheila would return to her old job there? Now that she had had time to think.

The letter crossed with one from Sheila herself, saying that things had gone well for Leonard in the end. He had

been cleared of blame in view of 'the particular circumstances' which looked, said Sheila, like an admission that
the department was underfunded and overstretched,
though they didn't say as much. He was to be transferred
to another area, a move which was felt to be tactful in view
of the feelings aroused in the local community. The other
social workers had returned to their work but she was sure,
now, that she wanted to be a teacher. However, she had
been unsuccessful in finding a place in college. She would
keep on trying; in the meantime, she had taken a part-time
job in Guildford Library, updating their list of charitable
organisations and services in the town and acting as a liaison
between them. She was finding the work satisfying, but
hardly stretching. She said that Cassie was being 'a pain,
always coming round and whining', was putting on weight
and looked a mess. There was a postscript which upset
Maggie more. 'I persuaded Leonard to come away with me
for a day or two after the hearing. We went to the Lakes,
a small hotel in Windermere. But I'm sorry to say that
nothing came of it, so you're stuck with me a bit longer.'

'Oh Sheila,' she sighed, 'we're all of us stuck with something or other. And what a great shame it is that you've
thrown away the one worthwhile thing you had.'

The envelope marked 'Maggie' duly arrived. With a sick
trembling in her stomach Maggie inserted the tape, and
holding Cake firmly for comfort she listened to Harriet's
quiet voice telling her calmly of her death. The voice was
husky with emotion, but Maggie didn't cry. She sat, motionless, Cake's fur warm beneath her chin, hearing her friend's
message from beyond the grave and not knowing whether
to be grateful, or ashamed.

# TWENTY

She packed a few clothes and her painting things and headed off into the mountains. Cake she left in the care of Madrilena to whom she also entrusted her plants. Like an animal going to ground she drove all one endless rainy day through the foothills of the Cordillera, arriving at last at a modern parador three thousand feet up in a bleak amphitheatre beneath the highest peaks, the Picos de Europa. Here she had already booked a room, which was fortunate as it was still crowded. When she had unpacked she sat on her small balcony, glass enclosed against the winters which she knew to be harsh and long, and watched the rain clouds tear themselves to pieces against the rocky peaks, finally dispersing at sunset to allow a dying blaze of gold and pink and turquoise before the darkness.

At nine o'clock she went downstairs to a solitary meal, choosing thoughtfully from the elaborate but comfortingly remembered menu, deciding on baked fish to start with, then roasted leg of kid which was tender, like lamb, but with a stronger flavour. But there was too much for her appetite and she pushed it away unfinished. She drank one glass of wine and two cups of coffee, then returned to her room to read one of the paperbacks she had brought with her from the big bookshop in Vigo. In the silent room, with only the distant voices and footfalls of other anonymous guests, she felt isolated, far removed from reality. Just as the Maggie she had come to know recently had surprised her, so this solitary inhabitant of the spacious room designed for two – with twin carved beds under white coverlets, a huge bathroom with double basins, bidet and separate toilet cubicle – was as unfamiliar to her as the view from the balcony had been, and as bleakly lonely and desolate.

She had not stayed in a hotel since Robert had died, apart from the night spent in a small pension on her way to Gondomar. Although she could afford it, the extravagance of the parador now seemed excessive. Together on their holidays, she and Robert had revelled in the space and elegance, the cool comfort and generous proportions. They had raided the little fridges for drinks each night, nibbling the packets of nuts which they knew would be replaced next morning. They had filled the drawers and wardrobes, run huge hot baths and long cool showers as their taste dictated and dampened all the thick white towels indiscriminately. Now, her small presence, her meagre possessions, seemed to fill but one corner of the space provided. She had used only one of the towels, and would continue to do so though doubtless they all would be renewed next day. She would have preferred a single room but there had been none available. Compelled to fill the demanding space she cringed instead in an armchair set against the wall, the long curtains drawn across the shuttered windows, one small lamp burning beside her. Eventually, unable to concentrate on her book against awareness of the yawning space around her she undressed and slipped between the taut and chilly sheets and turned out the light. She had opened the curtains and one of the shutters, but barely a glimmer of light intruded from the sky, from the uninhabited slopes outside. For a while, fancifully, she managed to delude herself that Robert was lying in the other bed, also staring into the darkness before drifting off to sleep, that in the morning they would plan the day's events or their onward route before going down to indulge themselves gently at the elaborate buffet breakfast. The comfort she

223

gained by such imaginings was outweighed by the inevitable desolate realisation that it was not so. Her other loss, that of Harriet, further impinged on her senses, weighing her down with a numb and wordless grief that she longed to dispel with sleep. But oblivion evaded her and she was compelled to spend the night in fitful snatches of uneasy dozing and repeated visits to the bathroom. Eventually, at five o'clock, she got up and put on a cardigan and her dressing gown, opened a miniature bottle of whisky from the refrigerator and drew her chair towards the window to await the dawn.

It came gently, subtly, touching the westerly peaks of the shallow declivity with a soft apricot sheen on the bare grey rocks. The colour strenghtened through orange to gold and the blue of the sky deepened with it. There was no trace of the clouds of yesterday. The flush of colour slid lower as the sun rose, until the burned brown-gold of the short grass on the lower slopes turned to fire and she saw the boxlike structure of the hotel roof thrown into shadow across the ground below. Facing west, her room was still dim and cool but she sensed, with an animal longing, the warmth in the early rays. She showered and dressed quickly and made her way along deserted corridors and down wide stairways to the main entrance where the reception desk was already busy, passed a pile of suitcases being stowed in the belly of a vibrating orange coach from Frankfurt, and stepped into the sunlight.

The air was intoxicating, the warmth on her face a benediction. She walked, briskly, round the environs of the hotel, a small oasis in a desert; past neat flowerbeds dazzled with dew, lawns where sprinkers played, a group of yellow loungers drawn companionably around an ornamental pond, on one of them a book, damp and curling, abandoned and, presumably, forgotten. She looked up at the mountains, knowing that there were more beyond, higher, snowtopped, luring by their very invisibility. A spark of interest

224

kindled, to be followed by a positive enthusiasm. She had never been here before but she knew what there was to see. She had come to see it, to paint it, to have a holiday. And that was what she was going to do.

She went inside and attacked the breakfast buffet, ravenously, as if she hadn't eaten for weeks.

It was fun, being a tourist again, once she had decided to embrace the role. She and Robert had always spurned coach excursions, preferring to travel independently. Now it seemed sensible to join in with a day trip to Covadonga and let somebody else negotiate the precipitate roads and the tourist traffic while she chatted desultorily with a retired school teacher from Wigan about comprehensive education and juvenile delinquency. They stopped at Cangas de Onís to view the Roman bridge and drink morning coffee, then proceeded up a narrow valley to climb eventually to a broad terrace above a ravine, and the basilica dedicated to the Virgin of Covadonga, the Virgin of Battles to whom was attributed the triumph of Pelayo over the Moorish hordes. Maggie found it bleak and sterile. She responded more positively to the shrine in a cave cut into the face of the cliff from which Pelayo was supposed to have hurled his boulders onto the invading armies. Banks of flickering candles dispelled the gloom of overhanging rock and dripping ferns, and the Virgin smiled benignly on pilgrim and tourist alike, all lit by their refulgent flames. Then it was on again, to the Lakes of Covadonga, circular pools of blue set like eyes in a bleak and treeless landscape. Her companion offered her half a bar of Cadbury's chocolate which Maggie accepted gratefully. Their packed lunch, eaten outside the cave, had not been substantial. Returning the way they had come, she quickly fell asleep, leaving her neighbour to view the landscape in silence until the coach shuddered to a stop outside the parador.

Another day, seeking solitude, she climbed the shallow slopes nearby to find a viewpoint and quickly completed a few sketchy watercolours to her satisfaction while lamenting the lack of man-made interest in the scenery. The hotel was far from imaginative; custom-built for comfort and convenience, it had made little attempt to enhance its unique position. She decided to take a day and drive to Sotres, the highest village in the Picos where, weather permitting, she would get a view of the highest peak, the snow-topped Bulnes de Naranjo. The map showed no easy way to get there so she started early. Soon she had regretted her decision. Even the main road was narrow and winding, the traffic heavy and liberally mixed with road contractors' plant and heavy lorries. Every now and then road works completely halted the traffic while bulldozers cleared huge boulders blasted from the rock face to widen the road. The last ten kilometres to Sotres, winding high up along the side of a narrow gorge on an unfenced and stony road, held her rigid with fatigue and tension so that when she arrived, at last, at the grey and derelict village she was near to tears. Her neck and shoulders hurt, her back ached. She cursed herself for a fool, to tackle such a journey on her own, and was already dreading the drive back. Worse, the weather had closed in; low clouds had gathered where Naranjo should have been. The huddle of drab hovels, their roof tiles weighted down by stones, with chickens pecking in piles of refuse and the gentle donk of cowbells from dark stone shelters, which would otherwise have enchanted her and brought out her easel enthusiastically, simply looked abandoned and neglected. However, there were two modern hotels with cafeterias, built to accommodate climbers and walkers, and in one she ate a hot Asturian stew of beans and sausage with a glass of beer, which refreshed her spirits. She took her paints from the car and walked a narrow stony track which led out of the village, grey boulders and dull green grass under a misty grey sky. A woman knitting in a doorway tried to sell her oiled woollen socks, a cable-knit pullover of vast proportions. Beyond the furthest house a group of men, some of them in carpet slippers, sat on a row of stones along the path, putting the world to rights with gestures and complaints, and one of them gave her a toothless smile as she passed by.

She set up her easel on a hummock overlooking the village. The scatter and tumble of the rooftops made a picture worthy of her enthusiasm; for an hour she sketched in shapes and angles, then began to apply the paint, a rosy wash here, a spread of grey there. Sotres took shape on the paper; absorbed, excited, she didn't notice the change in the light until sharp shadows fell across the scene in front of her. Startled, joyously, she turned round and there, across the valley, huge against a clear blue sky was the great round shoulder of Naranjo, gleaming white and silent. It had the awesome presence of a giant brooding over the sunlit scene stretched out below: it looked almost close enough to touch. She put down her brushes and sat on the damp grass, her arms around her knees, and stared and stared in delight, emptying her mind of everything but its grandeur. Regretfully, at last, wishing she had time to make a sketch, she took a photograph instead then packed up her things and turned away, back towards the village, glancing now and then at the scene behind her, imprinting it for ever. The group of men were still there, still talking, with never a glance at the view they had come to take for granted. Then she got into the car and began the long, weary journey back.

The school teacher from Wigan, who had called herself Jessie James and seemed impervious to the smile that Maggie couldn't repress, asked her to join her for dinner.

'It's so good to be able to travel out of season – not always be tied to the school holidays,' Jessie told her as they studied

227

the menu. 'You'll get used to travelling alone. Personally, I prefer it now. I've tried going with friends, but they never want to do what you want to do.'

'I suppose so. I've never tried it. My husband and I liked exactly the same things. It was always very easy.'

'Then you were lucky.' They gave their order to the attendant waiter. 'I've known a number of divorces come to a head after the annual holiday.' She nodded darkly. 'Either that, or Christmas. Of course I've not been married, so I can't speak for myself.'

There didn't seem to be much to say to that, but Jessie was clearly determined on conversation.

'Do you have a woman friend to come on holiday with? I know you married ones tend to forget about your female friends, until you find you need them.'

'But that's not so,' objected Maggie. 'I never did. Harriet and I –' and then she remembered. 'Oh dear.' She stared bleakly down at the tablecloth, seeing a bowl of fish soup placed in front of her and automatically picking up her spoon.

'Are you all right, love?' Jessie was leaning towards her anxiously, her dependent bosom just clearing the top of her plate of garlic prawns.

'Yes. I'm sorry.' Maggie sipped the soup, added salt and pepper. 'I'd forgotten for a moment, it hardly seems possible. I've just lost my closest friend. Harriet. She died, quite recently.'

Jessie slapped a sturdy hand across her mouth. 'Oh my goodness. I didn't mean to upset you.'

'You didn't. It's not your fault. Tell me, where else have you been on holiday? Do you like the beach?'

That set her companion off and for the rest of the meal Maggie was able to nod and smile and murmur her interest, while her heart howled out for Harriet.

\* \* \*

She stayed for a week, feeling the solitude strengthening her into a new self-sufficiency. She grew accustomed to the vast reaches of her room, which had been lonely in a way the house in Gondomar had never been. But now, returning from a walk or a painting trip or a coach excursion to Léon and its marvellous luminous cathedral, it had begun to feel like home, the single bed to welcome her and offer her sleep.

But Lilli would be returning soon, from England. She would expect to find Maggie there, Maggie told herself, but what she really meant was that she wanted to be there, too.

The first thing she saw when she drew up at her house was a pile of rubble in the road outside the next door building, which had remained deserted and semi-derelict since her arrival. Now she saw two hefty men carrying a rusty bath out through the front door and heaving it onto a skip with a tangle of lead pipes and a lavatory cistern. A chicken was having a dustbath in a heap of plaster dust sending an acrid cloud up into the air. Seeing it settle onto the bonnet of the car, Maggie pinched her lips with annoyance. Whatever was happening was clearly going to take a very long time, and clearly it was not going to be convenient to her.

She took everything indoors and threw open the doors onto the terrace, ignoring the dust rising from the road below. She gave a smile of pleasure at the carefully tended geraniums, freshly watered and with their leaves still damp from what looked like a good wash. Madrilena had been doing her job conscientiously. She decided to collect Cake, and her post, at once and walked back up the road to the garage. With a juvenile lurch of the heart she saw that Marcos's white van was parked on the forecourt. She had not thought of him all week; her physical needs seemed to have gone on hold while she grappled with the deeper emotional loss. Now an irritating automatic response, like the bark of Pavlov's dog, twanged its presence in her body.

She went to the office where Señora Vara sat enthroned behind her majestic till. She was thumbing through some greasy invoices but called out 'Madrilena' when she looked up at last and recognised Maggie.

She asked, 'Will you be doing the other portrait now you're back?'

Maggie hesitated apologetically. 'I did tell you, Señora. I don't think I will be able to do another one. I did explain this to you before.'

The woman snapped her lips and her eyes flashed, as haughty as Madrilena's but more daunting. 'Do you want more money?' she asked.

'No. It's not that. I just don't want to do it. I'm very sorry. *Lo siento*. Ah – Madrilena . . .'

The child had run out of the house, carrying the cat in her arms and some letters in her hand.

'Señora Maggie. You're back. And here is Cake – he is very fat, you see? I gave him chocolate drops, to keep him here.'

Maggie did see. Cake looked positively bovine, sleek and round and somnolent in the slim brown arms. 'And you have all these letters. See – there is a card from England. From London.'

Maggie took the card, a floodlit Tower of London with a beefeater imposed on the corner. She turned it over, it read, 'I will tell you everything when I return. Wish you were here! Lilli.' Maggie smiled.

'Will you bring the cat back home and have some tea with me?' she asked Madrilena, who looked at her mother, who nodded reluctantly.

'One hour, no more,' she instructed her. Obviously, Maggie was to be *persona non grata* now that there was no portrait to be painted. But she didn't mind, was so pleased to see the child, to see Cake, to be home again, even if the demolition men were now thumping something tinny and hollow next door, accompanied by whistling, crashes and the occasional Latin oath.

'Is Marcos here?' she found herself asking Madrilena.

'No, but he was here yesterday. His van is broken, he had to take the bus.'

'I see.' She ignored the disappointment. After all, she had managed perfectly without him. And Lilli would be back tomorrow. Lilli, Madrilena and Cake, undemanding and demonstrative, were all she needed. She took the tea onto the terrace and the cat onto her lap, sinking her fingers into his abundant fur and smiling at Madrilena, who was sipping her tea solemnly, an arrogant, graceful, smouldering little princess.

They greeted each other enthusiastically, with hugs and kisses, and Lilli gave her a present, a tin of Tartan shortbread wrapped in a Jacqmar scarf.

'You shouldn't have – but that's lovely!' She opened the tin and set it beside the coffee pot. 'So – how was England?'

'Wet. And cool. The summer is over, if they ever had one.'

'And how was Miriam? And Pepe?'

Lilli's smile slipped and she fingered her throat thoughtfully, watching while Maggie poured. 'They are both well. And happy.' She spoke carefully.

'And?'

The words came out in a rush. 'And they are going to live in Zimbabwe. With Joseph. He and Miriam are married, I went to their wedding. Joseph is black, like . . . like a playing card.'

'As the Ace of Spades. I see.' Maggie sipped coffee, bit into a piece of shortbread. 'And does that matter?'

'It should not, but it does.'

'That he's black, or that they are going to Zimbabwe?'

'I don't know. Oh Maggie – I don't know!' She looked so distressed, so puzzled, that Maggie had to laugh.

'Oh dear. How one's prejudices do hang out sometimes! But it can't be helped. Tell me, is Joseph a nice man? Did you like him? Will he look after your daughter well?'

'He is rich, certainly. And older. He is nearly forty. Too old for her. But he seems kind. And Miriam is happy. She tells me not to worry. I suppose in Zimbabwe they will have lots of black babies.'

'Not necessarily. I mean I don't think they will necessarily be black.'

'But it is so far away.'

'Yes, well, there is no answer to that.'

They sat in silence. 'I'm sorry,' Maggie said at last. 'I'm sorry you're upset about it, but perhaps it's for the best. For Miriam. And we can't live their lives for them. You've always told me that.'

'Of course. I understand. It just takes getting used to.'

They were silent again. Then Maggie said, 'I have some news for you too, Lilli.'

'What's that?' Lilli looked alarmed. 'You're not going home? Not when I need you?'

'No. And I need you too, Lilli. Harriet, my dear friend Harriet, is dead.'

'Maggie!' Her long hands flew to her mouth, her neck. 'What are you saying?'

'She died. Much sooner than anyone expected.'

'But did you expect her to die?'

'No. But she did. She was ready, I think. I hope . . .'

'Oh Maggie. I am so sorry. So very sorry.' She reached out and pulled Maggie's head to her shoulder, and there, against the bristly blonde hair, in a waft of Madame Rochas, Maggie began at last easily, cathartically, to cry.

# TWENTY-ONE

There followed a spell of tranquillity like the stillness after a summer storm, when at last it seemed to Maggie she had reached that plateau of self-sufficiency she had come to find.

'I always measured myself against Harriet,' she said one day to Lilli, 'and always found myself wanting. Now Harriet's gone and while that's dreadful, it's almost a release. Can you understand that?'

'I think I can,' said Lilli. 'I am like that with my mother. Only when she dies will I truly grow up.'

'I think that happens to us all, up to a point.'

'Yes but with me it will be different.' Maggie thought, I wonder, isn't the best thing just to go, and leave them to it? The ultimate sacrifice of a parent, tactful euthanasia, to make way for their young? But at what point is one ready to go? Surely, I made my sacrifice when I left and came to Spain. Although, honestly, it wasn't a sacrifice, it was an escape. Not altruism, but selfishness. But I cannot blame myself for that, not for ever. Harriet told me so. And Harriet was always right.

Lilli was saying, 'My mother never seems to bother about me at all. I can do what I like, I always have been able to. Nothing seems to worry her. But, whatever I do is wrong. So I lack courage to make decisions. I do not want her to make them for me, but I want her to approve of them when I do. Surely, that is ridiculous? I am forty-eight years old.'

'But you always seem so positive. Your life is amazing, and you've done it all alone.'

Lilli shook her head. 'That is how it seems to you. Just as you seem to me to be emancipated, creative, fulfilled, yet you too are full of doubt.'

Maggie made no comment, returning instead to their theme. 'Perhaps I was lucky. My parents died too young, but I had Robert. And I was spared the prolongation of childhood, and also the reversal of roles when they become the dependent ones. But neither can I blame my parents for what I am. As Nigel Tyson would say, I made my own bed and therefore have to lie on it.' And she thought, with a revelation that was like a gift: then surely the same applies to Cassie, and to Sheila.

They were walking, stumbling rather, over the rough scrubby ground behind Lilli's house. 'I am getting fat,' Lilli had complained. 'I must get back to my dancing.' She had turned to look at Maggie critically. 'And you are getting fat too, Maggie. It is the contented life you lead.' Tetchily aware that she was right, Maggie had agreed that a walk would do them good. Their brisk striving soon turned into an erratic ramble over the difficult ground and conversation, as always, took over.

Now, after a silence spent wriggling beneath some rusty wire bordering a narrow lane deep with bracken and brambles, Maggie pondered, 'I suppose, as parents, we just do what we can, and whatever we do is probably wrong!'

'So, I must let Miriam go to Zimbabwe, and tell her that I am worried, but that she is doing the right thing. When really I don't know if she is and I don't know what it is, if anything, that I am worried about! Or whether it's for me I am worried, or her. Truthfully, Maggie, the part of a mother is not a happy one!'

'But I am happy, now, Lilli. Curiously, for a while, I am completely happy. For the first time I find I can detach myself from Sheila's unhappiness over Leonard, her diffi-culties in finding work, Cassie's dissatisfactions and petty tribulations . . . Perhaps it is the only recipe for survival.'

'So – make the best of it, Maggie. Maybe it is that secret lover of yours that keeps you so contented, yes?'

But it was not.

She took her easel up the hill to the church of San Miguel to paint the view towards the distant hills, and found Nigel Tyson there. For a moment she didn't recognise the hunched figure on the canvas stool for he wore an old tweed jacket and a battered hat pulled low over his ears. Finn was sprawled beside him, his head resting devotedly in Nigel's lap. His hand was buried deep in the dog's thick red fur for the wind was cold. The weather was slowly changing; leaves were falling from the oaks on the steep road up the hill and the view to the east was clearer, the heat haze of summer blown away by the gusting wind that presaged autumn storms. Not for nothing did the older houses have glazed verandahs and double doors. Maggie shivered as she set up her easel in the lee of an old stone wall. For the first time she, too, was wearing a light cotton anorak, tightly zipped to the neck. She had tied her hair back in a scarf.

She sketched in silence for a while, unwilling to interrupt the Major, but gradually something about his stance twanged at her conscience; the normally straight shoulders were slumped, the erect back disconsolately stooped.

She called out 'Nigel? It is you, isn't it?' and when he turned round slowly she said gaily, 'Well, so it is. I didn't think so at first or I would have spoken . . .'

He seemed pleased to see her, relieved even, as if relieved also of the burden of his thoughts. 'Well, Maggie, that's a surprise. A very nice surprise indeed.' He came over, stood behind her as she sketched in a stone angel in the fore-ground. 'You've been here quite a time I see. That's looking very nice. Very nice indeed. You've been away, have you?

235

I've not seen you around. I heard your friend had died. Tragic. Tragic. Can't say how sorry I am.' He coughed. 'Been feeling a bit low myself this week or so. Anniversary of Edna's death, same every year. Hide myself away, lick my wounds, you know the sort of thing. But of course, you'd understand that.'

'Yes . . . I'm sorry not to have seen you. I have been away actually. To the Picos. The solitude helped, I found, once I had got used to it. And I did some painting. It was a useful week. I feel much better –'

'I saw you once, a while back. With that young chap from the garage. In a van – I suppose it was his? I don't think you noticed me.'

'Ah. We must have been going to Portugal.'

'Portugal? I didn't know you wanted to go to Portugal. You should have said, we could have gone together. And in your car, if you preferred.' He looked at her sorrowfully; his voice was chiding.

'I didn't particularly want to go to Portugal. I've been to Portugal before, with Robert. It's not so different from Spain only the language is more difficult. It hadn't occurred to me to go until Marcos suggested it.'

'He suggested it, did he? Well, seems a bit peculiar to me but *chacun à son goût*, don't they say?' He looked put out, shrinking back into his jacket and smoothing his moustache.

'Nigel!' She spoke playfully, immediately regretting it. 'Surely you're not jealous? He's young enough to be my son!'

'Exactly. Didn't like the way he monopolised you at that dancing jamboree either.'

'He didn't monopolise me. And I did apologise to you afterwards. I didn't know he was going to join us.'

'Hrmmph. If you say so. Bird in the hand's worth two in the bush, remember. You can rely on me.'

236

'For what?' Her amusement was tinged with irritation.

'Well – to look after you. You know the sort of thing.'

'No. I don't really'. She glanced down at her picture. 'I'd really like to finish this before the light goes.'

'Sorry, I'm sure.' His voice was piqued. He stomped off, picked up his chair and marched back towards the road followed by Finn, who wagged his plumed tail at Maggie. 'Come and see me sometime, Maggie,' Nigel called plaintively when he reached the gate. 'You'll find everything shipshape and Bristol fashion now, I promise you. Young Sophia's a good little worker.'

'That's good, and I will,' she called back. 'Do you want a lift home?' she added with compunction. But he was gone, striding up the hill with his chair under his arm, his hat jammed like a teacosy on the huffy teapot of his face.

He arrived next day with a bouquet of flowers from the florists in Baiona.

'Can't say how sorry I am about my behaviour yesterday,' he flustered, handing her the flowers with a nervous stab at his moustache. 'Don't know what got into me. Put it down to the time of year.'

Or the time of the month, thought Maggie, putting the flowers in water. Like a moody woman with premenstrual tension. She hadn't liked what he had said, not because he had no right, which he hadn't, but because it underlined the nonsensical and compromising position she had put herself in with Marcos. She didn't like to be reminded of her helpless subservience to the demands of her body; no matter how she rationalised it, she could only appear to anyone else as a pathetic older woman grabbing at her youth in the shape of a toy-boy on the make. What Marcos got out of her she couldn't imagine, though he had matched her passion with his own; had really seemed to need what she had offered him so freely. In her new-found certainty she refused to be ashamed.

But neither did she wish to look ridiculous. Thrusting in the last spray of blue-grey eucalyptus she carried the vase up to the sitting room where Nigel was drinking sherry and playing distractedly with the cat. 'Stay to supper, won't you?' she suggested by way of appeasement. 'You may as well hang for a sheep as a lamb!' He didn't get the little joke at his expense, but accepted with a bow, and a pink suffusion of delight.

The building work seemed to go on and on, filling the air with dust and noise, the street with rubble and vehicles, blocking her parking space and frightening the chickens who liked to scrabble and quarrel below her terrace for crumbs from her breakfast. From her back garden she could see, through the first-floor windows of the adjacent house, that a partition wall had been taken down. Now the upstairs room ran from the front to the back of the house. A steel girder was supporting the ceiling, braced by two expanding metal rods. She hoped the whole structure wouldn't collapse, fearing that if so, she would surely go with it. She wondered if Señor Velasquez knew what was going on, and whether he ought to know. But Madrilena surprised her one day by saying that her uncle, who was Señor Velasquez, had bought the empty house and was having the work done himself. Maggie expressed surprise that he hadn't called to see her. He must after all have visited his new property.

'But he did,' said Madrilena. 'When you were away in the mountains.'

'We must go and see him one day in Vigo,' said Maggie, as she had said before.

Meanwhile the summer receded and autumn moved in, boisterous at first, almost playful as it tossed leaves and dried flowerheads, dust and litter across the street. It knocked over the geraniums on the terrace, spreading the dusty tiles with soil and shards of terracotta. The sour, catty smell of the foliage stained her fingers as she cut the last of the red blooms and put them in a jug on the kitchen window-ledge. The bed of petunias was battered and faded; one day, impulsively, she pulled up the lot of them, together with the marigolds, and flung them onto the builders' skip where they lay, a sad faded heap of summer, until some chipped bathroom tiles landed on top of them crushing them to death.

As the air got colder, Maggie discovered the drawbacks of the house. Cool and restful in the summer, it now proved as draughty as a colander, the ill-fitting doors and windows letting in gusts of chilly air and the tiled floors cold and uncompromising beneath her feet. For the first time she found herself longing for soft carpets, furry slippers, central heating. There was an electric fire in the dining room. She unwound the brittle flex and plugged it in beside the television. The living room was filled with the acrid smell of burning dust but the warmth was welcome as a spring day. Cake, astonished then ecstatic, sprawled on the rug in front of it purring enthusiastically and Maggie stretched out her bare feet, luxuriating in the heat.

Her heels were rough and dry, the soles of her feet hard and yellow from months spent in sandals on stony roads and hard tiles. She got a bowl of warm water, added olive oil and sat, massaging in the soothing balm until the skin felt softer. She cut and filed her toenails which were looking quite horny beneath their pale pink varnish, then pulled out a pair of Marcos's socks which he had left beneath her bed. They were large for her, but soft and white, and her feet felt snug and pampered. They were her Surrey feet again, enfeebled by years of sheepskin and Wilton pile and tall leather boots and nylons. When she went to bed, drawing up beneath her for warmth her pink soft feet – like prawns deprived of their shells – she decided to buy herself a hot-water bottle.

\*      \*      \*

She heard nothing at all from Marcos. His van was still parked at the garage, but she neither asked for nor was offered any information. Madrilena had taken to coming in sometimes after school for a cup of tea beside the fire. Maggie taught her to make it, with 'one for the pot'. The child was delighted, repeating the words solemnly, ladling the tea and pouring the boiling water carefully. They had soon finished up Lilli's tin of biscuits, and Maggie went to the hypermarket and stocked up with chocolate ones that Madrilena liked, and chocolate drops for Cake, who got fatter still.

The time of Lorne's exhibition was drawing near and he telephoned and asked Maggie to come to help him select and pack his pictures. She was pleased to accept, flattered that he should seek her opinion. In the event, he had already decided what he was going to show. Perhaps he merely wanted confirmation; a preliminary adulation to assure him of the exhibition's success? The portrait of Maggie was the largest of them all and she couldn't help the feeling that she was to be the star of the show by dint of size alone, although there were other portraits, as good if not better.

Chloe seemed surprisingly well. She was writing again quite energetically and even talked of approaching her publisher with another small collection. Maggie asked to read some of the new poems and tried hard to emulate Harriet's informed and enthusiastic comment. But after a while Chloe said, 'Don't try so hard, Maggie, it really doesn't matter.'

'What do you mean?' She found herself flushing, indignant at being found out.

'You don't like them, I can see. But that doesn't matter at all.'

'Is my opinion so worthless then?' she asked humbly.

'Not at all, everyone's opinion is valid. So long as it's honest.'

'Well, if you want me to be honest, I don't understand them. It isn't a question of liking them, or not.'

'Then that's all right. Only don't expect me to explain. I refuse to justify my work. It has to speak for itself.'

'That's an artist's prerogative, I suppose. I expect Lorne feels just the same.' But Maggie felt wistful, inadequate, excluded from the secret circle of creativity. Her own paintings she regarded as pleasurable expositions of a certain art, a certain craft, a certain technique which achieved a desired result. But there was no flair, no spark, no unique stamp or message. Defeated and despondent she turned to where Lorne was wrapping wads of newspaper round his pictures and stacking them on end in cardboard boxes. Doomed for ever to mediocrity, this at least she could understand.

Lorne called by the following day. 'I forgot to give you this yesterday,' he said. 'And thanks for all your help.'

'It was nothing,' Maggie said sadly.

'Nonsense. We all need some moral support.'

She took the cream envelope he handed her. It was an invitation to the opening of his exhibition on 15 November.

'Thank you, I should love to come. I've never been to anything like that.'

'I hope you'll enjoy it. I can't believe it's happening at last. It's been a long time. I'd forgotten the buzz one gets.'

'Yes. I'm sure.' She thought, There can't be much buzz in his life these days. Poor Lorne . . . 'Chloe will come, of course?'

'If she's as well as she is now, yes. It will help if you're there too, of course.' He looked at her, assessing her expression, saying quickly, 'But I would be inviting you anyway. You're my model, remember? You may even get your picture in the paper. You will wear your hair up, won't you? I want people to recognise you.'

'If you like.' Now she too felt a buzz. At last she was

241

to join the ranks of the Bohemians; of Parisian coquettes lounging on couches in draughty garrets, of café society, of Mimi languishing in Rodolfo's arms; a Mona Lisa, enigmatically frozen in time, preserved for posterity.

Her metamorphosis was complete.

'Will you sell it, do you think?'

'I shan't even try,' he said, and she wasn't sure whether to be pleased, or disappointed.

So it was that, lulled and complacent, she was entirely unprepared for Cassie's news.

'Anthony's left me, Mum. What am I going to do?'

'Nothing. For the moment, nothing. He'll come to his senses, I'm sure.'

'I don't think so. I've begged him . . .'

'Is there someone else?'

'He says not. He just doesn't love me any more.'

Maggie digested the unsavoury fact. 'But what about Robert? He can't just abandon him as well.'

'Well, he's not having him.'

'Of course not. But he has responsibilities . . . he must be made to meet them.'

'I think he will. Mum – can I bring Robert over for a bit? We haven't had a holiday. I can't stand it on my own.'

Maggie said quickly, 'Later perhaps. I don't think it's wise to leave the house at present. I'm sure I've heard that. If you leave, Anthony could move back in. The wife has to stay in the matrimonial home or she relinquishes her claim . . .'

'Maybe, in your day. It's different now. I have rights . . .'

'Have you seen a solicitor? You should check your position, make sure where you stand.'

'I don't want a divorce.'

'I'm sure it won't come to that, not when he has time to

242

think. Not when he realises what it would cost him. The thing is not to panic.'

'He says he needs space!'

'Then give it to him. Don't cling and whine. Just be there for him. Can you manage that?'

'I don't know.' Her voice was trailing miserably.

Maggie was certain she was beginning to cry. She said bracingly, 'Of course you can. You're a big girl now.'

Self-imposed distance made her helpless, powerless to offer more. What more *should* she offer? What could she do if she were there? It was Cassie's problem, one she must face up to herself. But she added cravenly, 'Have a talk with Sheila. She knows all about these things. And Cassie – make sure you don't burn your boats. Okay?'

Not like Sheila did, so that there could be no return.

She took the car and drove towards the coast, into a brisk westerly wind which threw leaves into her windscreen like a child in a tantrum. She couldn't rid herself of the image of Cassie's face, childishly screwed, crying for consolation at the slightest thing. Maggie had always readily offered comfort; too readily perhaps, though latterly it had become a conditioned response. Cassie was a mother herself now. Was it too much to ask that she develop some inner strength? Why must Maggie feel guilty because there was nothing she could, or felt inclined to do? It was enough that her peace of mind was shattered, that a coil of anxiety had wound itself tight around her recent happiness. She could not envisage a future for Cassie alone. It was not what she wanted for her. Anthony had been the best thing that had happened to her; it was not Maggie's fault that Cassie had not accepted the life he had to offer. Maybe it was Cassie's fault that Anthony had chosen to go. She should have tried harder. Perhaps she, Maggie, should have warned her sooner. But she had not wanted to interfere.

Or had she, rather, simply been remiss; like a mother letting her child wander onto a busy road, unattended? Just how far did her responsibility stretch? Was there no end to the claims to protection, to succour and repair and support, to apology for the sins of omission?

She realised, somewhere along the windy winding road, that Cassie had said nothing about her suspected pregnancy. It had clearly been a false alarm, which was just as well in the circumstances. If not, Cassie would certainly have said. She breathed a minimal sigh of relief.

Reaching the coast road she turned north, following the bay round to the village of Paxon whose golden church dome glittered against a backdrop of dark trees. She would drive out to Monte Ferro, a steep headland thrusting into the sea, so named she assumed because of the glittering ferrous stones which littered the ground like the scales of a great sea monster. In the strengthening wind it would be a bracing walk between the pines; there would be big seas coming in over the rocks which would put everything into perspective again. As she left the village her spirits rose; she began to hum, remembering the warmth of another hand on her own. She felt a passive pleasure at the memory. It was enough that it had happened. It need not happen again. It had been a step in her journey, nothing more. She denied the twisting echo of an ecstasy she had not thought to feel again, which had been offered to her like an after-dinner mint, the final delicious sweetness after a lifetime which had been a satisfying, wholesome but unexceptional meal. Too many chocolates made one sick. And fat. She would walk fast, down the hill and up again. Lilli was right, she was putting on weight. It wouldn't do. She would take herself in hand, buy some winter clothes, something smart for the exibition. No, not smart, something aesthetic, feminine, sensuous, as befitted an artist's model. She allowed a smile at her own conceit. She wished she could have shared her triumph with Harriet who would have understood and been glad for her and proud.

The wind was gusting, spinning in circles between high stone walls on either side of the road. A sheet of newspaper lay one minute against the foot of the wall; then it was up and flying, straight towards the car. It flattened itself against the windscreen, across her eyes, as a lorry thundered towards her down the hill. Gripping the wheel steady she tried desperately to assess the space, knew a moment of wild relief as the lorry passed her by with only a rush and thrust of air, and then the car hit the invisible wall and she was thrown forward, her head towards the windscreen. The car stopped and the paper slithered to the bonnet, but she didn't see it.

# TWENTY-TWO

It was Lilli's face she saw when she opened her eyes again in a hospital bed in Vigo; Lilli with red-rimmed eyes, her hair wild about her head, fingering the gold cross at her throat as if she were praying.

'Maggie,' she cried. 'You have come back!'

'I didn't know I'd been anywhere,' slurred Maggie, puzzled. 'Where have I been?'

'It is a long story. The police, the Varas, Madrilena running down the lane to tell me. That was yesterday . . .'

A starched nurse had come to the bedside. Now she bustled Lilli away, lifting Maggie's limp wrist and studying her watch. Maggie closed her eyes, perplexed, drifting gratefully off into a warm darkness.

She remained there for three days while they satisfied themselves that there was no internal damage, her skull wasn't fractured nor sinister blood clots forming underneath. They had stitched up the cut below her eye, assuring her that it would hardly show in a little while. Studying her purple and white, bruised and shocked and mysteriously aged face, she thought that any improvement would be worthwhile. She tried to smile encouragingly at herself, managed only a stiff cracking of dry lips.

'Your seat belt saved you,' said the policeman who came to see her and ask her about the accident. It hadn't been the lorry driver's fault, she said; she remembered clearly, now, about the newspaper. It was thanks to the lorry driver stopping, then radioing for help, that she was as well as she was already.

'I was going to break in and find your address book,' said Lilli. 'Should I have done it sooner?'

'I'm surprised the police didn't insist. But I'm glad you didn't, in view of the way things have turned out. The girls would only have rushed out here for nothing. I'll write to them, when I get home. After all, it's really been nothing to worry about.'

Even so, she felt shaken and enfeebled when Lilli finally left her under a blanket on the sofa with the fire switched on and Cake nestled reassuringly across her legs. She dozed fitfully, tried to read, nibbled the sandwiches Lilli had left then, stiffly, filled a hot-water bottle and took herself to bed.

The calendar said 5 November. Guy Fawkes Day, thought Maggie, evoking the pungency of acrid early evening fog, the crack and hiss of fire and gunpowder, the shattering explosions that had terrified her as a child, that her own children had enjoyed demurely in their muddy back garden while she held their Fair Isle-mittened hands and Robert had gamely set rockets in bottles, Catherine wheels on sticks, and handed round sparklers for them all to wave above the last of the chrysanthemums, the crisp dead clamber of the runner beans.

She felt much better. The bruises had faded from her ribs and cheeks, the scar, once the stitches were removed, retreating to a pale red line among the folds beneath her eye.

Nigel Tyson, surprisingly, had proved himself efficient and determined in sorting out the problems of insurance on her car, arranging for its repair and, in view of the time it was all going to take, obtaining a hired Fiat from a garage in Baiona. He was due with it that afternoon. She felt suddenly nervous, like a child getting back on its first big bike after hurtling to the ground. The sight of Nigel's pleased and guileless face, the crisp neatness of his moustache and his bouncy military bearing was reassuring and familiar and for once she felt happy to put herself unquestioningly in his hands.

He helped her tenderly into the car and drove her back the way she had gone the week before. 'Best to beard the lion in his den,' was how he put it. 'Lay the ghost to rest.'

'Why not just let sleeping dogs lie?' she asked wryly, but she knew he was right. When they got to the wall he slowed down and she looked long and hard at the scrape of metal on stone which might have marked her ending. 'There, but for the grace of God . . .' she murmured, but she didn't believe in divine intervention. It had been luck, that was all. Another time, another place, and luck might have been busy elsewhere.

On the way back she took the wheel, feeling the car light and responsive in her hands. 'I shall enjoy this,' she told him. 'You've been very good, arranging everything. I really couldn't be without a car.'

'I would have taken you anywhere you wanted to go, you know that, Maggie.'

'I know. And I appreciate it.'

'I'd do more, if you'd let me.' His words hung in the air while she searched desperately to divert him while seeming not to repulse. 'I'll let you know,' was all she could think of. It was hopelessly inadequate, sounding only as if he was auditioning for a role, being interviewed, unsatisfactorily, for a job. She reached out a propitiatory hand for his. 'You're a good friend, Nigel, and I'm grateful.' Somehow she knew this still wasn't enough.

Next day she drove to Vigo to buy her costume for the exhibition. She drove slowly, cautiously, scanning the verges for vagrant litter, braking needlessly at approaching lorries. A clumsy Renault Espace following behind, three rows of small heads behind tinted windows, hooted irritably and she let it pass, dangerously, on a bend. It bore the 'F' of France, the driver handling his heavy vehicle and its precious load with a reckless nonchalance, an internally combustible Gallic shrug of the shoulders.

She was exhausted when she got home. It had been a long day, the shops had been hot, dressed as she was in her raincoat over a woollen jumper and skirt. Her chest felt stiff, her bruised eye was aching. But she had found what she wanted; a long floral skirt in a light printed wool with a matching shawl, and a scoop-necked black silk jersey sweater with long sleeves, buttoned at the wrist. She had lost weight since her accident. The skirt hung smooth and flat; her breasts were just full enough, the skin above them brown and smooth. She looked well-preserved, mature, interesting. Lorne would not be ashamed of her.

She was trying on the clothes again in front of her mirror when she heard a rapping at the door. Leaving the shawl on the bed she ran down the stairs, lifting the long skirt in one hand, and opened the door expecting to see Madrilena arriving for her tea. But it was Marcos she saw, and his eyes when they found her lit with a dangerous and contagious fire.

'So Maggie, you are better, I see. I have just heard about your accident, I came at once.'

She was annoyingly pleased. 'Thank you. I am quite well now, I think. But tired. I have been shopping . . .' She nodded down at her clothes. 'Will you come in? I'm just changing . . .'

He slid into the hallway beside her, one hand immediately round her waist, the other finding her breast. 'Please, Marcos. These clothes are new. For a special occasion. Let me get out of them.'

'Of course.' He smiled suggestively, drowning her. 'I'll help you.'

She didn't want him to. She had thought all that was over, that the temporary derangement had passed, but his hands moving over her body, gently unwinding the skirt and lifting the silky blouse, told her otherwise. They fell backwards onto the bed, creasing the floral shawl, causing her to cry out as he crushed her ribs until the pain was submerged by the other more demanding pain of pleasure. Just in time she remembered to fumble in the bedside drawer, pass him the foil packet which he ripped impatiently with his teeth. 'Anything for you, Maggie,' he grunted, fumbling, and she sank back, gratefully, giving in with an easy conscience.

He kissed the scar beneath her eye gently, his breath warming her cheek. 'You are still beautiful. And still the sexiest lady I know.'

He smiled at her, eyes warm pools of syrup, tanned skin crinkling.

'And you, Marcos, are unbelievable.' She traced the curve of his lips with her finger, leaving the ambiguity in the air. Let him think what he liked, take her words as approval or castigation. She wasn't sure herself how she meant them to be, whether in Spanish they could in fact be taken to be ambiguous.

He went on smiling. 'And tomorrow we will go to Portugal again.'

'Portugal?' She tried to sit up. He moved off her, pulling up his jeans. She wrapped the shawl around her waist, still shy with him when, after the event, awareness of her age reasserted itself. She went to the bathroom. 'Why do you want to go to Portugal again? And it's going to rain tomorrow.'

'It is to be a treat for you. I planned it, as a surprise.'

'Well, you could have given me more warning. I might have been busy.'

She turned on the shower and stepped beneath it. He came and pulled aside the curtain. 'And are you, Maggie?'

'No. As it happens I'm not.' She turned her back on him, smoothing bubbles. 'But I'm not sure I want to go. We didn't see a lot last time. And it's not summer any more.'

'No. We can't make love on our island. But I will take you further, go "sightseeing" as you say it. We will be tourists. And on the way back I will buy you dinner. We will have tapas and drinks at the parador, paella somewhere in Baiona. There is a little restaurant with a balcony, white lace curtains overlooking the street and a man playing the guitar. You can picture this?'

She could picture it. She could see herself and Marcos, a handsome pair, sitting across a check tablecloth pulling apart the soft pink shellfish, their fingers dripping oil and devouring each other as they ate. And she could see it for what it was, ridiculous. And impossible. It would never do.

'Portugal, yes, since you seem to have planned it. But dinner, no. Now will you pass me a towel? I want to come out.'

He handed her one then dropped his clothes and stepped in under the water after her. She turned her back deliberately on his lean brown maleness and went into the bedroom to tidy up, restore the damage and regain her equilibrium.

'So, your van has been repaired?' They were eating omelettes in the kitchen. She hadn't intended him to stay, but he didn't leave. Finally hunger had driven her to prepare the food.

'Actually, no. I think it is beyond repair. I thought we could go in your car.'

The audacity of it. But he was smiling, persuasively, certain that she would agree.

'I haven't got my car, it's being mended.'

He was unprepared for that. His face fell childishly. She said, 'I have a hire car, but I would have to drive. It's only insured for me. And Major Tyson, I suppose, since he collected it.'

'Well, I don't think we want the Major to come as well. Do we?'

She rather thought not.

'Would you mind driving, Maggie? I only have one day . . .'

'Let's wait and see what the weather is like,' she hedged. 'There's really no point if it's raining. Now, do you mind if I ask you to leave? It's been an exhausting day. And I'd rather sleep alone.'

He left willingly enough, pausing at the door to say, 'Until tomorrow, *querida*,' kissing her on the nose as Cassie, as a little girl, used to kiss Robert, when she wanted to get her own way.

He arrived at nine o'clock. It was raining, but he would not be put off.

'I have brought the picnic,' he said petulantly. 'It is all arranged.' He was carrying a large plastic carrier bag, and his overnight bag once more containing a bottle of wine. She sighed, overridden by his determination. There was nothing else to do, the day stretched dull and empty ahead, hemmed in by rain and solitude. Lilli had her classes, Lorne was in Santiago, Chloe didn't need her, absorbed as she was in her writing. Nigel did need her, apparently, which was all the more reason for not seeing him.

'All right,' she said, rather disagreeably. 'Put the things in the car and give me half an hour.'

This time they took the coast road to the estuary then followed the river inland, passing the turning to the ferry. 'This time we will cross at Tui,' he had told her. 'We will make a little tour, then return across the ferry.'

She found the drive through the outskirts of the town complicated and tiring, though she had to admit that with the left-hand drive it was considerably easier. Perhaps it would be sensible to change her car. She hadn't thought of it before. There was a long queue at the crossing point; Marcos opened her Thermos of coffee and offered her a cup, holding it for her to sip between edging forward in the queue. He was being solicitous and charming, making no comment on her driving though she crashed the unaccustomed gears several times, and stalled once on a hill. But when she said that really, the weather was quite unsuitable for a picnic, hadn't they better stop for a proper lunch somewhere, he looked sulky again.

'Anyway, I have no escudos,' he said.

'But you told me in a frontier town they'll take pesetas.'

'It's too soon to stop here. I thought somewhere out in the country.'

'It's raining, Marcos,' she snapped. 'And it's going to rain all day.'

'Very well.' He turned away, staring out of his window as if washing his hands of all decision, sitting in silence. She drove across the two-storey International Bridge and into the Portuguese town, found her way to a car park on the outskirts and reversed neatly into one of the few remaining places.

'Now what?'

'We walk, I suppose. There's nowhere to eat here.'

Grumbling, he pulled on a shabby anorak. Somehow he doesn't look so handsome now, thought Maggie, tying a scarf round her hair, buttoning her raincoat. And I look like a suburban housewife again.

They set off towards the town centre. Ill humour didn't become him; far from being exciting she found the sulkiness tedious. She would have preferred him to flash and resist her. This way she felt like a mother with a recalcitrant child.

The thought of him in her bed curdled her stomach with embarrassment. Furthermore it was barely noon. Lunch would not be served until at least half-past two. She longed hopelessly for an English pub, a Little Chef or a Happy Eater with hamburgers and beans served all day long. Instead, in desperation, they resorted to a small museum with a cafeteria selling sandwiches and rolls and cold gazpacho, which had to do.

'I'm sorry, Marcos, if it isn't turning out as you had planned,' she found herself saying with surprising firmness. 'But I did suggest we didn't come at all.'

'We would have been better off eating my picnic in the car,' was all he said. His dark eyes were sullen, the ready smile had deserted his mouth. She wondered where on earth his charm had lain. Clearly, he was wondering the same about her. She had a sudden wild desire to giggle and knew that, one day, she would have to tell Lilli. The situation was verging on a farce. How on earth was she going to bring it to a conclusion?

Contrary to expectation the afternoon brightened up and she actually enjoyed driving the deserted roads in the light autumn air. The towns were shabbier than those across the river, greyer, dirtier, seemingly deserted. Graffiti and torn posters from distant political turmoil still decorated the walls. '*PIDE PIDE PIDE*' screamed out in fading blue from the side of a church whose single bell was tolling mournfully, swinging overhead in its cracked stone framework which seemed to promise imminent disintegration into the street.

But the countryside was neat and sweet, reels of summer hay still lying on stubbly fields like giant Swiss rolls, root crops in clamps along the road, scarred cacti spiking up and out between tangled hedgerows of hawthorn and hazel, brown leaves crumpled at their feet. Marcos began to sing

and, relieved, she joined in, grateful for his returned benevolence, her own indulgence. The sun felt warm through
the glass and she pulled off into a lay-by beside a ruined
barn, and they ate peaches and cake and drank wine, sitting
on his anorak on the grass.

'Do you use drugs, Marcos?' she asked him suddenly,
apropos of nothing in particular, or maybe because of a
niggling doubt that she had carried all along. 'Or rather,
did you ever? I know how it can happen, with students.'
That sounds, she thought, condescending, parental and
downright middle-aged!

'Why do you ask? Are you still worrying about Aids?'

She was taken aback. 'Perhaps I am. But I was thinking
about you. About all the waste, young people throwing
away their lives.'

'Do I seem to be throwing mine away? Remember, I am
learning how to save lives. I am well aware of the dangers.'
But he didn't answer her question and his eyes seemed to
evade her.

Changing the subject she said, 'I suppose Señor Velasquez
who owns my house is your uncle as well, since he's
Madrilena's.'

'Not really, and I've never met him. My mother is Vara's
sister; Velasquez is married to Elenor Vara's sister.'

'I see. Shall we move on? It's a long way to the ferry.'

Marcos glanced at his watch. 'There's time,' he said.

'I don't want to be late back. I am convalescing,
remember.'

'But don't let's hurry. It's a beautiful afternoon.'

He began to sing again, softly, caressingly, but this time
she didn't join in.

They reached the river at half-past six, after he had persuaded her to stop the car and walk to a little park on a
headland which, he told her, commanded a splendid view
of the river and Spain on the other side. The view in the

255

failing light, she thought privately, hardly merited the walk but he seemed to want to linger, pointing out the distant hills through which they had driven on that other journey, when they had stopped at the lonely farm. At last he seemed satisfied. They returned to the car and took their place in the queue for the ferry.

'I'll dump the rubbish,' he said suddenly. 'No point in taking it back to Spain.'

'But we didn't finish the wine.'

'Somebody will be glad of it,' he said, pulling things off the back seat. She remembered the tramp going through the rubbish, the supplicant on the steps of the church. It was as bad as London; life was full of the have-nots, living off the crumbs of the haves. She watched as Marcos pushed paper bags into the wire basket and set the still-corked bottle carefully on the ground. He seemed to glance around. There were several people, walking dogs or standing idly on the scruffy grass. She saw him open a packet of Ducados, dropping the wrapper carelessly and lighting up. The match flared briefly on his face, which vanished as he shook out the flame. He came back to the car and jumped in just as she was edging forward to the ticket office and passport control. Now he seemed anxious to be away. 'I hope we get on this time,' he said, counting the cars ahead. He seemed unaccountably pleased when they did, getting out and leaning back over the rail towards the receding shore. It was getting dark and she stayed in the car. They were the last to leave the ferry and he got in quickly, saying, 'Can you drive fairly fast, Maggie?'

'When we get through Customs, yes. But what's the hurry?'

'I think I should get you home. You look tired.'

'I'll be more tired if I have to rush. We'll take it steady.'

The man in the kiosk had been called to the phone. There

were three cars including theirs still to leave the area. Marcos fidgeted and fretted, flicking the cover of his passport and rubbing his hand across his face. 'Good God, what are we waiting for?' he swore at last. The official seemed to be in no hurry. He had replaced the telephone and was making notes, seemingly taking no notice of them at all though Maggie felt he was only too aware of the impatient line of vehicles. The front driver sounded his horn, but was ignored. The ferry had departed, unloaded, reloaded and was arriving once again on the Spanish shore when the official looked up casually, and waved the first two drivers through. He took Maggie's passport and glanced at the photograph briefly, seeing her short neat hair, the surprised innocent look captured long ago in a kiosk on Waterloo station. He returned it and held out a hand to Marcos. He flicked the pages slowly while Marcos hissed in exasperation. 'We are in a hurry,' he snapped at last. 'Could you let us through?'

The passport was returned to him calmly. 'Let's get a move on,' he snarled at Maggie. Intimidated, she stalled the engine, then moved away with a roar and a screech. 'Calm down,' said Marcos.

'How can I when you're so tense? What's the hurry anyway?'

'I thought you said you wanted to get home.'

'I do, but not that much.'

He turned in his seat. She could see in her mirror a line of approaching headlights. The cars from the ferry were already catching them up.

'We'll go back through the hills,' Marcos said suddenly. 'Turn off here.' He pushed at the wheel, sending the car veering off to the right.

'What are you doing?' Maggie was furious, shocked. 'I didn't even signal. You'll have us off the road.'

'Just keep going.' He seemed to speak through gritted

257

teeth, as if his jaw was clamped with wire. 'And quickly, please.'

He lit another cigarette. She could see the match flame trembling in his hand and the chill of unease turned quickly into a cold fear. A simple excursion was turning into something more, something threatening and sinister, beyond her experience or imagination.

'What's happened, Marcos?' she asked quietly. 'Is there some sort of a problem?'

'Don't ask questions.' He spoke harshly, adding, 'And it would be better if you dropped me off somewhere. I'll tell you when.'

'And go on alone, in the dark? I don't know where we are.'

'Don't you have a map?'

'There may be one, I don't know.'

He opened the glove compartment, pulled out a new Michelin map and unfolded it under the map light. 'This is the road.' She glanced down, seeing nothing. 'Remember, we followed it the other day? It takes you straight down to the coast road, near the turning to Oya. Then it's just Baiona and home.'

'But where will you be? This is ridiculous.'

'Trust me. Let's just say you'll be better off alone. Give my aunt her bag back, will you? And throw away the chicken first, so she thinks we ate it.'

So the lunch had come from Señora Vara.

'Will I see you again?' In her growing panic, she hoped not.

'Of course. Now just concentrate on the road. There are animals, sometimes.'

She fixed her eyes obediently, glancing now and then into the mirror. For a while a pair of headlights followed them, disappearing and reappearing as the road dipped and curved. Then they disappeared completely.

She saw a cluster of lights from buildings ahead. 'Stop here, please.' It was an order. She obeyed without question, sitting frozen at the wheel while he took his bag from the back seat. Her eye began to pulse painfully; she blinked several times in bewilderment, pain and fear. He leaned over and kissed her, gently, twice upon her cheek. 'Thank you, *querida*. I am sorry. Take care.' Then he slipped out and disappeared, walking away into the thickening dark. The headlights reappeared behind her and she let them pass, thinking to follow them down the winding hill between the eucalyptuses where the mists had hung like magic, promising a beauteous day. The other car seemed to slow, then pull away. Grateful for its company, she pulled out behind but, before they reached the woods, it had turned and driven off, fast, back the way they had come.

## TWENTY-THREE

Maggie lay on her bed, trembling. More than that; she was shaking from head to foot and whimpering in the feeble helpless way of an animal released from the clutches of a predator.

She felt like one. Shocked, violated, fearful and incredulous.

When the other car had turned, leaving the circuitous road ahead dark and unmarked, she had perversely begun to drive fast, when common sense dictated caution. But she was beyond sense. The situation had spiralled out of control, beyond the bounds of her comprehension. The little car swept lightly down the hill, brushing the verges of the descending spirals of the narrow road with Maggie's hands clenched painfully on the wheel, her shoulders hunched as she leaned forward, blinking and straining her eyes. There was no white line, no guiding glitter of Catseyes, nothing to keep her on the road but the grassy unfenced verges, the stacks of logs and ghostly peeling trunks, the knowledge of the drop below. When she could tear her eyes from the road ahead she looked in the mirror, fearing pursuing headlights without knowing what she feared. She had no thought for Marcos other than a stunned sense of betrayal. When she reached the main road, she picked up speed, dangerously exceeding the limits both of the law and her potential control of the car, propelled by a nameless need to get under cover. There was other traffic now, headlights dazzled her from both in front and behind, but she swept on, like a comet negotiating the stars, oblivious to the possibility of an accident, of illegality or stupidity. Wound up like a clockwork toy, she must race pell-mell until the spring ran out.

And now it had. She had found her parking space taken up by a pile of building blocks, neatly stacked. Some instinct took her further down the road, turning eventually into the weedy drive of a crumbling empty house. Here she finally abandoned the car like a sweating and trembling horse, its fuel nearly exhausted, and climbed, stiff and sweating herself, out into the cool quiet air of evening. Her knees were trembling, she had to lean against the door for a moment, breathing deeply. Her ribs ached, her eye was twitching now intolerably, but even so she half-ran up the road furtively, fumbling for her key. When she got inside she slammed the door against unknown horrors and bolted it, for the first time. She went upstairs and threw herself on the bed, pulling the coverlet round her, and then she began to whimper.

Sleep had overtaken her somewhere in the night for she woke up, stiff and cold, still wrapped in the inadequate embrace of the cotton bedspread, to hear Cake calling frantically outside her bedroom door. It was still dark; her clock told her it was two o'clock. She threw off her clothes, shivering, and ran a hot bath. While it filled she fed the cat. Then she sank into the hot suds gratefully, pulling them about her like a protective shell and lay still, forcing her body to relax.

It was all right. Everything was surely all right. Whatever it was that had happened, she had done nothing, seen nothing. Then why was she so agonisingly, astonishingly afraid?

Had it all been planned? Why had he insisted that they go out that day? Had it always been his intention to abandon her out in the hills, her purpose been merely as driver in some complex scheme he could not fulfil without her?

Curiously she felt neither hurt nor insulted. She felt angry; furiously angry. And mystified. More than anything, she found she was mystified. She wanted an explanation. She wanted to know what it was that she was frightened of. For the first time in her life she sensed some irregularity, the stepping over of accepted bounds. She felt exposed and vulnerable, touched by the dirty fingers of disorder, beyond the restraining forces of the law. Yet there was no evidence at all that anything illegal had taken place. It seemed she would never know the truth until she saw Marcos again. And she didn't want to see him again, not now or ever. She began to scrub herself, vigorously, until her hot skin was red and sore, as if exorcising him for ever from her body.

She stayed indoors all day, listening to the crash and thump from next door as the evacuated guts of the house were replaced with a rough and ready expediency by the two vociferous workmen. She hadn't shopped for days, the cupboards were bare and Cake had to make do with bread soaked in juice from the sardines which she toasted and ate without enthusiasm. Late in the afternoon she stripped her bed energetically and filled the washing machine. She swept the floors, shaking the mats in the garden. She didn't open the doors onto the terrace, nor into the street. She kept the television on loudly, paying no heed to what was on. And all day her thoughts whirled on a merry-go-round of questions to which there was no answer, leaving her sickened from their spinning and from a tangible sense of despoilment.

For nothing was the same. It wasn't just that Marcos would seem to have treated her abysmally. She had taken what she wanted from him, as he had from her. On an emotional level she felt no betrayal. But on a more rational level her security had been shaken. The niche she had shaped to fit her new persona had been chipped and scored so that she no longer felt at home, was uneasy and watchful, fearful of a knock on the door, the ring of the telephone and, worse, not knowing what it was she feared. She was frightened to go outside, fearful of breaking cover even to make contact with Lilli, who alone could reassure her with her ebullience, although what she would tell her she had no idea. What was there to tell, after all? Simply, that she, Maggie, who all her life had been upright, conventional, dependable and unsurprising, felt now that she was on the run.

At ten o'clock she telephoned Nigel Tyson. He was surprised, saying, 'Nothing wrong, I hope, to ring this late?'

'Is it late? I'm sorry, I didn't realise . . .'

'Not to worry. These darker nights seem long, that's all. What can I do for you? No more problems, I hope.'

'You could call it a problem, yes. The thing is, I don't think I want to keep the Fiat. I've driven it a bit but I'm not happy. I'm still so nervous – and rather stiff. I think I'd prefer to get rid of it. If I'm not going to use it, it seems silly to incur the expense.'

'It will be covered by the insurance, Maggie, if that's what you're worried about.'

'I'm not, I just don't enjoy driving it.'

'But you seemed to love it.'

Maggie sighed. 'Not now,' she said. 'I don't love it now. Will you take it back for me, Nigel? Tomorrow? I would be most tremendously grateful.'

'My dear, of course I will. Anything – I told you. I'll just have to speak to Lorne.'

'Why Lorne?'

'Because he had to drive me in to fetch it, and I would need him to bring me back tomorrow.'

'Oh Nigel!' Maggie was appalled. 'I'd never given it a

thought, how you'd managed it before. I just took it all for granted.'

'Think nothing of it. We were only too pleased to help.'

'But we can't bother Lorne again. I'll drive it back and perhaps you'd follow me in. There is one other thing actually. I need to get some shopping. Perhaps you would be very kind, afterwards, and take me to the hypermarket?'

'I should be delighted!' He sounded to Maggie dangerously so. She wished she hadn't had to ask but felt trapped, with no alternative. 'Are you sure you can manage one last drive?' he asked solicitously. I'll follow behind, we'll take it very slowly.'

She cringed, ashamed. 'I'm sure, yes. Shall I expect you about nine? I'm really grateful.'

No sooner had she replaced the telephone than it rang again and Sheila's voice exploded into the room.

'Mother? I'm just about at the end of my tether. You'll have to speak to her.'

'Sheila? Speak to who? And I really can't cope with anything else at the moment . . .'

'Sorry, only you did say you were getting better. And I'm sure you'll agree she's done the wrong thing.'

'Who has?' Heart-sinkingly she knew.

'Cassie, of course.'

'What's she done now?'

'She's only moved in here, lock, stock and barrel, all her things, all Robert's, I can't move for plastic and laundry. And she never stops complaining and worrying me for answers to everything. I can see why Anthony left.'

'Don't be unkind, Sheila, she's a pretty frightened girl.'

'She's not a girl, she's a grown-up. Or she's supposed to be. You don't know what it's like. It's all right for you safely out of it all, out there in the sunshine.'

Maggie listened to the rain hammering on the windows

and smiled sourly. All the same, there was some truth in it.

'It's not all sunshine and roses here at the moment I can assure you. However, I take your point. You're feeling crowded out, though I should just mention that it is my house, not yours. But apart from anything else, I'm not sure that Cassie has been very wise.'

'She says she can't cope on her own. It's pathetic.'

'Is she there now?'

'She's in the bath. She spends hours in there. Robert is romping about upstairs, he never seems to sleep.'

'He'll be dreadfully unsettled, make allowances.'

'I make allowances all day long. If I didn't have my mornings at the library I'd go out of my mind.'

'So how long has she been there?'

'Three days. But it seems like a lifetime. You'll have to talk to her, Mother. She can't just shelve the problem like this.'

'Has she seen a solicitor? I told her to.'

'Yes, but God knows what he told her. She doesn't seem to have understood it, anyway.'

'I'll talk to her. I'll ring, in a day or so. I have things to sort out here, about the car. And everything. Try and be patient, will you? Please.'

'Very well. Two days, or I may do something I regret.'

Maggie was relieved finally to park the Fiat on the forecourt of the garage. Checking it over she found the plastic carrier bag with the chicken inside and dumped the whole lot in a litter bin. As she slammed the door a physical memory of the nightmare drive raised goosebumps on her arms. Good riddance, she thought, handing over the keys. Nigel was explaining the situation in painful Spanish and loud explanatory English, endeavouring to get her a refund of the hire charge.

'They'll put something in the post,' he told her vaguely. 'Seemed to think you were liable for the fortnight but I told them otherwise.' He brushed his moustache crisply and opened the door of the Citroën. She got in gratefully, finding refuge in the flimsy seat, the rattly doors and draughty flapping windows.

'While we're down this way we could go and have a look at your car, see how they're getting on with it?' Nigel suggested. 'I know you're in no hurry to drive, but perhaps, in your own, you'll feel better.'

'I had been thinking it would be a good idea to sell it, get a left-hand drive.'

'That's not a bad idea. I wouldn't be without it. Why don't we go and look at some?'

'Not now. Let's just go and look at mine. I'm in no hurry to get home, no hurry at all.'

The Vauxhall was parked at the back of a workshop, its nearside wing stripped off revealing the wheel and axle like the broken bones of a skeleton. The bumper was bent and the bonnet badly scratched. She shuddered and turned away. The owner of the garage, wearing an oily overall but the unmistakable air of proprietorship, came over to them, speaking slowly in English.

'We have been fortunate to get a Vauxhall part soon. As you see we are working quickly.'

Maggie turned to Nigel. 'Is the insurance all sorted out so soon? I thought these things took weeks.'

He coughed. 'I pulled a few strings in London. Old-boy network, you know.' He didn't elaborate. She turned to the proprietor who was standing to attention awaiting her congratulations on the service he was providing.

'How soon can you get it done for me?'

'Two days, three days.' He opened his hands expansively; she half expected to be required to cover them with paper money.

'Three days certain,' she found herself saying firmly. 'I may have to return to England.'

She saw the shock in Nigel's eyes as he held the car door open. 'Home, James,' she said lightly. 'We'll skip the hypermarket, I'll get what I need at Spar. For the time being.' She smiled graciously at the garage proprietor who had picked up a spanner and was tapping it thoughtfully on his other hand. Her mind was in a ferment and she prayed that Nigel wouldn't question her.

So they've won after all, she was thinking. Come in, number one, your time is up. And the dreadful thing, just at this moment, is that I don't even know if I care.

Nigel said nothing at all on the drive home but he seemed to droop so that the silence was unbearable. She asked him in for some coffee, a bite of lunch, then remembered that she had no bread, no cheese. 'Coffee will do,' he said. 'Then perhaps I can help you with your shopping.'

'There's really no need. Thank you. I'm not an invalid.' She made the coffee while he hung about the kitchen looking miserable.

At last he said, 'Are you really going home?'

'I don't know. I haven't really made any plans. But there are certain problems. I needn't explain, I hope?'

'Of course not. Of course not.' He took the tray from her hands and carried it upstairs. They both sat staring at the empty cups. Then he said, 'I shall miss you dreadfully, you know. I'd come to rely on you. It's always a mistake.'

'Not always. One has to rely on people sometimes. Only in this case . . .'

'Oh I know. Rather jumped the gun, obviously.' He stopped. She noticed in alarm that his smooth cheeks were flushed, his eyes over-bright as he stared busily into his cup. She was startled when he turned to her suddenly and said, 'To tell you the truth, Maggie, I had rather hoped . . . well, we're both lonely, and you're a damned attractive woman and I'm pretty well-preserved myself, I think. Well, I had hoped one day we might make a go of it. If you know what I mean.'

She detached his hand, gently, from her arm.

'Oh Nigel. I'm sure I do know what you mean. It really is a great honour. But forgive me . . .'

'I know. There's no need to explain. Quite got the wrong end of the stick. Case of the early bird not getting the worm! But I had to say it. Had to be sure. You understand?'

'Of course. And I'm sorry.'

She thought, after he had gone, that one day, very soon, she might be like him. Set in her habits, rather pathetic in her aloneness, both laughable and tedious in her funny little ways.

'But I did try,' she told herself. 'For a while my star shone, blazing a trail in the dark conformity of the mundane everyday. Maybe I frightened myself. Maybe now I am running whimpering for cover. But I did try.'

She walked round next day to see Lilli, to tell her she was going home.

'For ever? You can't mean it?'

Maggie explained about Cassie. 'So now I've got the two of them camping out in my house. Running away from life. It can't go on. You can see that surely?'

'Then you must just tell them to go.'

'It's not as easy as that. Go where? To what?'

'Maggie, it is not your problem.'

'But it is. It is. And if I don't help them sort it out it will be my problem for ever.'

'So. You sort it out, and you come back here. I need you also, Maggie! And I wanted to teach you to dance.'

'Oh Lilli. Don't make it hard. I need you too. But I don't think I will come back.'

'Why not? Why not? You have been so happy.' Now her English seemed to fail her. 'It is the accident, he has shook you up.'

'Maybe, a little . . .'

'It's that man, he has hurt you, he has given you the drop.'

'The push.' Maggie smiled. 'No, it's nothing like that at all. Let's just say I've lost my nerve. Maybe, some day, I'll tell you all about it. When you come to England. You must come to England and visit me.'

'To God-al-ming. But it will not be the same.'

'And it's not the same here for me now, either. I can't explain it, not yet. But Lilli, I have to go.'

She gave her, then, the little jug. She had never envisaged it at home in England, it would sit more happily among the fans and feathers.

Lilli took it tearfully.

'When? When will you go? I am missing you already.' She sounded tragic.

'In a week I thought. I've told the girls. When I have my car, and after the exhibition.'

For how could she possibly miss the exhibition?

She walked home slowly, feeling already bereft, in exile. As she had done earlier she braced herself to pass the Varas' garage. She did not expect Marcos to be there but the white van still stood rusting on the cracked tarmac, presumably beyond repair. This time, there was a grey Range Rover of the *Guardia Civil* parked alongside and a green-uniformed officer walking interestedly round the van, studying the number plate and kicking at the tyres. Señor Vara was busily filling someone's tank, while glancing furtively at the officer. She looked away, not wishing to let him see that she had seen. Her heart thrummed at her ribs, guilt seeming to blaze from her cheeks, and fear, and anger that it should be so.

'Well, Cake,' she said, gathering him fiercely into her arms in the kitchen. 'It seems I have to go. And what am I going to do with you? I can't bear it. I simply can't bear it at all.'

# TWENTY-FOUR

The proprietor of the garage delivered her car himself on the afternoon of the third day, handing her the keys with a flourish that demanded applause. He walked her proudly round the glossy freshly sprayed bodywork.

'You see,' he said, 'you cannot see the edges.'

'No. You can't see the edges.'

'And the wheel, he is straight now, and the front guard.' He kicked the bumper briskly. 'You wish to take a drive?'

Maggie didn't wish at all but thought it best. She climbed in beside him and took the wheel. She drove eastwards out of town, turning away as she passed the garage in an automatic response, a denial of what she could no longer deny. The car drove easily and her hands were cool and steady on the wheel.

'Thank you,' she said when they arrived back. 'I must have your account at once, I am leaving soon.'

'Of course.' He drew out a creased envelope with another flourish. She went indoors and wrote out a cheque. It left her Spanish account dangerously low; she still had to pay for the ferry. Despite Nigel's assurances she felt the insurance money would be a long time coming. She hoped they hadn't jumped the gun, told herself that she had had no choice and stood at the door as the rattly pick-up that had accompanied the garage man roared off down the road. She had noticed that there was very little petrol in the tank, certainly not enough to take her far. There was nothing for it but to go to Vara, and have him check the tyres and water and oil as well. She would make arrangements about Cake at the same time, for there was nowhere else for him to go.

It was only two days to the exhibition. She had not said anything to Lorne and Chloe about her leaving. They had enough to think of at the moment, it would be easier to tell them, casually, when she was with them in Santiago, and by the time they had returned she would be gone. She sat in the car, awaiting her turn at the pumps, and couldn't believe that it was so.

There was a tap at the window and she looked up to see, with a shock like a punch in the chest, a brown-coated policeman trying to attract her attention. He was young, red-faced and plump; the fingers against the glass were chubby like a baby's.

She wound down the window.

'When you have your petrol I would like to speak with you, please,' he said in English. 'Please, pull over there beside my car.'

She hadn't noticed the police car.

'Of course.' She spoke coolly, as if addressing a traffic warden in Guildford High Street, bracing her trembling hands on the wheel.

'Fill it up, please, Señor Vara,' she said when it was her turn. 'And would you check the oil?' She sat rigid while the petrol pump ticked round, counting out the pesetas, the remaining minutes until – what? She moved away, fighting a reckless temptation to drive off, away and away into the mountains. Recoiling from proximity, she parked instead outside the office, got out of the car ignoring the policeman ostentatiously, and began to discuss calmly with Señora Vara the question of Cake's adoption by Madrilena. Her request was met with a noncommittal shrug; news that she was leaving elicited no response but that Madrilena would be sorry. Señora Vara would ask the child to call round some time to discuss it. At last there was no more to be said, no possible reason for delay. She went outside. The officer was leaning against her car with an exaggerated air of patience. After all, she was not going anywhere.

She asked, 'What can I do for you, Officer?' and he said, 'Is this your car?'

'Of course. Do you want to see my papers?'

She handed over her licence and documentation. He gave them back after a casual scrutiny, his round brown eyes calm and amiable.

She felt herself go slack and gently released her breath.

Then he said, 'We are looking for Marcos Barreras.'

Her mouth went dry, heart pounding. 'Yes?'

'You know him?'

'He works here sometimes.'

'And that is his van?'

She glanced across. 'I believe so. Yes, it is.'

He studied her, timing himself.

'His friends tell us he has an aunt in Gondomar. Is that you, perhaps?'

'No. His aunt is Señora Vara here, at the garage.'

'They say he has an English aunt.'

'They do?' Should she feel grateful or insulted; denied – or betrayed? Had Marcos been protecting or implicating her in their unlikely liaison? And was there perhaps a prurient comprehension in the dark eyes of the officer?

The silence went on and on.

'Why are you looking for him?' she asked at last, exactly as he had intended her to do.

'It would be improper for me to say, Señora Fairbrother. But there is a little question of drug smuggling to be sorted out. We think he can help us. Many of his friends have helped already.'

She held her eyes steady, her voice cool, as realisation crawled up on her like a horrible manifestation of the night. The litter bin, the tramp, the careful timing. She said carefully, 'Drugs? Surely not. That's big-time crime. Isn't Marcos just a student?'

'Every Mr Big has many Mr Littles,' he told her. His command of English was exemplary, she thought. Respect for him grew, despite her fear. 'Students are easy prey. They are always poor. We have big new drugs problem. They are coming in from South America, sometimes through Vigo, more often using the many *rias* along the coast. From there, Portugal is but a stone away.'

'I see. Well, I don't know where he is. Why should I?'

'Why indeed, Señora? But we have to ask, you understand? This is a serious matter. I can see that you appreciate that. Perhaps, if you do see him . . . ?' He paused, delicately.

'You wish me to tell you. Of course. But I am leaving soon, for England.'

He raised an eyebrow. 'Really? Why, in fact?'

'I have family problems at home.'

'We would prefer you not to go.'

'Are you putting me under arrest?'

'Certainly not, señora. But there is just this little question of the English Aunt. We think, perhaps, he will visit her again.'

She stood with pursed lips, twisting her hands together, thinking. 'I have no wish to see him,' she said quietly, at last.

'Perhaps not. That is understandable.'

'Will you be watching for him?'

'I can't say. We have other lines to pursue. But we can rely on you I am sure.'

'You can rely on me.'

'Very well. And thank you for your time. Permit me to show you to your car.' He opened the door, clicked his heels and gave a little courteous bow which strained the buttons of his jacket. 'Fasten your seat belt, please.' She over-revved then stalled the engine. In her mirror as she drove away she thought she could see a knowing and sinister smile on his chubby face.

She waited until it was dark, going repeatedly onto the terrace to scan the street below. The only vehicles there were her own and a few familiar ones belonging to neighbouring houses and shops. Two scooters leaned against a wall. A dog scurried sniffing along the edge of the road and the donkey brayed as always in the evening, a lonely cry in the dark.

Methodically, she had begun to pack. The trunk presented a problem. It had been Marcos who had carried it inside. Now, because of Marcos, she had to manage alone. The irony struck her forcibly, bringing sour angry tears to her eyes. She dragged it empty to the back of the car and heaved it in, casting anxious eyes along the empty street. Up and down, in and out she went, packing the trunk all anyhow, filling the corners and crevices with underwear and photographs, left-over foodstuffs, the socks belonging to Marcos which for some obscure reason still to be examined she couldn't leave behind.

She stacked her paintings carefully, and Lorne's birthday painting of Serenidad, interleaving them with paper, and wrapped Madrilena's portrait tenderly in a sheet, tears tumbling freely as she looked at the arrogant innocence of the dark eyes, the proud set of the head and latent sensuality of the mouth. She was fiercely glad she had the picture. It encapsulated the proud sense of achievement, the dignity of self-sufficiency, the whole feverish abandonment of the past six months. And it was of Madrilena, her first friend, who had brought her Marcos.

Who had brought her to this pretty pass.

'What a lot of nonsense,' she told herself, smoothing and

folding her clothes and filling a suitcase, the holdall of shoes, a plastic rubbish sack with the contents of the fridge. 'But I can't regret it, simply can't, not even now.'

She cooked the last of the eggs, gobbling down an omelette and salad, gulping coffee and chewing the remains of her breakfast loaf. All the while she was listening for the step on the threshold, the rap at the door. While she was being questioned she had felt again the uselessness of protest. If she was pushed too far, now, she would surely give in. She was innocent, she had no information to give. Except that she had dropped him off at the farm. But surely, they knew that already? Did they know it was she who had been with him that day? They hadn't asked her that. Why not? Were they leading her into a trap? Would Marcos come to her?

And if so, what would she do?

She had no intention of finding out.

It was late when she telephoned Lorne.

'I'm so sorry, you must have been in bed.'

'Chloe is. I'm working. No matter. What's up, Maggie? Are you ill?'

'Not ill. Just worried. Something's cropped up at home. I have to go at once.'

'At once? Tomorrow?'

'No, now. I want to try for tomorrow night's ferry from Santander.'

'Have you booked?'

'I'll take a chance. It's out of season.'

'Why don't you fly, if it's an emergency? I'll drive you . . .'

'You don't understand. I'm going home.'

There was a long silence.

'For good?'

'I think so. It has to be that way.'

'But why?'

'I can't go into it now. Let's just say I'm needed there. Maybe this was all just a crazy impossible dream. I've had my time. Now I have to pick up the threads again.'

The shackles.

'But the exhibition. You'll miss the exhibition!'

'I know. That's almost the worst part of all.' The ultimate sacrifice.

'I hoped you'd stay on, Maggie. I'm going to need you, one day . . .'

Responsibility pressed down on her, crushing. 'Oh Lorne, not you too. And that could be a long way off. You'll manage, I know you will. And I'll write. I need to go now, I'm sorry. I don't want to cry. Give my love to Chloe. I hope she gets published again. And best of luck with the exhibition. I hope they like it. I hope they like my picture!'

'Goodbye, Maggie. Take care . . .'

Goodbye. Oh goodbye.

She called to Cake but he was gone, out on his night-time prowl. Madrilena hadn't come to see her. Maggie hoped that having Cake would prove some consolation for her abrupt departure without farewell. She wrote her a short, affectionate letter and left it with the remaining tins of food outside the door together with his half-eaten tea, partly grateful that she could not say goodbye to Cake either while longing to hold him just once more.

She put two months' rent in an envelope in lieu of notice and worded a careful apologetic letter to Señor Velasquez. Deepest regrets, family commitments, happy time she would never forget – she hoped to return one day.

Did she? Could she? Another time, everything would be different, she would be different, with different expectations. And there were limits, it seemed, to how far one could cast off the chains of the past, the claims of the future. And once cast off, one could find oneself without compass or rudder, a prey to dangerous currents, claimed by every passing breeze.

'Better the devil you know,' Nigel would have said. 'Between the devil and the deep blue sea.' Perhaps there was more truth than she knew in his overworked, seemingly thoughtless platitudes. She permitted herself a grim smile as she sealed the envelope and addressed it to the house in Vigo. She would post it on the road.

She closed the empty wardrobe, snapped shut the final suitcase, switched off the water heater and unplugged the fridge. She stepped out into the empty street. A lorry thundered past with an overnight cargo of cabbages. There was nobody else about. The car was riding low, nearly scraping the road. She looked back once as she drove away, her heart dragging behind her, seeing little through her tears.

Then she turned her face north, towards England.

Retreating, ignominiously, under cover of the dark.

After four hours she had ceased expecting to be stopped and challenged, imagining that every pursuing headlight was giving chase. Sometime around dawn she pulled into a service station for breakfast and allowed herself a two-hour sleep. Then she was on the road again, forging towards the ferry with her brain in suspension, her emotions in limbo as she was herself. She reached Santander in the late afternoon and was able to get a cabin on the six o'clock sailing. She put through a call to Heathercote but there was no one there. She dragged her overnight bag from the back of the car and found her cabin, dropping wearily on top of the blankets and sinking into exhausted sleep even before they had left the harbour.

The Bay of Biscay was rough. Maggie had never been a good sailor and kept to her bunk even after she had woken sometime in the small hours. If she lay very still, she would not be sick. By morning she was compelled to rise and use

278

the little bathroom. She washed her face in cold water and applied some makeup. Her tan had faded; her skin which had filled and ripened in the sun now looked dried out and sallow, a pale sultana left to dry on the sand.

She staggered tentatively up the companionway to the big restaurant which was half empty in the grey morning light. Musak flowed indigestibly from concealed loud-speakers. Pouring milk into her coffee she thought suddenly of Cake. Would Madrilena have found him, how long would it be before he wandered back, scrambling up the vine to the terrace calling for her? How many chocolate drops would it take to hold him, how fat and lazy would he get? She resolved to get a cat as soon as she got home. And were there flamenco lessons in the Surrey commuter belt? She would find out, she must write to Lilli, she had left without saying a proper goodbye . . .

She went on deck and leaned on the rail, the damp wind gusting tearfully against her cheeks, ripping her long hair from its moorings under the scarf that Lilli had given her. Perhaps she should have it cut now. She could not quite see herself thus, in Godalming.

An elderly man leaned against the rails beside her. 'Pretty rough,' he commented, looking out at the wind-tossed waves. His English voice sounded unexpectedly strange, telling her she was nearly home. 'Have you been away long?' he asked.

'Long enough,' she said. 'Long enough.'

She longed to say, 'But I am different now than when I went away. I have done things I never dreamed of.' But he would think she was mad, quite mad.

It was 15 November. Lorne's exhibition would be open-ing, the press and the invited guests and the critics drifting into the arched and panelled room where the pictures hung. Among them, yet absent, would be Maggie herself, a silent evidence that she had once been there in person. She was grateful for that. But anger at Marcos for what he had denied her rose bitter in her throat.

She breathed deeply of the tangy air. Did she have any regrets? She had found things out about herself – one of which was how far she was prepared to go. Remembering, she found herself smiling. Marcos would always be her secret, something to get out and savour like a jewel when life wore her down. He had cheated her of the exhibition – but he had given her adventure. And she had survived!

She would never see him again, but she would certainly see Lilli, she would ask her to come and stay. She felt a pang of sorrow for Lorne, but there was nothing she could offer him but sympathy. Her biggest regret was Madrilena, but she had her portrait, and would send her letters, and photographs of England.

And now she looked towards England, longing to see the shore.

They docked in Plymouth on a drab November evening with fog hanging in swathes around the lights. The air was raw and sour. Once on land and through the long queue at Customs, Maggie found a telephone and rang the house again. Sheila answered, sounding brisk and competent, in control, the mistress of the house. She was surprised to hear that Maggie was so close already.

'I'll find a bed and breakfast for tonight,' Maggie told her. 'The fog's coming down quite thick.' She booked into a pub, bought herself steak and kidney pie and chips and ate it by a small coal fire, washing it down with a glass of beer, watching the locals playing darts. Their West Country accents sounded thick and rich and unfamiliar. She felt foreign, a stranger in her own land. The smell of Spain was still on her clothes, unaccountably on her skin. She went to bed early and sweated in a small centrally heated room beneath a floral eiderdown, listening to the empty bottles being stacked outside, the call of seagulls, the lonely hoot of a foghorn.

Already feeling homesick. And frightened of coming home.

When she drew up outside her house her first thought was surprise that it looked so big. She got out, closing the door quietly, unwilling to announce her arrival. The front garden was neat, the beds closely planted with wallflowers for the spring. Mr Blake had done his job well. Skittering leaves brushed her ankles, piling up against the gateposts, bundling damply beneath the shrubs.

Doreen from next door was sweeping leaves from the adjacent drive.

'Hello, Margaret,' she called, coming to the fence. 'welcome back. We didn't expect you quite so soon. Have you had a good journey?'

'Yes. Quite straightforward.' From here, to there, and back again. She was poised to tell her, 'I'm Maggie now,' but that would keep till later. Instead she asked, 'Are you well?'

'We're fine. You must come in sometime and see Janet's wedding video.'

Maggie nodded. 'Yes. When I'm sorted out.'

She went to her front door and knocked. Waiting, she took a long deep breath. After a moment Sheila opened the door, neat and businesslike in a pinafore, carrying a duster. A smell of meat and onions and polish wafted out. 'Hello,' she said, her eyes wary. 'Welcome home.'

Maggie stepped inside like a visitor, careful to wipe her shoes. She kissed her daughter dutifully, thinking, Where are the trumpets, the strewn flowers? Instead a red and blue tricycle stood at the foot of the stairs, a small stranger sitting astride it regarding her owlishly. She smiled at him, shyly.

281

'It's good to be here,' she lied to Sheila. 'It's been a long journey.'

'I'll make some tea.' Sheila bustled into the kitchen, sturdy, drab, filling the kettle possessively, opening the oven and peering in. Maggie stood in the doorway. She saw that things had been rearranged. Her Portmeirion storage jars were on a higher shelf, the teapot stored fussily in a cupboard instead of on the worktop beside the kettle. A twitch of resentment started up.

Then she heard footsteps on the stairs: Cassie, tumbling down, curly, plump and flushed in pink dungarees stretched too tight. She flung herself at Maggie tearfully, like a wet puppy, clinging damply.

'I *am* pregnant, Mum,' she said. 'What am I going to do now?'

Maggie took another deep breath, exhaling with it the last essences of freedom; of heat and lust, of oil paint, geraniums, eucalyptus and wine. Then she patted Cassie's back as she had done when she was a tiny child in the pink furry sleeping suit that Harriet had given her.

She said, 'I'm here now. We'll see . . .'